The Immortal Philosophers

CHRONICLES OF DYLAN EAGLEGOD

BOOK ONE

SUNSET IN THE VALLEY
OF NOW AND THEN

THE IMMORTAL PHILOSOPHERS
Chronicles of Dylan Eaglegod Book One
SUNSET IN THE VALLEY OF NOW AND THEN
by
ALEXANDER ANTHONY CASILLAS

Published in the United States by Four Elements Press LLC, New Jersey.

To request permission, contact
contact@fourelementspress.com

Cover design and formatting/design of book interior by
Mario Lampic

ISBN 978-1-965996-00-3 (Hardcover)
ISBN 978-1-965996-01-0 (Paperback)
ISBN 978-1-965996-02-7 (e-book)

Printed in the United States of America
Edition One

Published by Four Elements Press
fourelementspress.com
theimmortalphilosophers.com

THE IMMORTAL PHILOSOPHERS

CHRONICLES OF DYLAN EAGLEGOD

BOOK ONE

SUNSET IN THE VALLEY OF NOW AND THEN

by

ALEXANDER ANTHONY CASILLAS

FOUR ELEMENTS PRESS

CONTENTS

For all the parts of us longing for new beginnings.

"**D**YLAN LEFT ALREADY?" Joshua said, rushing down the front stoop past Walt. The pavement outside the Greenwich Village brownstone they shared was mossy and green from the shade of the maple tree and ivy running up the building's brick face, obscuring the sun and warmth of daylight.

"Yeah, I thought you knew," Walt said, his squeaky voice as irritating to Joshua as ever, but it brought a smile to Joshua's face the way Walt's feet turned in every time he was around.

"He did know," Chris said, joining them in the doorway to the hall. The mess of his uncombed hair and the gray bags under his eyes told of too much time spent inside.

"Shut up, Chris. I told him I needed him before he left," Joshua said, staring down the street as if able to catch sight of Dylan's car, but he knew Dylan was already long gone.

"You gonna be alright without him?" Chris taunted. "You're always needing him for something."

"Don't ask stupid questions," said Joshua, the impatience in his voice cutting. "He had to pay up before he left."

"Pay up?" Walt said, staring with a pinched face up at Joshua. "His parents own this place. What does he have to pay for? None of us pay anything."

"You're going to get stuck looking like that forever," Joshua said. "The uselessness of you all makes me sick. I'm leaving as soon as I'm packed."

"I'm on my way out," Chris said, but couldn't finish his thought or remember what he wanted to say. His voice had left him, both the audible one that originated in his vocal box and the mental one.

Head up to my room and pack my things for me, thought the voice of Joshua in Chris's head. It was a thought Chris was unable to distinguish from his own desire to pack Joshua's clothes and car.

"He can think he got away for now," Joshua said. "But he won't be thinking that for long."

CHAPTER ONE

LONE RIDING

I IMAGINED MYSELF RIDING horseback into the wilderness in the times before cars with my sole possessions bundled in bags strung to my saddle, rather than piled on the leather seats of my Jeep as I cruised down the Garden State Parkway. My journey wasn't to face the dangers of the wild, but at a young age I became an expert at maneuvering my life around my own very real dangers. It may have been a far stretch to consider myself a lone rider, but even modern day lone riders discover themselves one mile at a time.

My expertise at maneuvering my life around dangers came with sacrifice. Four years of closeted college life should have its own post-traumatic stress classification in the DSM-5, and I had a theory that moving to a vacation destination far away from the city for a summer would be as good as any other short term treatment plan I could hardly afford. Living in Manhattan made me reconsider my desire for personal space. After high school I wanted to be everywhere and to see everything, but graduating from NYU made me want to be nowhere, with nobody else around.

I roomed with grade school friends in an antique brownstone in Greenwich Village where each of us guys had our own rooms, and, though we weren't a fraternity, we were as toxic as one. We were always together, always in each other's business, and when we weren't together, we knew where each other went to the point of suffocation. In a place with as many people as New York City, where you could easily feel invisible within a crowd, I felt like I had a bullseye on my back the entire time I lived there. Some days I felt like a real life Jason Bourne, making it through day by day, as handsome as Matt Damon, hiding from men who wanted to know everything about me, and who would kill me if they found out a little too much.

The stakes may or may not have been that dire, but my friends were beacons of the insecure side of masculinity. While my masculinity made me fearless of things like sexual orientation, theirs made them harbor deep rooted homophobia. I feared them finding me out, but not as much as I feared what would result if they did. I would have ended up kicked out of the brownstone, and news would have reached my parents before the end of the day. With their thinking on the topic of gayness being more backwards than most, I knew I would have then been cast out. Familially, financially, and academically.

For those reasons, I further put to use my developed skills in the art of deception during my University years the way I used them in my middle and high school days. I mastered myself to fall in line with the delusional worlds of my parents and peers, and if it wasn't so, I would have been stuck in the streets. I knew how to handle the threat of living with people who wanted to control me, but all that did was prepare me to be so much more.

That was how I came to know the peace of traveling in a car alone, with full control of the radio, the road, and without the eyes of others everywhere. I had experienced everything New York City had to offer, and the hopeful ribbon of the Garden State Parkway felt like freedom from the neurotic pull of my metropolitan psychosis.

Joshua was my only friend completely against me moving away. Everyone else wished me luck, but they were all staying around the city for work. Joshua mused that I thought myself better than the Empire City, but I wasn't one to think of myself as better than anyone. He was just the cruel-cousin type, bent on making all of our days miserable, and that was a fact that the other four of us accepted. We were his compliant targets. Every day I had to wake up around him, every part of me hurt. But that part of my life was burning into the asphalt with every mile more I drove.

Driving South through New Jersey started out as urban highways the size of airport runways and rush hour traffic I knew well, but eventually the drive turned into the scenery of great bays and dense pine forests that I hoped to get to know better. The luck of employment brought me to the seaside island of Ocean City, New Jersey. Halfway through my final semester I landed a remote book cover design job for a publishing company, but movie art for theatre posters and blu-ray covers was what I really wanted to design. I wanted to see my art on all of the streaming services and to work with producers, animators, and actors. I wanted to be big time, but sometimes big time started in a Jersey Shore beach rental.

It was noon when I pulled up to the two bedroom bungalow on Sixtieth Street, Ocean City. The island sun was harsh overhead in the May sky, and in the heat the pastel painted houses that lined the streets looked like pastries baking along the roadside. The only relief from the heat came from the gusts of sweet and salty sea breezes that tickled my lips with the taste of the ocean instead of the sting of familiar city pollution. I messaged my new property manager as I crossed over the island bridge, and he messaged me back saying he would meet me at the house.

The rental was an old pale blue paneled bungalow with a rusty screen door for letting in the breeze and a bow window on the front face where someone had hung two flower boxes a long time ago that had since shriveled into petrified plant skeletons. The driveway sat beside the beach, between the house and the dune wall that climbed into a mountain against the sky.

The seashell-filled yard and the seagrass blowing in the wind along the dunes felt foreign to live beside. I was a long way from the communal study rooms, bathrooms, and spaces of the city. I moved to the land of private property, personal space, room to breathe, and time enough for thoughts of my own. Making me eager to get inside and settle in.

At the end of the street a sporty silver Datsun coup turned off the main road, cruising in my direction. The shore sun glinted off the paint as it stopped at the curb in front of my bungalow, and a serious thirty something year old looking Japanese man climbed out. He was wearing pale green pants and a white, buttoned shirt with green detailing along the button line. He came up from his car, pulling off his aviators and waving.

"Hey, you must be Ikkyu?" I said, crossing the yard to meet him.

"Yes," Ikkyu said, his voice low and smooth like the bubbling of the radio in another room. The seashells crunched beneath my feet no matter how soft my steps were, but Ikkyu's steps somehow weren't making a sound despite his bodyguard size. His rigid face broke into a smile that felt as warm as a long time friends'. "You sound like the Dylan from our call. It's nice to finally meet you."

He reached me and stood with the wide stance of a boot camp commander as he crossed his arms on his chest.

"I wasn't expecting my property manager to double as a bodybuilder," I said. "What gym do you go to on the island?"

Ikkyu laughed, "I go to *Sojun's*," he said. "It's down Boardwalk Avenue near the cafés and shops. It's indoor, outdoor. The only one like it on the island."

"I'll have to check that out," I said, starting to feel more interested in exploring more of the island. "Thanks for coming out here for me."

"Don't mention it," Ikkyu said. "John says you have a promising career with him, and I've seen your work. You've got talent," he said, nodding his head as if impressed with what he remembered.

"Thank you," I said. "I try to bring a lot of purpose to my work."

"Keep it up, and you'll make a name for yourself," Ikkyu said. "Eastman's the right person to work with. He's an investor, and if he sees something in you, he'll get his return. And you'll double and triple your own value by default. Most people hardly ever invest in themselves, even where you come from."

"Manhattan?" I asked, unable to think of a place more synonymous with investment, but, of course, he was right. "Most people do just get by on the grift. But I'm not from Manhattan. I'm from upstate."

"You're better off for it," Ikkyu said, but I wasn't so sure that upstate was any better or worse than anything else.

"Life is feeling far more complex than a one-skill-fits-all type of game," I admitted.

"Yeah, it gets like that," Ikkyu said. "But you learn to adapt."

"That's the plan for now," I said, taking in the sight of the weathered bungalow and thinking the place of my attempted metamorphosis could use some changes itself. "I can't wait to adapt to life here for a bit. The city takes a toll."

"It's unnatural for so many of us to live in the congestion of Manhattan," Ikkyu said. "I'd never go back to city life. Too elitist for my preferences. I'd get into trouble. What do you think about the island so far, though? Did John show you the pictures of the house and everything?"

"Well, the view of the bay from the bridge was beautiful," I said. "Driving through town was a breeze, and it looks like there's a lot to do down here. But this is the first time I'm seeing the house. John didn't show me anything."

Ikkyu let out a few drawn out laughs and started up the yard.

"Come on then," he said. "Let me show you your new home."

"Thanks," I said, following him. "Do you work for the company too?"

"In some ways yes," Ikkyu said. "But I have a lot of other responsibilities that are also connected to Eastman in different ways."

"You sound busy," I said, hoping to be able to strike a work-life balance that would let me enjoy time outside of work. Living alone and working alone would be things I would have to get used to.

The single story bungalow opened up to a main room that came furnished with a hardwood coffee table between a tv and a futon I foresaw myself taking many afternoon naps upon. The kitchen was a hallway straight ahead of the entrance with a portrait-like windowed view of the dunes and sea grass in the backyard along the far wall above the sink, with the cabinets and appliances fit like puzzle pieces around the counters.

The bathroom next to the kitchen had a large window with a view of the backyard behind an old claw bathtub that promised the most brilliant bathing experience I could imagine. The dark colors of the stone on the floor and into the shower were soothing sinks for the orange glow of the lighting.

Next was the main bedroom, which sat complete with a queen bed and wardrobe. Above the headboard of the bed were hung six square paintings of the sky at different times of the day, starting on the left with sunrise and ending on the right with sunset. Ikkyu said the paintings were a gift from a friend from long ago who the house reminded him of.

The second bedroom, which was destined to be my office, was the smallest room of the house. It was empty except for a twin bed footed with a chest. Through the doorway between the kitchen and the bathroom was the cramped laundry room with the door to the backyard making up the far wall.

"It's perfect," I said to Ikkyu after seeing the entirety of what Ocean City bungalow life had to offer. I had more space for myself than I ever had in the city, and the footed tub was a welcomed bonus. I wasn't sure what to expect from the place before I arrived, but it turned out to be everything I wanted it to be.

"John wasn't sure how long you'd need the place," Ikkyu said, laying the keys down on the coffee table. "It's yours for as long as you want it. As long as you're good with John, John will be good with you, which means you'll be good with me."

"Thank you," I said. "For now, this is exactly what I need. It's perfect for me to figure out what's next."

I picked up the keys and wound them through my key ring for safe-keeping.

Before Ikkyu left, I handed him an envelope full of the first few months' rent I had tucked inside my jeans pocket, but he took a look at it and laughed.

"Company expense, John told me," Ikkyu said. "Your rent is paid directly by Sunrise Productions."

"Company expense?" I asked. "The cost would be nearly half my monthly pay," I said, unsure of what to make of the expense.

"Must be a job perk," Ikkyu said. "You know John and the details. If you need anything, call me."

I followed Ikkyu out through the screen door to see him off. My Jeep was sitting in my driveway, shining in the sun beaming on the yard. Letting out my first guest felt like something so foreign to me, and I was suddenly conscious that once he was gone I would be alone in my own home.

"I mean it," Ikkyu said, holding up his finger as he reached his car. "Even if you get lost, give me a ring. I can't have John's star designer go missing on my island. He'll never let me forget it."

"You'll be my first call," I said, laughing at the thought of needing help, but fearing the thought of needing it all the same.

I watched Ikkyu take off down the street. It felt good to feel good about a friend, even if he wasn't quite my friend yet. The island sky was a crystal clear cobalt blue without the wisp of a cloud anywhere while the sun warmed me to my core. I tried to imagine the barren and shelly yard with a bit more life. The house and us both needed a bit of sprucing up, so I made a plan to check out some of the shops along the main street for supplies, but all of that had to wait until after I sorted my old life into my new home.

CHAPTER TWO

EL CAFÉ HERBÍVORO

MY COFFEE WAS A DARK herbaceous brew, like liquid oregano on my tongue with sweet dark-caramel notes and a spiced aroma that brought the jungle theme of the Puerto Rican café to life around me. The comfortable dark wooden table-tops and leafy green plants hanging along the walls made the café feel like a full tropical rainforest inside, and just a block away from the beach. I took my coffee black in the windowed front corner of the place, where I decided to call my office for the day. The combination of liquid stimulant and semi-tribal instrumental music became a panacea for productivity that I found intoxicating, and as an added bonus, while I worked, I kept my eye on the barista behind the espresso counter who charmed everyone who walked into the place while he worked.

The café was bustling with a crowd of groggy Philadelphian and Manhattan elite. They were the exact people I was looking to escape, but they proved to be the perfect morning entertainment as I watched their stressed out souls walk in over my laptop, looking disheveled and desperate for a cup of vacation mode coffee. They waited in line half awake and fixed on their phones with cash and credit cards ready at their sides to trade for that sweet, sweet caffeine high, but in the far off reaches of the Jersey Shore, neither my metro-misery nor theirs proved a match against the magnetism of Antonio.

I took his name when I picked up my coffee order. He was tall, mid twenties, with dark, clean-styled hair and the sharp features I couldn't help but fall for. His smile would have put most Manhattan models to shame, and he flashed it like it was magic. He moved with the grace of a master of his hands and words, turning out drinks, talking, and making people smile. He had a genuine intrigue about him that had been impossible to find in the city, making me feel more confident in connecting with someone here. He was the type of guy I would have loved to have talked to, but with guys in the city I never really saw the possibility of anything more substantial happening than a potential hook up. That's how it was in the city, and I rarely took the opportunity to hook up, as a matter of practice and out of fear of being found out.

I was never afraid to let the beast between my legs rest for a while between bites, but I never judged those who did otherwise. People should live how they want and do what they want in their lives. My calculations of the rate at which people moved through Ocean City on a weekly basis during vacation season made me curious if Antonio was one to give it up to the tourists or to nobody at all, and I wasn't sure where I fit in that equation either. I was more than a tourist, but I wasn't sure if I yet qualified as a local.

You can say all you want about stereotyping, but gays don't have to toe the line of social acceptability when it comes to sex. Most sex for gays is done behind a tight veil of secrecy and shallowness, with great care given not to let feelings slip through the cracks of our callousness. This reality tears apart the hopeless romantic and destroys the sex feign from the inside out. Who ends up better off in the long run is hard to tell, but most people's lives appeared more full of misery than much else as far as the general dating scene seemed, let alone the gay dating scene. But the more I observed the way Antonio carried himself, the more I wanted to discover more about him.

It took effort to pull myself out of the trenches of my lust and turn my attention back to my work as the morning progressed. *Personal thoughts are for personal time*, I told myself. It was a refrain I used throughout my college years. It was one of the few useful remnants of my Greenwich Village days. I used it to keep my thoughts focused on my studies, yes, but more so on my reputation.

Coming back to the refrain taught focus for the objective and the overcoming of personal distraction. If I felt the need to get diagnosed by a psychiatrist, or psychic even, they would tell me that compartmentalizing my thoughts in such a restricted way was a bad method of avoiding emotions and overcoming obstacles, but it was all I had to work with.

My assignment for the day was to design the cover of a novel about an ordinary Japanese twenty-something guy who became the hero of his own story after falling into trouble with Yakuza gangsters. The story featured fast cars, wealthy friends, and the average amount of drugs and girls for a big city gangster thriller. The author of the book, I was told, was a modest man from an English speaking island who spent time in Tokyo, and his publisher was none other than well known former movie director, John Eastman. I met Eastman at an event at NYU and worked on part-time projects while I finished up my final semester, making the gangster cover my first full-time project.

Eastman fawned over the Action & Adventure style movie-case-like book cover designs I created for him. He would send me a pitch, and I would send him a design. It was usually that easy. For my first full-time job I planned on sending him two designs. One design to please Eastman, and another to please the author.

Eastman always contracted for the author to have the final approval of the design, and my goal was always to give them a design I wouldn't have to do much work to if they sent it back with tweaks. I hadn't been asked to make any major design changes for Eastman in the past, but I wanted to give this author two options. Going the extra mile pays off in every business, especially the production and marketing business.

By noon, I was already thinking about eating food. The peanut butter banana smoothie I had that morning was wearing off and the caffeine surging through my veins was making me start to feel empty inside. I didn't think my first cup back into the depths of coffee addiction after a month-long cleanse would be so powerful, but my body felt like a furnace running out of burning fuel. Plus, I wanted to try to figure out Antonio.

In the straight world it's easy to walk up to a member of the opposite sex and ask them out as long as you feel you have a shot. I watched the interactions like a sociologist, if not like a sociopath, throughout my high school and college years. Guys trying with girls, girls trying with guys. People would shoot the shots they wanted to shoot. Sometimes they made them, other times they didn't. The Greenwich guys got what they wanted and enough to refuse, despite being vile. Bottom line, sex was selfish. Guys and girls alike were more likely to shoot their shots until they got what they wanted out of their nights. Sex was at the top of the agenda, but money, power, and lust were top of mind.

In contrast, the gay world is instinctively timid when not

in the insulated safe spaces of Pride parades and gay clubs. My approach to sex was more strategic and drawn out by necessity. I was one to meet up for a number of dates over the course of a couple of months and learn about a person in a more thirsty way than I sometimes think a straight person can understand. Even for us gays, the inside lives of another gay is something of an enigma. It is the learning of the ways of another person who is more your equal in experience than most of the people who surround us most of the time. Those similarities and differences between us fascinated me in ways that were romantic in a fairytale sense. And, though I might not have fallen in love with the guys the way lovers sometimes do, I was able to see and love who they were by their own standards, which is a rare feeling for gays in a straight world. Only at that point of understanding would sex be of interest to me in both a selfish and selfless way, us both knowing we wouldn't be able to pursue anything more substantial after, but not allowing anything to break us away from the intimacy of each other.

It was that same thirsty and inquisitive motive that brought me to my feet, across the café, and on my way over to Antonio. He was behind the espresso bar in his tight, black t-shirt and khaki shorts finishing up with the customer before me, joking about something I missed, but their laughter made me smile too. When he called me up this time I was struck again by the way his eyes glistened like the crystalline brown of Tiger's Eye.

"Hey," I said, approaching the counter. "I was wondering which coffee I should try next. What's your favorite?"

Antonio's customer service mask broke into a softer, more cautious version of himself, as he considered my intentions before speaking.

"That was really smooth," he said, bringing his hands to his hips.

"The coffee was, yeah," I said, placing my mug on the counter. "Can you recommend something just as smooth?"

The corners of his mouth peeled into tight triangles of amusement that told me he enjoyed the game of conversation I was nearly failing at playing.

"Our café Rico," Antonio said, throwing a thumb at the menu behind him. "I think you'll like that one. It's our smoothest, most full bodied, single-sourced Puerto Rican dark roast with notes of pecan and brown sugar. It's also my favorite."

"That sounds really promising," I said, trying not to seem too impressed. "I'll take it."

Then Antonio smiled, in what looked like a confirmation of his interest.

"Where are you from?" Antonio asked.

"Small town in upstate New York," I said. "But I just graduated from NYU. I moved down to the island for work. How about you?" I said, wanting to know more about him, but also aware of the line of eyes forming behind me, all wishing me away so they could order.

"Are you working here today?" Antonio asked, nodding to my corner seat up front by the window.

"Yeah, for the next few hours," I said, feeling good about my chances with him.

"One second," Antonio said, and in a quick move he lifted my mug from the counter and carried it over to the dish bin. His other hand was already around the handle of a clean mug from the rack on the counter by the coffee pot. His baristas worked around him through the steam of their espresso machines, and he worked around them, like the cast of a production. While he filled the clean mug with café Rico, he thanked his team and cheered them on.

"Here you are," Antonio said, returning to the counter and handing me the fresh coffee. "I'll come over to your table in a bit, and we can talk about that coffee. Did you want to order anything else?"

"Yeah, I'll try the Seitan Jibarito" I said, smiling with success.

"Great choice," Antonio said, writing down my order with a smile of his own. "I'll bring it out to you in a bit."

"Thanks, I can't wait," I said before taking my coffee to my seat and feeling free of the fear I had found it so hard to escape on the streets of New York.

The next few minutes consisted of me staring out the front window of the café while mentally replaying my interaction with Antonio. The feel of the conversation was flirtatious enough for me to be confident about his interest in me, and the coffee was just as he explained. Outside, the morning was turning to noon, and the day was looking bright and clear over the ocean. Across the street were a row of shops selling candies and beach themed junk that I couldn't promise myself I wouldn't buy, while tourists in beach attire strolled past the windows making their way down the side streets, up the ramps, and onto the sunsoaked boardwalk.

I watched them disappear over the beach dunes and down one end of the boardwalk or the other. For the first time in so many years, time felt slowed down to a pace I couldn't immediately recognize. It felt like that of my childhood self, staring up into the canopy of a tree and watching the leaves shake for however long I wanted to lay.

After a while of watching island life outside the window with my mug of first class coffee, I got back to work on the dark city street scene of the Action & Adventure cover. I was at the point where I could start touching up the figures of the gangsters, cars, and the Japanese metropolitan public. The skyscrapers were sleek and clean lined, but I still had to review them for the crispness I desired before overcasting a rainy day city haze.

The second cover was on my plans for the next day, and for that I was playing off the Lennon-esque title and the feature of love-hotels in the novel. Pastel pink, yellow, and purple neon circles on a white background, with the title stepping across diagonally. The author's notes wanted an example with the feel of the dreamy, almost delusional, perspective of the narrator, and I hoped the second cover would resonate with him before he picked the Action & Adventure style. The story made me wonder what kind of trouble the author experienced while writing it, but having mingled with a few literary types during my time browsing galleries in Greenwich Village, I found that it was rarely the case that the authors were truly the ones getting into the kinds of troubles they had their characters fall into.

"Here's your Jibarito," a familiar voice said, pulling me back into the café from my computer-screen coma. Antonio was standing at my table without his apron, smiling down at me. So, I resigned my laptop to a place on the bench and cleared the table for Antonio to sit with me if he wanted.

"That looks delicious," I said, entranced by the Jibarito. It was a delicious looking sandwich of flattened plantains for bread with a pickled veggie slaw and slices of seitan, cheese spread, tomato, and onion.

"This is our best seller," Antonio said, setting the ceramic plate on the table in front of me.

"It looks like I'm going to love it," I said, offering him the other chair with a wave of my hand.

Antonio hesitated with surprise, but said, "Sure," before pulling out the chair and taking a seat with me. "Thank you," he said.

"Of course," I said, watching him retrieve his own Jibarito from where it sat on the table next to us, making it seem like eating together was his plan all along, and giving the meal the feel of an impromptu first date.

"Buen provecho," Antonio said, holding up his Jibarito before crunching down on a bite.

"Buen provecho," I said, lifting my sandwich up to him before having a bite of my own.

The sandwich was an explosion of flavor. The plantains for bread were a hearty and satiating alternative to regular sandwich bread, and the flavor of the slaw was of fresh cilantro, garlic, and spice that burned my tongue, while the seitan melted between bites of umami richness.

"What do you think of everything so far?" Antonio asked, watching me with amusement as I chewed.

"Everything is incredible," I said when I finished. "I never heard of a Jibarito before today, and I wouldn't be surprised if this is the best one out there. I ate at some of the top places in the city, and this competes with some of the best."

"Ah, is that what you do for work?" Antonio asked. "You're a restaurant critic?"

There's a trademark cynical side to gays that make us want to get to the bottom of what won't work for our preferences, and it sounded like food critic would have been a big miss with Antonio.

"I'm more of a food enthusiast, for fun," I said. "I work in cover design in the book publishing industry."

As I spoke, I watched Antonio's eyes widen, with interest I hoped.

"You were right, also," I said, chewing on my thoughts more than my food.

"What do you mean?" Antonio asked, his handsome face turning serious and making him appear more handsome by default. I would have been nervous if I wasn't enjoying my time with him so much.

"The coffee is super smooth," I said, holding up my mug to take a sip.

Antonio laughed, and I couldn't help but love the roller-coaster of it as it left him, hearty and bubbling.

"We've been working hard to grow that one to perfection," Antonio said.

"I've been going down to Puerto Rico," he said, in a storyteller kind of way I could listen to for hours. "I worked with our farmers on producing a soil blend for this plant to help achieve a well balanced, cocoa-nutty flavor. This is the first batch of our most successful attempt. The farm only produces enough beans for our shop for now, but we have a strong family-partnership. I'll have to pass on the compliments."

"That's an awesome project," I said. "Not many coffee shops actually work with the farmers that grow their beans. The flavor difference is unreal. It sounds like you do a lot of work for this place."

Antonio felt like a person who was whole. Like he had a sense of self figured out. Those were new thoughts to me, having come from places rampant with rural conformists and shallow city power seekers. Antonio's work was genuine, and his food and coffee were excellent. I took another sip to try and taste the Puerto Rican terroir through the rich liquor to taste a bit of what Antonio meant.

"Owning this shop was a dream of mine," Antonio said, "So, the work is part of the dream."

Antonio struck a smile as if for a professional photo, making me laugh as I enjoyed his performative personality.

"That's really impressive," I said, smiling in admittable admiration. "The town clearly loves this place. You guys have been busy the whole time I've been sitting here. So, where'd you move from?" I asked. "Unless you've lived here your whole life?"

"I've spent my adult life living in South Jersey," Antonio said. "But I spent a lot of time with my family down in Puerto Rico when I was younger. My family owns the coffee farm, so I kind of have roots in both places."

"That sounds like an amazing childhood," I said, zooming out of my life to wonder what it would be like to have roots in vastly different places. "My parents traveled a lot, but only to resorts in remote places, mostly without me. I haven't seen much of how people actually live around the world, aside from New York. I didn't really agree with the fast paced superficiality of city life. I just wanted to graduate and get to somewhere like here so I could finally put down roots, I guess."

I hadn't thought about it that way before, but Antonio's life was inspiring new thoughts in me.

"I think you picked a great place, coming here," Antonio said, sitting back in his seat. "You'll be able to find what you're looking for. I know a few of the business owners along the street, and we all get together every now and then, if you'd like to meet some good people."

"That sounds great," I said, unsure if Antonio was putting

me in the friend zone or closer to the zone I wanted to be in. Either way, spending more time together and having mutual friends couldn't hurt. Antonio took the final bite of his sandwich, and I followed suit, savoring the treat before it was gone.

"Will you be in here tomorrow?" Antonio asked, nodding at my laptop.

"Sure," I said, happy to oblige. "You want to do the same thing then?" I asked, pointing at our lunch plates.

"Yeah," he said, after giving it a second's thought. "I'll see you here tomorrow, and we can have lunch. Enjoy the rest of your day, Dylan." Antonio said, getting up from his seat and taking our plates.

"Thank you," I said. "You too. I'll see you tomorrow."

After Antonio took our plates back to the kitchen, I couldn't think of anything else but him. I did what I could to finish up the dark city street on the Action & Adventure cover by combing through the pixels of the entire piece and touching things up here and there until I couldn't look at my screen anymore. My mug was drained, and I was ready to leave my final review for the next day. So, I turned my attention to the back cover.

Back covers are hard to mess up, and the only way that you can effectively mess one up is by trying too hard. It was my practice to keep to the theme of the front, without being extra. Publishers love to throw writing over the art on the back anyway, so I give them enough space to do it. Down the middle of the back cover I threw a cloudy, near white space, the width of a paragraph, that grays into blackness at the edges, where tiny neon star-specks hung suspended like stars in the city sky at night.

When I was satisfied with my work, the clock showed past three-thirty, and the only people in the café were a couple of laptop workers like myself and two baristas. A hard day's work felt good after the move the day before, and I was looking forward to getting back to the bungalow to finish up organizing my things.

I paid my bill for the sandwich at the register and packed up to leave the organic comfort of El Café Herbívoro with the promise of returning the next day for lunch with Anotonio. The sun was strong in the May sky, and my skin was still unaccustomed to the abrupt change of season. Antonio's skin was smooth and tan while mine was still its winter pale in the rearview mirror of my Jeep, and I hoped my LED bleached glow would soon transition to the UV gold I turn when taken enough sun.

When I returned home, the bungalow was warm from the afternoon heat, so I decided to open up some windows to let in the fresh ocean air. There was a smell to the house, but it was not a terrible stink. It was just one of those odors left over from the previous renters. It cleaned out while I worked out on the floor beside the coffee table with the breeze off the ocean billowing through the bay window and sending the long curtains dancing above me.

A few sets of pushups, squats, long planks, and sit ups, along with a good stretch were enough to get my blood pumping and take away the discomfort of sitting in a seat all day.

After, I decided to put together my desk and desk-chair for my office in the spare room. Officiating my settling in as I pushed the desk up against the spare room window. All ready for the next morning.

While I still had a good few hours worth of sunlight left, light, I headed onto the beach for a jog. I went out through the laundry room door and into the small roped off back yard. It was my first time out back, and I was stopped by the beautiful smell of the pine trees in the humid air of the afternoon. I breathed it in, delighted by the thought of making use of the stone fire pit and pair of long driftwood logs for sitting around with new friends.

I crossed the bleached shell yard to the path that led up the dunes along the side of the house, where the beach lay beyond. As I ascended, the soft shhhhushhhhhh of the ocean waves came to my ears with the breeze, transporting me to another world of sensation. When I reached the top of the dune, the beach sprawled out like a blanket for what looked like a hundred yards of white sand before where the waves crashed like person sized barrels into the shoreline. Then, the sea dominated the horizon until it met the sky in indigo brilliance.

The balance of the view was photogenic perfection. The bright green of the long grass on the dunes, blowing with the wind, the powdery tan of the sand, the blue-green of the water, and the bright blue of the sky, pocked with fluffy white clouds overhead. I took it all in, telling my brain to save the memory like a postcard from an old friend and offer the memory up to me when I needed to feel the kind of awe inspiring peace and balance that only nature can offer.

I ditched my shoes at the top of the dune, where I decided to pull off my t-shirt in order to start off the summer's tan. The sunlight was warm on my skin, but the sand was like hot coals against the soles of my feet, so I sprinted down the beach as fast as I could to reach the cooler, wetter sand by the water.

I couldn't resist jogging into the waves up to my knees and

splashing water onto my body just because I could. With it still being so early in the season, the water felt like ice washing over me, leaving my skin tough with goosebumps, but it felt so good. I wanted everything shore life had to offer.

I listened to the ocean's rhythm as I jogged along the shoreline, passing families and fishermen still out enjoying their afternoon at the water. Friends sat on picnic blankets in shorts and sweatshirts eating and drinking while music pumped out from phones and speakers nearby. Life guards were packing up their bright red gear and laying down their guard chairs while the sun continued its golden descent over the bay side of the island. I didn't know how long the beach was, but it felt like I could have run for hours. The limitless expanse of the beach felt even better than the endless ribbons of the U.S. highways.

Back at the bungalow the air in the house was as fresh and fragrant as the salt in the ocean breeze. Dinner was the last of the leftovers I packed from the city, which I followed with a long hot shower. My soft skin pulsed with the little bit of sunshine it soaked up during my jog, and I reveled in the way that there was nobody else around to tell. My mind was free to replay my day at Antonio's café.

CHAPTER THREE

Storm Sailing

THE BEAUTIFUL SKY of the day before clouded over in the night, bringing a day's worth of rain to my New Jerseyan slice of paradise. Along with the rain, came the gift of a morning headache, which I immediately tried to melt under the hot shower tap. There's a science behind getting rid of a headache, and I had perfected a method with an eighty-percent success rate for alleviation before noon.

First, I let the hot shower water beat the top of my head for six minutes, followed by an abrupt switch to cold water for two minutes. Two minutes sounds like a short time, but standing for two minutes naked under a cold tap shrivels the mind, body, and soul. It's awful, but I can attest to the fact that it also shrivels the creeping hand of a headache beneath the scalp. The longest two stoney minutes of my life were followed by a medium to hot wash and rinse with a quick towel off.

After showering, my headache removal method hurried me to the kitchen for some breakfast and tea. My usual breakfast for a morning like this was some kind of oat bowl with nuts and seeds, which suited me fine because the fridge was empty except for half a container of oat milk. So, I made a mental plan to stop for groceries either before or after my rendezvous with Antonio.

I feasted on my oats at the coffee table while the steam from my tea evaporated in a dense cloud of perfume in the cold morning air. The tea itself was a bright, floral, black tea with a sweet malty fragrance that reminded me of overripe peaches. That specific tea had become my go-to for headache removal, though I could never explain why it worked so well. I assumed it had the right level of caffeine and flavonoid balance to kick mental pains to the curb, but any regular tea might do. And when I finished the tea, my headache was a memory.

The sky outside the bay window was dark, and the clouds looked to be getting more aggressive over the island than when I first woke up. I hoped the worst of the storm was overhead with clear skies behind it, but I still had a day of work to complete before I could set foot outside. That was if the weather turned around.

After cleaning my breakfast dishes, I brought my laptop to my desk and returned to working on my book covers for Eastman, wanting to try out my new office before meeting Antonio for lunch. I started with an in-depth final review of the Action & Adventure cover. I even had the chance to compare my artistically designed storm clouds with the ones nature had corralled outside my office window, and I didn't want to miss the opportunity for inspiration. When my digital clouds started to look as menacing as the ones outside, I felt good about sending the cover in for review.

The final design was a dark blue-black strip of city street, lined with sky-scrapers, with one scraping the sky higher than the rest. Eastman described such a tower being featured in the novel, so I made sure the book browsers would get the picture. The yakuza gangsters in their day suits were getting into their black SUV at the curb to peel-out after the bright orange sports car speeding down the flooding street. While the warm lights in the windows of the buildings of Japan's metropolitan landscape were the beacons of life, tucked away in their own private window framed pictured worlds.

I cast the protagonist's face as a faint ghost across the front of the cover as he overlooked his world. From his metro-city, to the island of his birth, which lived in his mind at the top of the cover. It was the island of his home, of his memory, and of his curse, depicted as a canopy of green leafed trees during the brief orange window of sunset before twilight.

I could relate to the hero's struggles with a tormented mind, so I knew exactly how to portray it. When your mind is plagued with something, the sickness lives in your head until you beat it back with all your might, like a cartoon granny with a broomstick kicking out the cat.

Satisfied with the first cover, I turned my attention to designing the second cover, starting with a blended off-white and silver toned background. After dusting off the background by adding some depth between the pixels, I added powdery pink, purple, and golden wispy rings that faded in and out in an indiscriminate pattern that made them look like the pronounced rims of blown bubbles. The Lennon-esque title looked at home in the dreamscape that I wrapped around from front to back, letting the book browser know that this was the book for feeling a little psychedelic.

I managed to get both of the covers saved in files and sent to Eastman before my noon deadline to meet Antonio, and headed out into the spitting drizzle of the day to go see him. Driving through the storm flooded island streets felt like sailing my Jeep up a river. Before leaving the house I was under the impression that storms slowed down island life and kept everyone home, but it seemed like every local and out of towner was sailing with me through the streets as they would have any other afternoon.

While I worked, I tried to keep my thoughts about Antonio to a minimum, but my mind was a merry go round of questions as I drove down the avenues. I wondered what Antonio drove, what he had driven, what he liked to do with his freetime, and what else he'd like to do with me. I still didn't know how old he was, but I guessed he was around twenty-five, compared to my twenty-two. The last thing I wanted was to get ahead of myself, but I believed my excitement was harmless. If things started going south, I had a plan to retreat and find a different coffee shop to lunch at. The red flags while getting to know a gay are the shallow tips of dense banners hiding below the surface, and I knew how to avoid their bearers.

I pulled into the driest spot in the lot around the back of El Café Herbívoro and braved through the rain on my way up to the front door. The café was a warm welcome of delicious aroma filled with the cacophony of coffee shop sounds I always found relaxing, but one look around the coffee shop had me glad that I set up my desk back at the bungalow the night before. The crowd that was usually lined up for take out and on their way to the beach, had lined up, and then taken a seat. Every table in the place was taken by groups of the unbeachable would be sunbathers. They crowded around plates of Jibariots and pastries, mugs and to go lattes, and phones, enjoying the warmth and ambiance of the tropical rainforest atmosphere inside.

In line I was able to get a view of the baristas bouncing around behind the espresso bar. I scanned their ranks in my search for Antonio and found his grinning face in the kitchen door window. But before I could smile back, he was out in the lobby coming my way. Instead of his café t-shirt and pants that he wore the day before, he was wearing a pair of dark-washed blue jeans and a fit sage sweater that gave him the look of a rainforest tour guide brochure model. The only accessory missing was the wide brimmed hat, because he was even carrying an umbrella with him as he blew past me on his way to the front door.

"Are you ready to eat?" he asked, leaving me in his wake.

"Extremely," I said, taking his lead out the door, as I was also relieved to get away from the crowd and be alone with him. The day before proved to me that public places still felt awkward for gay flirtation, but I was determined to set a solid date by the end of our lunch date.

Outside, Antonio stood under the awning, rummaging through his café branded bag for the pair of tin foiled bundles he pulled out a second later.

"One for me. One for you," he said, holding one of the silver bullets out for me to grab.

"Thank you," I said. The special treatment was starting to make me feel spoiled. "I'm afraid I might get too used to this kind of service."

Antonio looked at me and shrugged.

"What's there to fear from that?" he asked, in a way that might have been flirtatious, but I couldn't tell. He was linguistically good at straddling the line between innocent curiosity and showing interest.

"I guess I'd be afraid that you might get tired of me before I get tired of you," I said, hoping he was leaning more towards interest. Despite what I said, I was approaching a new neural network of thoughts and feelings that opened me up to a new side of myself, and in those thoughts of exploration I couldn't hear fear. I only heard free.

"I don't think you have to be afraid of that at all," Antonio said with a sly smile. He popped open his black umbrella to reveal the green café logo printed on top, and he hoisted it over his shoulder while I started to unwrap my bundle.

"I thought we could take a walk, if you'd like?" Antonio said.

"I can't refuse a walk under that umbrella," I said, nodding up at the logo.

"These umbrellas are a big hit," Antonio said, in defense.

"I don't doubt that they are," I said, impressed with his branding, but unable to contain a laugh about how over the top it was.

Over the marsh, still closer to the mainland, dark gray sheets of haze were rushing toward the island as downpours, but overhead the drops were only intermittent drum beats on our umbrella as we made our way south along the avenue.

Being under the umbrella was like being in our own private covered coach. Antonio held it low, so it came down around our heads. Our shoulders bounced off each others' and back together again like Newtonian friction balls in their cradle as we walked.

"What do you think of the wrap?" Antonio asked.

"It's good," I said. "But what is it?" I had taken a few bites, but my mind was where our shoulders touched, the cadence of our walk, and the spiced scent of Antonio's cologne.

"This is the BarbieShroom," Antonio said, holding his out.

"Barbecue... mushrooms?" I asked, before taking another bite to investigate. The barbecue sauce was savory and spicy on the fried little arms of the long mushroom stems that were crispy against my tongue.

"Grilled and barbecued oyster mushrooms with cashew-ranch, arugula, cilantro, and diced tomatoes," Antonio explained, and as I chewed, the flavors came through as he described.

"As a professional food critic," I said, to which Antonio rolled his eyes. "This is incredible."

Fresh cilantro and spicy arugula gave a punch in the after-taste. While the creamy ranch and diced tomatoes tamed the party with texture and sweetness.

"When I was telling people I was leaving the city," I said, "Everyone told me I'd miss the food more than anything else. But since leaving I've never eaten better. This wrap alone would make you a fortune in the city. You'd be able to have all the coffee farm land you'd need."

Antonio was smiling over another mouthful of BarbieShroom.

"I've thought about it," he said, staring into the shop windows as we passed them along the sidewalk. "But life wouldn't be the same. I'm too busy to even think about Manhattan life. Besides," he said. "The distance hasn't stopped New Yorkers from making the trip down to tout my merchandise back home with them."

"You're right," I said. "I thought I was escaping them by coming down here."

"Ah, so that was the motive for your move, then?" Antonio asked, looking closer at me than before. Our faces were close when we both looked at each other between bites as we talked. His energy was magnetic.

"Yeah," I said, smiling with relief. "I wanted to be free of all of it."

The wind tunneling down the street blew harder and started whipping one way one second and another way the next, swaying the umbrella in Antonio's hand. He held on and kept walking, unphased by the change in the world around us in a way I admired. I always considered holding an umbrella on a windy day to be a lot like walking a dog in the way you could always be swept off your feet and dragged down the street.

While we finished our wraps I browsed the windows of the canopied shops we came upon. One was wall to wall surfboards. Each board was a different type of wood, color, and size. In the toy store window were a dozen silly sand sculptures, surrounded by treasure chests full of beach toys.

Next was Beach Babes' Books and Shades Incorporated in big pink swooshing letters across the glass, matching the seventies beach themed decor. In their window was a flying inflated toy shark over a sandbox where a couple of mannequins were sitting in their bikinis and sunglasses with books in their hands. Giovanni's Room was one of the books, Meditations by Marcus Aurelius, the other. I wondered if any of my covers were on the store's shelves, and I hoped an email from Eastman was waiting for me in my inbox with a great review of the work I sent him earlier.

"That window should be on display at Bergdorf's," I said, finishing off my wrap and tossing the wrapper into the trash can as we passed the bookstore.

"It should," Antonio said, looking back at Beach Babes'. "I'd be getting a nice check if it got there, too."

"You set that up?" I said.

"I helped," he said. "My friend Janté owns that bookstore. She has a creative eye for displays. She helps me keep El Herbívoro up to date, and I help her out with setting up her windows. We work together. A good window can turn a business around in a place like this."

"Wow," I said. "Well, you proved that theory. You guys definitely caught my attention. I'll have to stop in and see if they have any of my covers one of these days."

"That's right," Antonio said. He had finished his wrap and was walking with one hand in his pocket and the other on the umbrella. The drops on the umbrella top created an aural sphere of comfort as the shop fronts turned to home fronts while we walked down the sidewalk of the slick, long island avenue.

"I have to see your work," Antonio said. "We could use a good graphic designer in our network. Do you freelance?"

"Yeah, I do," I said. "I'd be happy to hear some proposals and help people out."

"So, how is the scene down here?" I asked, desperate to move on from the topic of work and into something more relevant to the non-friend zone topics.

Antonio looked delighted I asked, and for that I was relieved. Until he laughed at me.

"This is it," he said, nodding down the street. My eyes landed on a gutter, a gushing storm drain, and the wet bark of a tree.

"What do you mean?" I asked, not understanding.

"During the off season," Antonio said. "There aren't many guys around. So, this is pretty much it." He looked over at me. "You and me," he said.

"Then the season starts," he continued. "Soon more families and friends will come down for the summer, and everyone is out and about and as wild as could be. There are two very different worlds here, at two very different times. It all depends on what your flavor is. Tourists, or locals."

Antonio turned very matter-of-fact, meaning he was testing

me now, despite not giving me a picture of exactly what he wanted.

"It sounds like the wild tourists bring the city here with them then," I said. "That's how it is in Manhattan."

After one look at him, I couldn't hold back smiling at our gay dance around directness. It was clear to me that Antonio was a guy who could handle himself through any conversation and situation he could possibly imagine himself getting into, and somehow that made me feel like I didn't know myself at all.

"You should let me take you out on a date," I said. "I owe you a meal, and I could use a night out to get to know the island better."

If he said no, I felt I would know where I stood for sure, but it seemed like he was already offering me a shot.

"Yeah," he said. "I'd enjoy that. I know a place you'd like a lot."

"Yeah? That sounds great," I said, pulling my phone from my pocket to get his number. "How does Friday night sound?"

"Friday night's great," he said. "How about I pick you up at six, and I'll show you one of my favorite restaurants and then some other parts of the island?"

"Yeah, that sounds perfect," I said, curious about the restaurant. "What's the name of the place? I can make the reservation at least, and what's your number?"

He gave me his phone number and I texted him with my name.

"The place is called Chado," Antonio said. "It's a sushi place with a flair that I think you'll like."

"That's amazing," I said. "I actually just finished a cover design for a book set in Japan, so I had to do some research on Japanese architectural and artistic style to help the book connect with people."

"I like that attention to detail," Antonio said. "You really put a lot of thought into your work as a designer. I respect that," he said, and we both slowed our walk down to pay closer attention to each other as we talked. It didn't escape me how I reverted back to work talk after scheduling our date, but we both seemed to share a business-like nature.

"Yeah I do," I said. "It's important for me to have the author feel that the cover is a great visual conveyor of the purpose of their art. The better I become at connecting with people through my work, the more work I'll get, and the further my viewership will become. Once I start doing cover art for movies, everyone will see my work."

"What a vision for fame," Antonio said. "I love the way you talk about your art. I admire that kind of passion."

"Thank you," I said, seeing something in Antonio that reminded me of how I viewed the world. Then, without warning, the clouds let loose a thick curtain of rain over the avenue.

"I think it's time to turn around," I said, eyeing Antonio for confirmation. I didn't need life experiences on the island to know that when rain gets bad, it's better to not get stuck in it.

"Yup, it's time," Antonio said, and we turned around and started back towards the café with the wind at our backs, pushing us along as we passed the home fronts and storefronts. The flags whipped on their poles, while the street lights bobbed on their strings, and Antonio was struggling to keep the open umbrella steady in the violent turns of the shore wind, as cars passed us in the street.

"It's probably going to be like this all night," Antonio said of the wind and rain.

"You think so?" I said, the small shelter of the umbrella wasn't enough to keep us comfortable, so we were rushing along with only parts of us staying dry.

"I was hoping it would pass before night," I said, burying my hopes for a walk on the beach later that night.

"No, this is going to be a long one." Antonio said. "It's best to just stay in and stay warm on nights like these."

"That's fair," I said. "Close the umbrella. We can run."

Antonio zipped shut the umbrella, and we were running past the crying storefronts gushing with currents of water from their roofs and onto our feet as we splashed. My shoes were soaked, making my toes squirm in my socks as I ran. We passed Beach Babes' Books and Shades Incorporated, the toy shop, and the surf shop. Then the café was in sight.

As we came upon El Herbívoro, we slowed down to a walk before clamoring into each other on our way through the door. The café was as packed as it had been when we left it, and everyone was staring at us in the doorway as we dripped rain onto the door mat while the door swung shut behind us. We looked like a mess, but it felt like we were, perhaps, long-time friends. Smiling and laughing at each other after a drenching adventure.

"I'll text you about Friday then," I said, feeling proud despite our silliness. We beat the storm, I landed the date, and the flavors of lunch were still swimming around my mouth with powerful taste.

"Please do," he said, shaking his umbrella over the floor mat. It rained like a cloud. "I'll be waiting."

"You won't be waiting too long," I said. "See ya soon, Antonio."

"Bye, Dylan."

Back in my Jeep, my mind felt like a wet fish. I was thrilled by the excitement of something new, but I was too physically uncomfortable to enjoy it. My clothes were soaked down to my skin as I struggled to get the heat to pump through the air vents.

"Wooo!" I cheered, as my nerves took over with the thrill of the cold on my skin.

The heat from the vents couldn't come out fast or hot enough. My seat was already soaked before I even reached the road, squishing like a damp sponge every time I hit a bump.

To my luck, the roads weren't as busy as before. I followed my GPS to the only supermarket on the island, and vowed to make it as quick a trip as possible. The store itself looked like it had been remodeled in the seventies, with big red letters on the front that read 'SUPERMARKET' next to a logo that looked like the family crest of the people who owned the place. The beat up carts strewn about the parking lot told me everyone on the island had already come and gone for the day, considering the storm. I felt bad for the cart guy running in a handful of the many carts at a time against the storm. I took one from the parking lot to help him out, but it was too wet to use, so I swapped it out for a dry one inside.

Aside from myself and the workers, there weren't many people inside either. In the produce section I felt like a spoiled child walking into Willy Wonka's chocolate factory chocolate room. The rainbow of bright fruits, berries, and veggies made me hungry and excited. The produce section is a paradise where everything is edible and the flavor varieties are beyond imagination. Produce is the fruit of life on Earth, and us twenty-first century humans are lucky enough to enjoy so much of it.

I filled my cart with as much fruits and vegetables as I thought would fit in the fridge and moved on to the other sections. My next stop in the store was to the dry beans section. Dry beans were usually tucked into the "International" food aisle for some reason. I always felt beans should have their own section, with scoops and bags for filling with a variety ten times what most places have in stock. Despite our tremendous access to great food, there are so many varieties of fruit, vegetables, nuts, grains, and beans that don't make it to our shelves.

After picking up some kidney beans, I threw a big bag of rice under the cart and chose a box of quinoa and a few different types of noodles. I picked up a few cans of stewed tomatoes, tomato paste for sauce making, and a couple of other things to use for daily cooking. Then I finished off my supermarket run by picking up a carton of oat milk and making my way to the register. Even after shopping, my clothes were still dripping while my shoes squeaked around the store under me.

On the way back home the road was visibly more flooded. I wondered if the tides had anything to do with the way the water came up some streets and not up others. Down the bay side of the island the flooding was worse. As I passed the bayside streets I noticed that there were no dunes along their waterline. Instead there were docks with boats thrashing nearly above their bulwark s, threatening to cascade onto the streets with one strong wave.

Where the storm drains were full, the bay, ocean, and rainwater crept into the middle of the street where they combined with the capacity to set small cars asail down the flooded avenues. I wanted nothing more than to be out of my wet clothes and in my warm bath.

Thankfully, I was back at the house before the heat in the Jeep started feeling hot, which I appreciated in a way only New Yorkers could understand. In the city it could take you hours to get down a few blocks, but on the island the drives were quick. In Ocean City, a drive was a drive, not a stop and go flirtation with madness, death, and frustration.

Finally inside my little blue bungalow, I got to work putting the groceries away while my mind was already set on taking a bath to the sound of the storm outside. Once everything was put away, I ran to the bathroom to get out of my wet clothes. I wasn't sure how Antonio was coping with the drenching, but I hoped he was seconds away from relief if not already dry.

While the tub filled with hot water, the bathroom grew thick with a fog that coiled up and out over the sides. The cold air in the room sunk as the steam grew thicker, fogging up the rain specked glass of the back yard window. I left the light off to exist in the gray light of the stormy night, and peeled my damp clothes off my clammy skin.

When there was a good amount of water in the tub, I lowered myself in. The faucet was still gushing out a hot gurgling waterfall as I sank all the way down. I had been in many bathtubs before, but never one with enough room where you didn't feel cramped. I didn't want the sound of the faucet to stop when I cut the flow, but the rain on the window and the thunder overhead were welcome replacements to the sound of the spout.

I was eager to lean back along the steep incline of the tub wall and close my eyes. I filled the tub so that the water ebbed at my chin while my skin hummed with heat below the water. Baths were always best at the temperatures just before burning. Even the air around my face was thick and hot with the humidity off the water's surface. I embraced the heat, matching my breathing to the pace of my blood surging through my dilated arteries and blood vessels. The force was exhilarating.

The combination of the water around me and the sound of the thunder rolling in the storm above made me appreciate how water could be a small strike of pleasure in a cup, a storm in the sky outside, and a long stroke of full bodied ecstasy in a bath. Water could be a bitch if it got too hot, but my bath was in the perfect zone for numbing the body and mind. Before, I wasn't able to imagine a life outside of what I knew, but inside the womb of the stormy-gray room, I felt the shreds of a future for myself beginning to form.

After what felt like the entire afternoon, I was hesitant to leave my water cocoon, even as the water cooled. But, like a butterfly, I knew when it was time to go. While the tub drained, I soaped up and rinsed off in the shower. My body was warm from skin to bone, and by the time all the soap was down the drain, I felt more clean and comfortable than I had felt in years. The filth I felt under the peering eyes of city life finally felt washed away.

After showering, I decided to lay out on the futon in my sweatpants with a joint to stretch out my mind and think. The thick stream of smoke burned off the end of it against the gray of the clouded sky on the other side of the bay window as I pulled it to my lips and took a hit. I imagined what it would be like to be up there, inhaling clouds. I thought maybe it would feel like a lungful of marijuana. A bright, bursting, floral aroma.

The quiet of the night was fresh in the dim house, making me eager to find out what I would discover at the nearer end of the joint as its burning end crackled and popped as I pulled in its smoke. The weed sent my mind into a whirlpool that brought me first to my least favorite place.

I fell back into the corridors of the Greenwich townhouse. I recalled the firm images of the faces of my roommates, who for so long had been a single call away from ruining my entire life. However, my fear of being found out also allowed me to breeze through my majors, sacrificing as much of my social time as I could to office hours with professors or attending guest lectures by the global corporate elite. Anything the guys would be disinterested in.

From the whole university racket, I came to understand how corporate success carries with it the stench of shit from all the ass kissary that it requires. I knew how well I could play the game of their two-faces for every situation type of world, but I couldn't stomach how the route to where they were was always behind where some devil checks in souls the way ushers take in coats. If there ever was a way to circumvent the bullshit, while still playing the game, I'd be an ace of the system.

The club I joined outside my small circle was the Buddhist club. I was lured into the club by a cute and modest gay offering to make students cups of a more traditional matcha tea than found at most of the thousands of fast-food coffee shops around the city. The matcha we drank at every meeting was a patch of sweet grass on my tongue in the middle of the concrete jungle I was beginning to more accurately understand. Throughout the meetings they talked about sacrifice and letting go of attachments, which forced me to sit and look at my life from a distance.

I never pursued anything with the cute gay, but four years of listening to Buddhist thought gave me a scornful perspective of the city and the people in it. I began to see the skyscrapers that used to be marvels to me become dangerous beacons of desire pulling me away from what truly mattered.

To me, New York City became the biggest market of desire I didn't even realize I was experiencing until I ceased to engage with it. My peace was disrupted by signs and sounds and attitudes abound. It's an immortal place. It's the city that leads the way and carries the weight of global desire. Signs stand in the place of species of trees and animals that used to inhabit the land. Signs on cars, on walls, in the sky. There are signs on signs on signs. There are even signs that are three-dimensional art screens that are lab tested pictures of desire.

These are real life boxes we can't 'x' out with the touch of the tip of our finger, and unlike our personally tailored social media existences, the experience of the city is a shared one. The Buddhist lectures showed me that the only way to preserve my sense of self in a city of so many, was to turn inside myself and away from the temptations of the outside world.

When I wasn't playing pretend around the guys, I spent my city days in as close to silence as the city ever lets you get. I worked with headphones on without music playing in different cafés all throughout the city. The headphones told people to leave me alone, even when I didn't want to hear music. This obstacle allowed me to focus on my work at all times. The sunny days of spring and summer brought me to the grassy fields of Central Park and to the Hudson waterfront benches where I watched the river's gleaming currents in all their littered glory.

The lounge was smoked up from the lively tip of the burning red end of the joint, and I took it in like a pro. If there was one thing I appreciated about the guys and our access to money, it was the unlimited access to the best of the best weed that New York City had to offer. Afterall, there were limits to the access that I could refuse.

So, who was I at the end of my last hefty drag? If we are what we desire, then I was a man in a new place more full of desire than I ever allowed myself to feel in Manhattan. The best marketing teams in New York failed to sell me on the Empire Dream, but this shore town's coffee guru was giving me dreams of something I might eventually be sold on.

Lightning struck the other side of the island, snaking across the darkening sky like a luminescent serpentine dragon. I applauded the inevitability of everything as I aligned the afterimage of the bolt with the butt end of my roach until the image was as faded as the joint into the smokey air around me.

A boom of thunder barreled over the house like a train, shaking everything with the shock of a bomb. And for a few lagging seconds, the energy in the room was manic. It felt like a sleeper stirring awake in a panic before settling back to the familiar rhythm of before. But minutes later, the room was still alive. I laid down and closed my eyes to focus on the feeling of the storm, and let go.

CHAPTER FOUR

ROAD BLOCKS

I SLEPT LIKE A GOD RIDING my futon through the stormy night. It could have been the weed, or maybe it was my anxious city-mind, but my dreams took me to places I had never before thought to conjure up. The commonality between the string of them was the handsome dark haired guy who followed me from dream to dream, like the soul of a lover across lives. My dreaming mind couldn't quite capture the memory of Antonio's face, but the feeling I felt around him in the dream was the same I enjoyed while awake.

Between the dreams and chasing raindrops with Anotonio the day before, I was feeling pretty good in the dim gray morning light of the lounge. I felt a sense of power staring up at the pitched ceiling, but still felt too tired to actually sit up. However, my habit of getting up and promptly getting ready eventually prevailed, and I was soon staring out the bay window in horror at the scene playing out at the corner of the street.

A dozen flashing trucks jammed the end of the intersection, from corner to corner. Police trucks, bucket trucks, and fire trucks sat like buildings, blocking my one way off the street. I thought construction traffic in the city was bad, but even there they had the courtesy of leaving lanes clear for passage. There was too much money on the line every second in New York, and people weren't shy about letting you know how much you cost them. I considered what might have happened if I were to take the Jeep for a drive on the beach to get to the street on the next block, but I couldn't convince myself that it would have been a good idea.

My plans for the day had originally been to stay home, but it was a bummer that I couldn't entertain the idea of Puerto Rican coffee for breakfast. The mess of the broken poles and downed wires looked to be at least a day-long fix. The bucket trucks had their necks extended with workers high up near the powerlines, while another crew worked on clearing the pole debris, but the scene was moving at a snail's pace. I didn't blame the workers for taking their time with the live wires, as long as I had power.

I was only days into my first full-time work week for Eastman, and I wasn't ready to mess it up on a count of not having power. In the worst case scenario, I would've simply been forced to don a reflective orange vest and get out there to help them restore my livelihood.

All of the lights in the house were off, just as I had left them before falling asleep. A day without work would have been a tragedy. I wanted my work out there. In a world where you can do many things that only matter a little bit, you might as well aim to inspire as many people as you can in the small ways of your work. Perhaps, deep down, I wanted nothing more than to be eternal, and that morning was a reminder that without power, I would be nothing.

After lifting myself from the futon I checked the lights in the bathroom, hoping to start my morning routine. To my delight, the bathroom light burned away the discomfort of not knowing if I'd spend the day looking up at the ceiling.

The warm glow bathed the floor and walls in an antique glow against the slate gray of the yard outside the back window. Broken branches and loose strands of sea grass littered the yard from the wind, but the storm had since tapered down to a drizzle against the glass. I loved the natural world being just a window glance away.

Without checking, I knew that Eastman had a new assignment for me in my inbox and a reply to the covers I had sent him the day before. Working for Eastman was like clockwork. Every time I brought him something, he was there to challenge me again. Every new job was a chance to improve myself, and I loved it. Starting new covers also meant that I was still well employed.

Eastman and the author loved the covers. Eastman was ready to print two different designs if the author wanted, but the Action and Adventure cover took the prize. The author said that he wasn't sure how I had achieved it, but that I was able to put into design what he felt he failed to put into words. It was as if I had plucked the images from his mind, he said. Eastman said that it was by far my best cover yet, and that his bets were paying off on me. The key, I figured, was to continue to be someone who I myself would bet on, hoping everyone else would be more likely to take notice and follow suit.

Once satisfied with reveling in the past, I turned my attention toward the future. My next job seemed to be one where I could again incorporate a cityscape, but this time a much older looking city than 21st century Tokyo. The novel's title was Jazz Americano. It was the story of an aspirational young Black and Puerto Rican nine-teen year old in the segregationist world of the 1940s United States.

The main character braved gig tours into the deep south by rail with his brothers in jazz, all the while spreading the jive of their craft. From their home in Harlem, the young musician and his crew played in clubs from Boston down to Florida and everywhere in between. Given the vast differences in settings and emotions described in the brief, I had a lot of design brainstorming to conjure up. The smokey jazz club settings were an alluring direction for such an aesthetically seductive novel, but I had to do my research.

Eastman was always good at having the author include the novel descriptions of the most significant settings in the story, and there were a few of the warm colored, smoke filled, booze serving jazz bars that immediately came to mind from my previous research in American history of the time period. There were also the descriptions of the train cars that carried the musicians from place to place, with the train cars also segregated by race. The trend I found most interesting was the difference in the descriptive language between the world outside the jazz club and the world inside the jazz club. The world outside of jazz was cold and isolated in a way that made the comforts of jazz feel all the more rich.

The music, the smoke, and the drink made all the difference for people in need of comfort in a world where their comfort was made illegal and their discomfort was legislated and reinforced by a class of people obsessed with racial superiority against their own countrymen. There is no greater national sin, as there is no greater national poison. The mechanisms of exploitation are always turned upon those with too little power to do anything about it, and segregation was a physical experience of that corruptive violence.

I wasn't sure of it, but I believed Eastman was testing me

once again by upping the bar with the complexity of the novel. And I was ready to blow him away with something special. Traveling city bands were apparently as much the rage in the 1940s as traveling pop stars are today. The novel portrayed the jazz brothers as proud representative celebrities of their home cities. People knew their names. People knew their sounds.

They had reputations for being cooler than cool. The smoothest talkers, and of course they were fawned over everywhere they went. The Boston bands, Harlem bands, and the bands of all the cities from Boston to Nashville and down to Miami would make the rounds up and down the coast. One of the most interesting settings was Jefferson Street in Nashville, Tennessee, where the railroads were at the heart of the musical exchange between the coastal cities.

In the backdrop of the music, the main character was tasked with maneuvering around the obstacles of the segregated world, which meant conforming with the very real sense that his life could be taken by any white face at any time, especially south of home. The pervasive state of white supremacy in America was almost dependent on lynching Black people for daring to speak out against injustice. The brief explained the way the lynchings came in both physical and social forms, and always were in effort to cancel the advancements toward the equality of Black people. In the segregated world, every white person was charged like a deputy to harass everyone who wasn't a part of the privileged class. That was a social expectation. Everything about the era felt like dystopian fiction, to the point where vanilla ice cream was not sold to Black Americans except on the Fourth of July. Worst of all, some of the same hatred was still alive in the 21st century. Memories might not reach as far as time, but the memory of hate spans generations.

From the brief, I admired the way the main characters packed themselves onto trains with their gear and chests full of hollowed out books stuffed with reefers. Some were for the band, some were for the fans in the seats of the clubs. Most of their clothes were full of hidden inside pockets lined with flowers where they would stash enough, until restocking with the bigs of business after their gigs.

Some of the greatest musicians of the time had an affinity for the plant that sank them into the vibes of the music, to play a little smoother to the rhythm of their sound. They were traveling genies, arriving in tin cans billowing smoke and soothing tortured souls with the magic of musical salvation. These bands were the harbingers of culture, but they were also targets of local, state, and federal violence. These were the times where police across the country were expected to shut down clubs because of the color of the clients' skin. Every day was a struggle in America for these jazz musicians.

Listening to the stories of my own grandfather from that time period were siestas into a world of slow-rocking chairs, wraparound porches, and sweaty pitchers of iced tea in the shady forests of upstate New York. He allowed for my 21st century curiosity to guide us through my questions about his youth as I hunted for exciting insights about the world when I was around him. I wondered what stories the jazz men would have told their grandchildren. The good memories, for sure, but what about the bad?

My thoughts on the jazz cover quickly became a few digital sketches boasting all of the warm and bright metallic tones of the brass instruments and the jazz club decor. The feature of the train felt like it deserved a spot on the cover, but I didn't want it to take up too much space. I wanted to catch the detail on the nose of the engine car up close to the point where it looked like it would chug right off the page.

In a quick draft, I threw the train nose on the right side of the cover as if it were about to shoot off in the direction of the buyer's ear. With the rest of the cover I wanted to capture the crew and the club, and I couldn't think of a better way than to have the band members walking off the train, dressed and ready to perform with their instruments in hand, right onto the jazz club stage. With the left side of the cover as a progression into the life of the jazz club scene.

In the sketch draft, the stage was lit with lights from above. I made a note to use a warm orange toned color for the light to keep the palette consistent with the warmth of the club. The stage itself was to be the color of dark roasted coffee beans. Between the stage and the left side of the cover, I sketched out a sea of tables full of attendees with crimson colored horseshoe shaped booths lining the back wall that wrapped around the club to where I started sketching out the bar.

That first draft session took me well into the afternoon, when I decided to get up from my work for the day. I had accomplished a lot on day one, and I was feeling good about the direction I took. Throughout the day, thoughts of Antonio came in snapshots of memories from the day before. Getting up from my desk allowed me to explore these thoughts a little further. It was hard to believe our date for Friday was already the next day.

While I waited for my tea kettle to boil, I got out a nice white tea that was picked earlier in the spring. It was a Silver Needle that our Buddhist Club professor had gifted us all. It was a large bud selection of fuzzy, silver leaves. They were picked and dried in a shaded covered fruit garden. The production of the tea created a floral, green grape, cream, and treacle-like perfume that released once the boiling water hit the leaves.

With my mug snug under my chin, I checked the bay window for the day's roadwork progress. The number of emergency vehicles that were gathered earlier had halved in number. The new poles were up, and the wires were all attached. Only a few construction and police trucks remained on the scene, and it looked like everything would be cleared up in no time. The officers that were still on the scene were directing cars on and off the street, so my night was opening up with new possibilities.

Back in the kitchen, I took my first sip of the Silver Needle and sank into the ecstasy of the smooth, thick, amber nectar I was thirsty for. I swirled the tea around my mouth to taste the full flavor of the sweet dewy brew before pulling out my phone. There was a new message from none other than Joshua Bailey, my old roommate and oldest, most loathsome friend of all time.

"I'm down in Ocean City bro! Where's ur spot?!"

Dread washed over my mind like a freezing towel as I tumbled down a trip of desperation and fear before coming to the conclusion that I couldn't, under any circumstance, message Joshua back. It was true that if I didn't message him, my whole network of people back home would hear of my negligence. Joshua's parents would find out, and, in turn, my parents would find out. Then that would cause them to be curious and ask questions, but one thing I didn't have to worry about was my parents coming down to check on me in person. There wasn't a force on Earth that could bring them to visit their son face to face. Our relationship was phone and expectation based, not actually relationship based. Though, having only been a few days out on my own, I was already struggling to justify my fear of their upstate wrath.

I wanted to be happy living two separate lives for a time, but my old life was threatening to pull me back in for more experiences I had been dying to live without. I was in a good place. I didn't have to worry about losing anything in a material sense if my parents found out, but I still wanted them in my life until I figured out how to come out to them in the best way, considering their predispositions.

But nothing could compromise my date with Antonio. I was not letting anyone get in the way of that. It was rare to find such an interesting guy, especially in a small town like this. I didn't feel desperate, but the thought of messing things up with him and having no other guys on the island to even meet was a scary thought. Plus, I wanted something real, and I wanted to start it off right.

I decided to ignore Joshua's messages and the calls as they eventually came rolling in while I finished my tea, gazing out the kitchen window at the swaying pine trees along the back fence. The house was heating up from the day's sunshine. I wanted to let some air into the house for a nice breeze, but felt committed enough to go for a quick swim in the ocean to get away from my phone and from my thoughts. It wasn't uncommon for Joshua to call and message back to back, but it bothered me more than ever before.

I ran across the hot sand and down to the beach with nothing but my bathing suit. The breeze from before died down to intermittent gusts of warm humid wind that felt like a second skin. When I reached the cold, wet sand I could tell that the water was going to be freezing, but I didn't slow down. I was on a mission to conquer the water. I wanted to see what life would be like on the other side.

I high-kneed over the first couple of waves before diving in when it got deep enough. I pushed myself forward against the icy current as it tumbled over me, numbing my skin with shock. Every part of my body was screaming at me to turn around and run up the beach, to run to the sun, but I swam on, coming up for air and dunking myself under again to continue on. My arms and legs were paddles and propellers, and I willed myself forward. How long I planned to swim for, I didn't know, but I turned around when I reached about fifty yards out and swam back up to where the waves were crashing at the break. It was exactly what I needed. As I approached the shoreline, I rode in a wave taller than a bus that came out of nowhere. Then I dove under the water in the direction of the sea to swim out and do it all over again.

After a few back and forths, my body was warm with adrenaline and an electric joy from the playfulness of the ocean. Not even the way the wind blew at the shore was a comparison for the strength with which the ocean moved me along, crashed down over me, and offered up tremendous waves for me to ride and dive into. Every second in the ocean brought a different experience. Each wave deserved and demanded special attention as they grew up and rolled into curls, where one unaware second could lead to tragedy.

Floating on my back, over the deep water where the waves started forming up into hills, I stared up into the clear blue sky. There wasn't much to not be thankful for with the depths of the sea stretching down far below me.

When I returned to shore, I wasn't sure how much time had

passed, but the sun was still hot in the sky. Beaded with ocean water, I climbed up the incline of the beach, letting the sun dry me while I soaked up its UVs, hoping my skin would start tanning enough to show Antonio that I wasn't a hermit who never left his house. City life preserved winter paleness even in the most active city lifestyles. But I liked how, as the water droplets dried on my skin, small crusts of salt were left in their places. Where I found the rough crystalline patches, I rubbed them in, exfoliating my arms and hands until all I felt was powder.

I dreaded returning to my phone, so I decided that the shower would be my best next move. For the first time in a long time, standing there on the empty beach, I felt a power running through my body. It was a feeling I remembered feeling as a kid. Every inch of my skin felt charged with electricity. My stomach felt like a hot bowl of sloshing soup, and I could feel the tendrils of something more attempting to burst out as I climbed the hot dune.

After the ocean washed it away, the veiled depression that Joshua evoked in me returned the moment I picked up my phone again. I had a list of notifications from him. Text messages, half a dozen missed calls, and voicemails all proving to me that he was not giving up. He was staying in a house on the other side of the island with his family for the next two weeks as part of a family retreat.

I couldn't think of a worse situation to involve myself in while trying to get more involved with Antonio, but even without getting involved, my situation became a lot more complicated. Joshua and his cousins were spending the afternoon at the vegan café with a tropical theme, according to one of his messages. Two of his cousins and his mom were all newly vegan and loved the place, another message informed.

Joshua had a family with eight first cousins, two parents, and an extended family of two aunts, two uncles, and all the other cousins they towed around with them on vacation.

Leaving the bungalow without being seen by one of them seemed to be an impossible feat. I was upset, angry, and horny, but I didn't want to risk being seen by Joshua after only just escaping his irritating antics. But, despite the millions of scenarios that swarmed my mind of Antonio and I running into Joshua's family at the restaurant, I had to go to dinner.

To try to loosen up the knot of stress in my stomach, I warmed up a cup of lemon water and agave before my shower. And in the mess of Joshua's notifications I didn't notice until I took my first sip that I had an unread message from Antonio. He wanted to confirm our "date" tomorrow, he said, and I couldn't have been more excited to answer him back.

CHAPTER FIVE

TAKEN BY THE WAVES

ANTONIO AND I MESSAGED back and forth until I fell asleep, finally unafraid of the big bad Bailey bunch. Thankfully, the messages from Joshua slowed down to a trickle overnight, with the morning awarding me not a single message from him until eleven. I figured by the evening time he would stop completely, but after consideration, I determined that it would be useful for me if he were to continue his persistent updates on his movements around the island, just so that I wouldn't once find myself in the same place as him.

Though, it was the whole Bailey bunch that I had to worry about being found by, which made the next two weeks of his stay look to me like a nightmare realized. I had a long fourteen days ahead.

Once the clock came to five-thirty, I would be at Antonio's will. I didn't tell him about Joshua or go into detail about my anxieties over the Bailey bunch over text message. I avoided all such conversation, though their presence was at the top of my mind as Antonio explored ideas for after dinner. I was afraid the restaurant sounded too much like somewhere the Baileys would get a kick out of going to for a fun Friday night out.

"I'm going to make sure you have a great night," Antonio messaged. "You have a lot to celebrate." Antonio was making the night all about me, in a way that no one ever had.

By the time five o'clock came around, I'd completed work for the day, pushed through a quick run down the beach to get the blood pumping, and showered myself into a date-ready, groomed, and handsome looking beach boy. With the start of a nice tan coming through. I finished myself at the bathroom mirror, checking my hair and taking the opportunity to clean up my eyebrows. The final steps were a quick floss and an oral swish and rinse, and I was feeling good in my beige pants and blue button up.

I hadn't yet seen Antonio outside of work, so I had no idea what he would be wearing, but I was confident I wouldn't want to take my eyes off of him when I saw him. By the time I left the mirror, with a kiss to myself for good luck, I was confident he wouldn't be able to keep his eyes off of me either.

Antonio pulled up to the bungalow in a black hybrid Toyota Avalon. I knew the type because I almost picked one up before I saw the Jeep. It was a nice ride, and it shined in the island sun on the curb. I could see him in his car from inside the house through the bay window of the lounge, but he wasn't looking to see me. His attention was on his lap. Then my phone buzzed.

"Here!" Came through on my phone screen.

Yes you are, I thought, and I said good night to the bungalow on my way out the door.

Outside the sky was bright blue. The sun was shining at us from the bay side of the island, having crossed the sky over the course of the day. Antonio's car sat idling at the curb, and I let myself in beside him.

"Hey," I said, as I got in. I closed the door and took a closer look at him with my heart drum rolling in my chest.

"Hey," Antonio said. "It's good to see you."

"It's good to see you too," I said, unsure of my words and how they came out with my heightened nerves. I couldn't deny that my attraction to him was electric in all the proper places, and that it distracted me more than I thought possible.

He looked even better than in the days before. His hair was neatly styled with gel and pushed up in the front, the way the New York models do.

He seemed a lot more relaxed than I felt, but he was inspecting me the way I was inspecting him. There was a tension between us that I couldn't ignore. I expected, at any moment, the resistance holding us back from each other would snap, sending our heads forward and smacking together.

"You look great," Antonio said, after too many moments of silent staring at each other.

"Thank you," I said. "You like the vibes?" I asked, pulling at my shirt's neck. "I wanted to look the part of wealthy beach-house owner while I had the chance."

"You're killing it," Antonio said, and I already had him laughing in his seat. He was wearing a pair of tight fitted beige shorts and a black silky looking button up with a golden shimmering calligraphy that I couldn't identify.

"Thank you," I said. "That shirt looks great on you. I didn't know if you'd still have on your barista apron."

"No," he said, "I could never. This night is for pleasure, not business." And like a movie star he took the shifter in hand and looked at me squarely. "You ready?" he said, squinting an eye.

"More than ever," I said, buckling my seat belt before he pulled onto the street.

For an island guy, Antonio took care of his car's interior. It was a chore keeping beach sand out of fabric, and there wasn't a grain of it in the whole interior of his Toyota.

"These poles here were the reason I couldn't make it over to the café yesterday," I said while Antonio waited to make the left hand turn onto the avenue. The new poles at the corners to the main road were fresh looking wooden trunks, still green with weather-treatment. "I was tortured with the phantom flavor of your coffee for the last two days."

"Oh, yeah," Antonio said with a laugh. "It's hard to forget good coffee once you have it. I'll have to send you home with some home brewers next time." He was glancing at the upturned orange dirt at the base of the poles. "A lot of these older poles have been going down across the island as they try to replace them all, but these new ones should hold up. Better to start fresh with the new move. You shouldn't have to worry about any other storms taking out your power," he said, and turned left onto the main road. "But the weather has gotten more severe out here over the last few years," he added. "Hurricanes like never seen before. I'm sure you remember hurricane Sandy?"

I knew exactly the storm he was talking about before he finished. Hurricane Sandy was a bad "SuperStorm" as they called it at the time, because three storm fronts met to form SuperStorm Sandy on the Jersey shore in the fall of 2012. It devastated Caribbean islands on its path of destruction Northward, and even impacted communities up in New York. In my own community, families with summer beach homes were freaking out and flocking down to Jersey with truckloads of repair supplies after stocking up at the local hardware stores once the storm passed over us.

"Yeah, I can't forget that," I said. "I was in high school at that time. I remember one of my friend's cousins posted a video of himself on Facebook standing out in the street over in Mystic Island, leaning against the wind and rain in a tank top and boxers. Big American flag in hand, flapping like a bat."

"I saw that, too," Antonio said, laughing with me. "People do crazy things during crazy times."

"Yeah they do," I said. Both sides of the street had decent traffic flow, with the dinner rush beginning for the locals and early season vacationers.

"So how've you been since last night?" Antonio said as he drove. He kept his attention on the road, but seemed eager to turn the conversation to me. My focus on getting ready for the date had kept my mind off of Joshua and his family, but Antonio's question triggered the reality of the looming presence of the Baileys. But I didn't know how much I wanted to share about them out of sheer embarrassment, and I wasn't afraid to admit that to myself.

"I had a great day," I said. "I was mostly focused on work. I have a new cover I'm working on, and it's really coming along." Diversion away from my fears felt like the best route to take.

"That's great," Antonio said. "You have to remember to show me your work when I drop you off. I'd love to see this latest one. What style are you going for this time?"

"I'll remember to show you," I said, happily receiving the honor of welcoming Antonio into the bungalow. "Right now I'm working on a nine-teen forties' jazz scene cover for a historical-fiction novel about a jazz band that traveled up and down the East Coast, singing their sounds with pockets full of jive."

"That sounds like a novel I'd want to read," Antonio said.

"Jazz and jive are a hell of a combination."

"I couldn't come up with a better way to end the night," I said, feeling bold and hoping Antonio couldn't hear the panic of my heart.

"That sounds perfect to me," Antonio confirmed, catching a look at me from the corner of his eye.

"Is the restaurant nearby?" I asked, unable to beat down the grin plastered across my face.

"Yeah," Antonio said. "It's just a few blocks further. You'll notice when we get there."

"Okay," I said. "Sounds like a challenge."

About a minute up the road I saw the building, and I was stunned. It wasn't a challenge at all. We pulled into the rocky parking lot, and along the waterline was a raised Japanese style temple resting on stilts. I felt like we were on our way to dine in a different century, making me feel underdressed compared to the formality of the past. The red painted logs constructing the ocean view restaurant were as iconically Japanese as the pitched roof of old Japanese architecture that topped the building. Around the restaurant walls was a wrap-around deck, with tables along the sides and around the back of the building. A number of customers and waitstaff were congregated at the front doors, making the place appear to be crowded. I could discern a good amount of tourists and locals in the mix out front, making me believe the place had to be good. The waitstaff was dressed as authentically as the building looked, each wearing a spectacular ornamental gold, red, or black kimono. I hoped the sanctifying presence of the place was enough to ward off the evil of Joshua and his family.

"I was not expecting this," I said, in awe. Antonio parked

in an empty spot out front and turned to me. I couldn't pull my eyes away from the place.

"Aren't you glad I didn't spoil the surprise?" he asked.

"Absolutely," I said, nodding my head. "But, I wouldn't have believed you even if you described it."

"My friends' family own the place," Antonio said. "They've been here on the Jersey Shore for generations. They moved from Japan during some of the earliest years of Japanese immigration into North America, settling here for the bay and the ocean. They appreciated the seafood bounty as much as every other group that's called these islands home."

"That's incredible," I said, as impressed with the history of the shore town as I was with Antonio's stature of acquaintances.

"Is your friend going to be here tonight?" I asked, eager to meet the people Antonio called friends. My lack of friends to share didn't bother me at that moment, but it was a truth that did make me feel insecure.

"Yes," Antonio said. "The two owners are siblings. Brother and sister. They'll both be performing live music tonight, too. You'll see. Come on."

With the car snug in a spot, Antonio cut the engine and opened his door to leave. I followed him through the parking lot and up the large wooden staircase that led to the patio, feeling like I just landed in Disney's Epcot, having never been to Japan, myself. Everything from the wood, to the presence of the building seemed more authentic than all of franchise-era America. Following Antonio up the front red-stained wooden steps felt like walking up a monument.

When I reached the deck, I scanned the faces in the crowd for any sign of resemblance to the Bailey lineage, just to be sure of no surprises before taking in the magnificence of the building up close. The same red stained wood used for the steps was also used to construct the actual building. The stain went deep, but I could still make out the rings in the weathered wood from the trees that the trunks used to be.

I waited with Antonio in the line leading up to the outdoor hostess stand, trying to get a view of the inside, but I couldn't see anything beyond the wall of people except the dark vaulted ceiling of a dark hall when the dark wood doors opened.

When we reached the host stand, the hostesses were gathered waiting to help us. Three of the women wore red kimonos, while the woman standing at the head of the stand set herself aside from the rest by wearing a silk white kimono with textured pink trails of what looked like flower petals snaking down the sides and back of her dress. Antonio greeted her with a wide armed hug and stood back to introduce me.

"Kana, this is Dylan," he said. "He's a new to towner. I couldn't let him go his first whole week without trying your food."

"That would be cruel! Don't you dare," Kana said to Antonio with a laugh before turning to me. "Welcome to the island," she said. "It's a pleasure to meet you." She clasped her hands at her chest and tilted her head with warmth. "My name is Kana. My brother and I run this place together with our staff. Antonio is family to us, and so are you. Welcome."

She was measured and deliberate in how she spoke. She had the glow of young adult-hood with the seriousness of a widow, but any ounce of uncertainty in me was kept at bay by her hospitality.

"Thank you so much," I said. "Your restaurant is beautiful."

"Ah, thank you," Kana said. "Ikkyu will appreciate hearing that when I tell him. Antonio spoke with me earlier about arranging a table in the center near the stage, so you'll both be up front for the show."

"Ikkyu is your brother?" I asked Kana. "And Ikkyu is your friend?" I asked Antonio, surprised by the connection.

"Yes...," Antonio said. "He's my friend and her brother. Do you know him?"

"Yeah, he's my landlord for John Eastman," I said.

"Ikkyu does a lot across the island, you'll find," Antonio said. "It's like that on small seasonal islands like this."

"Yes it is," Kana said. "I'm sure Ikkyu will be all the more pleased that you're here then, Dylan. Let me take you to your seats. You're going to enjoy this very much." Kana passed me a smile that let me know I would find out what was so special about what she meant and gathered two of the wood bound menus from the stack on the hostess stand.

"Best seats in the house," Antonio confirmed.

"Follow me," she said when she was ready, pushing open the heavy wooden front doors.

Kana led us into a narrow dim hall with a high vaulted ceiling and dark walls that felt like the way into an exclusive backroom event space. At the end, the hall opened up to a large open dining room, lit by the light from the windows that lined the far and side perimeters of the room. The view of the ocean just beyond the wrap around deck gave the room the feeling that we were on a ship, or simply floating above the ocean.

I noticed the diners weren't the normal beachwear wearing beach crowd. These guests were tucked into tables enjoying their drinks and food in neat outfits, making the expensive room look all the more exclusive. Collared shirts and summer dresses were everywhere, and I was relieved to discover not a single Bailey face among them.

The layout of the room was a series of nesting squares,

with a stage in the middle of the room, ringed by a sunken level of tables that sat low to the ground, while the two outer rings had the usual tables and chairs. We followed down one of the four pathways through the two outer rings and into the center square around the stage. Kana stopped at one of the floor tables inside the recessed section and kneeled down to place our menus on the low table.

"Front row seats for the show," Kana said, stepping back from the table to let us into our booth. "For our most front worthy guests."

"Thank you, Kana," I said, eager to sit and look at the menu. I assumed they had sushi, which I loved, but I wanted to see what else there was to try.

Antonio took a moment to speak with Kana in hushed, what I assumed to be, Japanese. There was nothing pressing about their tone, so I didn't think anything of the content, but the fact that Antonio spoke English, Spanish, which I had heard him speaking at the café, and Japanese blew away my expectations. At the end of their short back and forth, it looked like Kana affirmed something Antonio seemed concerned about, but I couldn't tell if it was serious or casual. Kana departed a moment later, leaving Antonio and I alone. With Kana gone, Antonio's attention was finally, undividedly, given to me, and he looked like he didn't want it any other way.

"Here, let's sit," Antonio said. "Take off your shoes."

I watched him proceed to slip his feet out of his shoes before sliding them into the shoe cubby built into the side of the partitions that separated the booths. The table was low, like low low, with a booth that I had to step down into. I watched Antonio step and slide into the seat of the booth like an Air Force pilot settling into a fighter jet while I slipped my shoes off, stored them away, and settled into the booth across from him. The below floor seating and the half walls at our backs made it feel like we had our own private room across from the stage.

Chado, I remembered. The place was already better than any of the five-star restaurants my parents treated themselves to. Joining my parents for nights out to such places would start with high hopes, but upon reaching our destination I would clam up into my shell, overwhelmed by the crowds, and become drained from the exposure of managing myself around them in public.

"This might be the coolest place on the island," I said. "Ten times better than the cafés here."

Antonio feigned shame, bowing his head. "You're not wrong," he said.

"You'll reach this level one day, I'm sure," I said, enjoying the banter. "When did you have the chance to learn Japanese on your busy schedule?"

"I learned from Kana and Ikkyu," Antonio explained.

"That's impressive," I said, always baffled by the acquisition of languages. "You must have spent a lot of time with them over the years?" I said, feeling more open to asking long-answer questions now that we were settled in for dinner. Antonio took a second to consider, looking above my head as if counting the number of years.

"I've spent a lot of time with them," he said. "They're practically family to me."

"That's great you got to learn so much from them," I said.

"It's been an experience like no other," Antonio said, smiling at me with a definitive nod. "I'll show you why. One reason is their taste in tea. Their selection here is phenomenal. Do you like tea?"

Antonio pointed to the top of the menu where the drinks were listed. Under "Cha" was a list of teas written with both English and Japanese names.

"I do like tea," I said, recognizing some of the names. "I've heard of Sencha before, and I drink white tea. But I haven't heard of Gyokuro, Kabusecha, Shincha, or… Genmaicha. I've had good matcha back at NYU, but I'm sure it's nothing compared to what they have here."

"Well, whatever you'd like to try, I'm sure they'll send you home with pounds of it, just so you never have to drink bad tea ever again," Antonio said. "They believe, in the least, everybody deserves to drink good tea."

I laughed at the thought of myself walking out of the restaurant with bags of tea leaves in my hands, hoping the tea would be as good as the Silver Needle in my cupboard at the bungalow.

"And what do you believe?" I asked, prodding him to see what would come out. "Everybody deserves good coffee?"

"No," he said. "Mine is, everybody deserves to drink Puerto Rican coffee!"

Despite my involuntary eye roll, I liked his humor.

"Okay, Mr. farm-to-mug," I said. "Which tea should we try?"

"Hey, being farm-to-mug is a lot of work," Antonio said. "Sencha's my favorite meal-time tea, and I usually like to finish the meal with a bowl of matcha and a plate of assorted mochi with fruit. Everything on the menu was created by Ikkyu and Kana. But you really can't go wrong with any of their recipes or their teas."

"Let's start with the Sencha then," I said, my stomach starting to feel hollow. The smell of food in the air was thick and enticing. "This menu is huge," I added, thumbing through the few pages of listed items. Every dish was an entirely different Japanese meal. "How did they come up with all of this?"

"Generations of knowledge," Antonio said. "Now, I did say that I'd bring you here for sushi, but order anything you think sounds good. I've had it all. You can't go wrong."

As I read the menu items, I couldn't believe two people created every dish. Some of the recipes, surely, had to be passed down from parents and grandparents. Antonio's group of savvy friends were exactly the type of people I would have loved to have acquainted in New York City, and I was starting to feel robbed of my time there.

Getting lost in the menu descriptions was like a dream. Everything sounded delicious, and, while not everything was vegan, most of it was. The Japanese meals seemed to use meat and fish as an additive rather than the main feature of individual dishes. The variety of rice, noodle, and sushi dishes flummoxed me with the momentary indecision one experiences when hungry to try everything but required to choose only one option.

"Sushi sounds good," I said, unable to detach myself from my days long desire for sushi rolls draped with pickled ginger. "I'll try the shiitake and sweet potato rolls to start, and I'll have the spicy miso ramen for my meal."

"Great choices," Antonio said, making faces over his menu in amusing contemplation. "I think I'll have the same thing. It'll be like we're sharing a meal like at home."

"That's a great idea," I said, his charm sincere and endearing. I wasn't sure what to make of him. It wasn't my very first date, and I doubted I could have been his first date. But everything about the experience felt new. And for some reason, I felt like Antonio felt the same way too.

A second later, Kana returned to our table. Her white and cherry blossom pink kimono folded around her knees as she knelt beside us.

"Have the two of you decided?" Kana asked, her voice level and smooth. While Antonio was more of an energetic goof, Kana carried herself ready to be speaking keynote at a status quo business seminar if the desire enticed her. Their friendship seemed like it would be awkward, but they both had deeper, more serious sides to them that I sensed I'd learn more about.

"Of course," Antonio said, closing his menu, and offering me the first go at ordering with an open hand.

"I'd like to start with a sweet potato roll and a shiitake mushroom roll," I said. "And I'll have miso ramen with tofu for my meal. I can't wait to try your recipes."

"Well, thank you," Kana said. "Ikkyu is in the kitchen getting ready to prepare the dishes for the two of you. The recipe for the miso ramen was a labor of love by the both of us. I can't wait for you to try. And Antonio?"

"I'm having the same thing," Antonio said. "I'll add a pot of the premium sencha along with an order of kanzake."

Kana clasped her hands in her lap and bowed her head in approval.

"We'll start serving right away," Kana said. "I'll be back around with your tea and kanzake. The sushi will be around shortly."

"Thank you," I said, and Kana got up to return to work.

"My pleasure," Kana said, before walking away, smiling at her guests as she made her way through the inner dining square and back up to the front of the restaurant.

"What was the other thing you ordered?" I asked Antonio. I

wasn't sure what kanzake was, but I was up for trying new things.

"It's warm rice wine," Antonio said. "The kanzake they serve is some of the best sake in the country. Kana and Ikkyu have their own distillery here on the island."

"Wow, they don't cut any corners here, do they?" I asked, again surprised by my hosts.

"Not at all," Antonio said. "We all want to share tradition with society. We want to offer people elevated experiences in dining, or in coffee drinking. Everything is considered for the pleasure of the guest."

"That's very different from most other businesses in America," I said.

"It is," Antonio agreed.

"How do you manage that contrast when big business says it can't be done without charging obscene prices and alienating half the market?" I asked.

"It's simple, I think," Antonio said. "Our business models are designed to produce the greatest quality for the greatest masses. By taking a lot of the production and manufacturing on for ourselves we're able to cut costs and keep quality. We also don't need millions in profits to make investors happy."

"Well, the proof of all of your success is clear and all around us," I said. "Maybe making customers happy is the best investment a business can make. I've never thought of opening a business myself, but I suppose my art is a business. I'd have loved to design this restaurant setting for a cover. I love the raw red wood logs, the dark table tops and floors, and the heavenly light from the ring of windows around the room."

Antonio smiled and looked around, as if testing my observations. "If you were to create a cover in the image of this restaurant, what would you try to convey?" Antonio asked.

The question prompted a second of contemplation. It felt like a trick question, and that feeling was reinforced by a sly smirk that spread across Antonio's lips. However, I was privy to the meaning of my work, so I wanted to think about it. Luckily, Kana came with our drinks and took her time handing them out.

"Here you are," she said, kneeling beside our table with a bamboo tray propped on her hand, carrying an assortment of pitchers and cups. First, Kana rested what looked like a cast iron tea kettle onto an iron circle that sat depressed into the center of the wooden table. Then she placed down a smaller tea pot made of a terracotta colored smooth clay. The pot looked squished, with a flat reservoir and an attached handle off to the side rather than on the back of it. Then, Kana rested a similar looking empty pitcher beside the tea pot. The pitcher was made of the same clay and in the same flat style, but it had a wide rim and an open top, with a depression for a spout with no neck. Two small porcelain sip cups followed. I wasn't sure of the purpose for so many vessels, but I was excited to find out.

"And here is our house sencha," Kana said, extending out her hand to place down the tight lidded clay bowl onto the table beside the tea pot. "I'll allow Antonio to brew to his heart's content," Kana said, giving Antonio a look that said she didn't want to bother with his particularity.

"Wonderful," Antonio said, smiling at her, exposing a hint of mischief in his intent.

"This is the kanzake," Kana said. This time, she placed down a set of a stone pitcher and cups collected on a stone serving dish. The tall vase-like pitcher looked like it could fit nearly a whole bottle of wine.

Antonio and I both thanked her before she hurried away

to another part of the restaurant.

"I would attempt to capture the experience of the place, if I were to create such a place in art," I said to Antonio, after Kana left us. "That's what I do for every cover I create. I emphasize the experience of the novel, or the experience of a particular place in that novel. This would be a setting to tell a great story."

"Ah," Antonio said. "What type of story would be set here, do you think?"

"Hmm," I said, looking around and taking in the salty rich smells and the murmured sounds of the restaurant. "Easily a mystery, or something magical. It's an enchanting place. Enchanted places always have secrets," I said. The temple design gave the inside of the building a sanctuary like aura, like the clean feeling of a well maintained and perfumed church.

"How would you portray mystery in a cover using this place?" Antonio asked. I didn't know where to begin. I was about to protest, but then I thought better of it and decided to see what I could come up with.

"For a mystery, I would frame the stage at night in the center of the cover. The world outside the windows would shine in a dim haze of moonlight. The stars would be as visible as the lights on passing ships. The dining room would be empty, and the stage would be lit. I might add a clue to the mystery if I think it would look good. The title would be in the dark red of the roof peak, with the author's name along the bottom of the stage."

"'That would be fantastic," Antonio said, looking impressed. "And what type of story are you designing for yourself, here on the island?" Antonio asked.

"I'm not sure," I said, enjoying the way he asked. "Haven't thought much about it."

My lips registered my reply as a big fat lie before the words left my mouth. The answer was clear to me once I met Antonio. I craved a romance story, but I couldn't tell him that. I needed to remember back, past the inconvenience of Joshua, past the joy of meeting Antonio. I had to remember back to when I was riding in the Jeep alone, cruising down the Garden State Parkway, with the road like a ribbon as far as I could see. Back to when the road was my long gray ticket to freedom.

"I just wanted space to figure out how I want to be in the world," I said. "I'm not sure what that genre would be, but it would definitely have some action and adventure."

"Oh, yeah?" Antonio asked. "Like skydiving?"

"Yeah, or no, not skydiving, necessarily," I said. "I've been jogging along the beach and swimming out into the surf and swimming back in. I've upped my morning workouts, and I think I'll be ready to try paddle boarding again. I love going jet skiing. That's adventure and action."

"That's about as much action and adventure as you'll get on this island," Antonio said. "Now, Puerto Rico is an island full of action and adventures. You would love it there. There's a place for everybody in Puerto Rico."

"It sounds like a great place," I said. "I'd love to go. I want to see the rainforest and the beaches. My grandfather used to tell me about the rainforest, and how Roosevelt expanded the protected forest. El Yunque?"

"El Yunque," Antonio confirmed. "It is a spectacle to experience. It's just as mysterious as here, though."

I didn't know what Antonio meant by the last part, but he seemed to quickly back away from the subject. His attention refocused on the tea before us, which he reached for, smiling as if it had just arrived.

"Well, this isn't an interrogation," Antonio said. "Let's

drink. This tea is what we should be discussing."

Antonio held up the small clay container and removed the lid to display to me the collected vibrant green strands of soft needle-shaped Japanese green tea leaves.

"I've never seen green tea like that before," I said, perplexed by the complexity of something as simple and settled as tea always was to me. The emerald strands appeared to shine with an oily finish, like a fresh bag of roasted coffee beans.

"Have a smell," Antonio said, extending the bowl my way and up to my nose. The scent of the tea was the scent of fresh green leaves and lemon zest, with a warm buttery nose feel. The tea immediately took me to a bright sunny field with rows of tea plants shaking in the wind against a clear mountain sky, but I couldn't ignore how close Antonio's hand was to my face. Another smell of the tea brought the scent of Antonio's skin to my nose, turning me into an anxious mess. The slightest notion of intimacy was enough to pump my heart rate into panic attack range.

"Now, I'm not sure I've ever had a proper cup of green tea before," I said, pulling away from him. Antonio lowered the bowl and shook a good portion of leaves into the handled clay teapot. "I've never had one that smelled anything like this."

"I believe it," Antonio said. "Tea is so much better than the typical American experience of it. Tea here is synonymous with brands etched into peoples' minds. This tea has hundreds of years of cultivation and expertise, meaning this tea has a history older than this entire country."

Antonio poured water from the cast iron kettle into the clay teapot and over the leaves. The green strands swirled around the pot as the waterfall of steaming water filled the reservoir. Antonio then placed the lid on top and sat back in his seat. The scent of the tea had already hit my nose as the dry leaves awoke with hydration, and the steam lifted its essence into the air.

Antonio only let the tea steep for a few seconds before he grasped the handle of the teapot and tilted it sideways, pouring out a clean looking green liquor. It collected into the clay pitcher, releasing torrents of steam as it settled. Then, from the pitcher, Antonio poured us each a serving into our small tea cups.

Once in the sipping cup, the tea stopped steaming and looked cool enough to taste. I lifted mine to my lips, admiring the thickness of the swirling greenish yellow liquor. It smelled like a clean coastal mountain breeze. When I sipped, the flavor of floral lemon biscuits tingled over my taste buds, and at the tip of my tongue and in every crevice of my mouth the tea flooded over, was tinged with bitterness. After I swallowed, the walls of my mouth were left with a tight bitter sensation that invigorated salivation. The aroma from the sip was so strong it lingered on my breath.

"Now I see why there's been so much hype over green tea," I said, adapting to my post-sip self.

Antonio laughed, and I was feeling refreshed and relaxed at the same time, in a way that was different from caffeine's familiar effects on me.

"This is just the beginning," Antonio said, refilling our cups with the tea still steaming in the pitcher. I was ready for another full cup. The flavor felt like a mouth full of hundreds of years of mountain top bright summer days. It was different than matcha.

After the second cup of tea, I felt ready to taste Kana's and Ikkyu's warm sake, and Antonio was happy to oblige. So, he poured us each out a healthy portion into the stoneware sake cup beside my porcelain tea cup.

"Now, sake is competitive based on how robust and distinct its flavors are," Antonio said. "The flavor profile is typically bright, floral, and herbal. We sip if we like the flavor, and we shoot it if we don't. If you serve it, you're always watching how people take the second cup."

"I'll be sure to sip," I said, looking around for Kana and Ikkyu.

Antonio cracked another smile for me, and I felt good about it. If all I had to offer were a few laughs and an artist's perspective, I was going to get what I could out of it.

Antonio took the sake all at once like a shot. I took it slow and let the liquor swirl around my mouth to try and pick out the flavors Antonio had referenced, but I couldn't taste anything beyond the alcoholic burn. After it raked my esophagus, leaving it raw and throbbing, I found the flavor in the aroma that came up from my sake warmed stomach. The seconds of agony turned into numb pleasure once the sake kicked in.

"Another?" Antonio asked.

"Sure," I said, enjoying the feeling. "But I'm shooting, not sipping."

Antonio laughed as he poured. "It's a dangerous game," he said. "You looked like you were about to cry for a second."

"Well, after tasting the tea, you kind of led me into a trap by telling me to pick out the flavors in the sake," I said.

Just then Kana returned with a pair of servers in matching red kimonos who were holding out trays with our sushi plates and ramen bowls. Kana served us from the trays. She set down the steaming bowls of noodles, vegetables, and broth before each of us and placed our sushi plates beside them. Everything was stunning. The sushi was vibrant and fresh looking, and the creamy looking ramen smelled like savory miso and Thai basil.

"Are you gentlemen enjoying yourselves?" Kana asked, kneeling to be at our level.

"Yes," I said. "The sencha and sake are the best I've had."

Antonio watched me as I spoke, smiling as I did, so I looked to him for his answer.

"Everything is great, Kana. Thank you," Antonio said, lifting his chin.

"Wonderful," Kana said.

Antonio went to say something more, but the building became dark, so the only light came from above the stage and from outside the windows.

"Ah," Kana said, gathering herself. "Enjoy your meals, and enjoy the show."

Kana departed with the two servers to the main dining room, while servers along the outside of the room started pulling curtains closed to black out the windows, making the light outlining the stage look all the more bright, until that too dimmed into darkness.

In the next second, Kana and, who looked to be, Ikkyu were illuminated on stage. Kana's white and pink peddled kimono dazzled under the stage light, and in her hands she held an instrument that I recognized as a shamisen, a type of three stringed guitar style instrument played with a large paddle to pluck the strings. I had no explanation for how quickly she had gotten on stage, but before I could question Antonio, Ikkyu let out a commanding breathy note from his long wooden flute.

I recognized the sound from so many of the video games the guys and I played that took place in Japan, but I couldn't remember what the instrument was called. Ikkyu's kimono was a dark gray with mint colored accent welting. I didn't want to look away from the couple, but something made me look over at Antonio. He was staring back at me hard, and as Ikkyu let out another breathy command from his flute, Antonio reached across the table and grabbed my hand. Then he nodded up at the stage. Stunned by his hand in mine, I followed his command.

Kana strummed her shamisen with the corner of the paddle, and pink sparks burst off the strings. I wanted to look at Antonio to confirm what I saw, but I couldn't look away. Ikkyu matched Kana's strum with a turbulent fluttering from his flute that sent plumes of green smoke out the mouth of it. The two of them together started playing fast, and every strum produced sparks, while every breath that ran through the flute produced green smoke that glowed like microscopic LED pixels, shimmering three-dimensionally in the air before him.

I imagined the audience was just as stunned as I was, because not a soul made a sound in the entire place. For all I knew, the whole universe was focused on Kana and Ikkyu performing what I could only explain as magic. The cherry blossom sparks and soft green smoke grew brighter as the song picked up from a back and forth duel, to a duet where Kana started strumming up and down for a waterfall effect like the back and forth of a harp. While the green smoke pouring from Ikkyu's flute pooled around his feet with its low wallows.

As the song progressed, Kana's sparks turned into silk like strands that sprung from the strings of her shamisen as she strummed them. The magic dispersed into a soft pink glow around her that became a haze that took over the air of the stage. Then Ikkyu's flute took the high lead in the song, and the magic flowed faster out. His magic grew to cover the floor of the stage with its iridescent glow and poured over the edge into the walkways as it crept outward. Then, the music grew heavy.

The new solemn tone of the flute caused the magic to move differently. The green smoke gathered in heaps around the stage and rose, collecting into the images of green figures that plumed into animation in the air of pink haze. It was hard to think of doing anything other than watching the display with the comfort of Antonio's hand still around mine atop the table. The sake made me loose, but not loose enough to keep me from being able to count to twelve. That's how many figures grew to stand around the stage. As Kana and Ikkyu played faster, the figures spread out their arms and started spinning from the waist like tornadoes. The pink mist grew dense around them, until the magic spun into a vortex of green and pink clouds, while the music roared and cracked with the electric energy of a lightning storm.

After a bit longer, the music died down, and Antonio released my hand. The magic that had been all around the room a second ago was gone. I didn't know what to make of it all. I looked to Antonio for answers, and a second later the lights came back on inside the restaurant. The blinds were opened. Kana and Ikkyu stood for a bow that beckoned more than an applause. Every seat in the room erupted with clapping. I joined the impressed lot, still unsure if they saw the same display I saw.

Then Kana left the stage, while Ikkyu knelt down center stage with his flute. As the applause quieted, Ikkyu started playing mellow tones that occupied the background of the returning restaurant conversation. I turned to my food for comfort from my hunger while I took a second to process the performance. Antonio was watching me stuff my mouth with a roll of sweet potato sushi blanketed with pickled ginger. The crunch of the ginger as I chewed told me it was fresh, and it was delicious.

"That was magical," I said, deciding to break the silence before too long. With the lights on and everyone going back to their normal behaviors, I started to wonder if what I had seen in the dark was real. I had a creative mind. I could have conjured up such a scene on a book cover, but the magic felt different from imagination. It felt already imagined and plopped into the real world. I had nothing to do with it but observe it. It was like the source of the mystery I imagined.

"You liked the music?" Antonio asked, bringing his hand to his face. The same one he held my hand with during the show. I almost forgot that detail through the mental struggle of trying to rationalize what I had seen, but it was his hand that cut the visual connection that I had with the magic at the end of the performance. My face must have betrayed the thoughts that were failing to form in my mind as a response, because Antonio looked at me with a concerned look, without offering any form of support. I didn't want to sound too outlandish, but I didn't want to discredit my experience either.

"Yeah, I did," I said. "What exactly was that?" I asked. "A fog machine?" I expected a laugh or explanation, because there was no fog anymore, but, instead, Antonio reached across the table for my hand again. I let him wrap his fingers around where he held a minute before. Then he held his other hand out like a bowl between us.

"Look," he said.

In the bowl of his hand sky blue magic started pooling like liquid. I could see it. I could hear it. And I could feel it. The liquid magic appeared from thin air, but it had more than just a visual presence. The magic hummed with energy.

It hummed like the buzz of a bee in my ears. I could feel it growing stronger as it grew brighter. A sensation emanated from it like the force of magnetic waves that I felt separate the molecules of my body as they pulsed through me.

"What?" I heard myself say. My head was spinning, and I felt like I needed something in my stomach. Upon releasing Antonio's hand, the magic disappeared, but the sensation remained. I could still feel the magic buzzing with power in the pool of his palm. Then he reached for my hand again.

This time I gave it to him, ready. As I became accustomed to the sensation of the power tearing apart the molecules of my body, I wanted to once again see the source of the effect. When Antonio took my hand, the sky blue magic flicked back into my vision, and it felt like Antonio walked me into a dream that showed me how little I knew about reality. I wasn't sure why he was sharing it with me, but I was already taken by the waves.

CHAPTER SIX

THE ATOMIC ROOT OF EVERYTHING

"THIS IS AURIC ENERGY," Antonio said, sounding more serious than before. Everyone in the restaurant was back to their own business, leaving Antonio and I locked in conversation in our private recessed booth.

"Like electromagnetic energy?" I asked. "That's what it feels like."

"Ah, you feel it," Antonio said, looking impressed. "You're somewhat correct. Aura is the energy of life. It's electric, magnetic, spiritual, mental, and metaphysical. It's probably a bunch more things too, but you get the point. It's like the essence of everything."

As Antonio talked, the auric energy swelled in his hand without spilling over his palm, until it rose into a bright blue ball the size of a baseball. The auric ball was bright and seemed to be made of light, but grew smokey around the edges, where it dissipated into tendrils of mist. I held my free hand nearer to the ball to see if I could feel any heat or chill, but didn't feel either sensation.

"What would happen if I touch it?" I asked, feeling more intense electromagnetic waves as my hand got closer.

"It will do whatever I make it do," Antonio said.

"Interesting," I said. "Tell me more." Dozens of questions filled a que in my head that I wanted the answers to all at once, so I decided to sink into my bowl of ramen and let Antonio talk.

When I pulled my hand out of his, the aura filling his upturned palm flicked out of my vision like a lamp flicking off in a room.

"Life is submissive to will," Antonio said. "That is one of the key principles of aurics, as we call it."

"Got it," I said. Life is submissive to will. I liked the principle, even if I didn't fully understand it. "But isn't it also true that without life there would be no will? So, it would be that will is submissive to life."

"You're right," Antonio said. "But life without the will to live is not life at all. Life is what you will it, and that is especially true for those who know how to wield their will the way we do." Antonio said. Before continuing, he took a sip of broth from his spoon and licked his lips. "It's really as simple as that."

"Okay," I said. "So, who is 'we?'" I asked, taking my first spoonful of noodles. Each soft strand dripped with warm salty, miso, sea herb flavored broth.

"There are a lot of us out there," Antonio said. "I don't have exact numbers, but some will good. And some will bad. Some just will to live a life somewhere in between if they can. Kana, Ikkyu, and I are on the good side of the spectrum. Ikkyu's wife Zenda is here on the island. There are many of us good Immortal Philosophers all around the world. I'm the newest member of our group, but there's a lot of other good guys and bad guys and associated groups out there. More bad guys than good guys, of course. I don't have exact numbers for the bad guys either. It just ain't easy for us in most places."

Antonio took another pause. This time he went for some noodles, undoubtedly feeling more hungry as we progressed into the evening of reality shattering conversation.

"When did you join?" I asked, taking advantage of his pause and asking the first question that I could articulate. I poured myself some more tea and kanzake from their pitchers while he chewed his noodles.

"I've been with them my whole life," Antonio said. "I'm the youngest Immortal Philosopher, by far. Everyone else is older. Our group is led by Aurelius. You know him as Eastman, but a few of our members are even older than him."

"Eastman, too?" I asked, starting to see more of the connections that brought me to Ocean City in the first place. "And, how old are you?" I asked, figuring out what to think.

"I was born December twenty-ninth nineteen eighty. I'm only thirty-nine," Antonio said. I wasn't shocked that Antonio was older than he looked, but it was shocking that he looked no older than my twenty-four. "And yes, Eastman too. Though he's much older."

"Kana and Ikkyu must be around your age though?" I asked, emphasizing the 'around.' Everything about the immortals was a mystery. For the first time in a long time I didn't know what to expect. It felt like I was sitting down with one of those book fair books about dragons or fairies, learning about the secret history of new mythical creatures.

"One of the ways we use aurics," Antonio said. "Is to will the preservation of life. There's a lot that goes into it, but it's a long, if not endless, life. Ikkyu and Kana were born around the year fourteen hundred in Japan. Aurelius was Roman. Second century AD."

"They've been around a long time," I said, not understanding what a person would do with so many years, or what those years would do to a person. It was impossible for me to conceptualize, so I accepted them as immortals with powers of gods who lived normal lives forever. My knowledge of ancient history wasn't anything to brag about, so the dates didn't mean much to me. "Roman and feudal Japan sound like interesting time periods to come from," I said.

"You have no idea," Antonio said. "Our time right now isn't too bad. Safest period in history, if you think about it. I'm still on my first run through of life. I haven't had much opportunity to live outside of the world of the Immortal Philosophers. I didn't grow up normally, unlike you."

Antonio slurped another mouthful of noodles.

"What do you mean?" I asked, not fully believing I had a 'normal' upbringing, but more interested in learning more about his life.

I watched him mull over his response to get a long look at his eyes. Antonio was the one thing I couldn't keep my mind from returning to no matter what Antonio threw at me. His Ronaldo-like physique and looks were something I couldn't ignore. I imagined the feeling similar to that of viewing a work of art and being brought to a place of pure admiration. Antonio's soft charm, clean shaven, sun tanned cheeks, playful mouth, and dazzling eyes turned me into a reveler. It was a captivating feeling I wasn't sure I'd ever be able to shake, even if the two of us had eternity together.

"I was very powerful at a young age," Antonio said.

"Is that normal for people like you?" I asked.

"It can be," Antonio said. "But usually only when encouraged or taught. I was very attune with my aura and was able to use it even as an infant. I was a newborn living in an orphanage. It was run by nuns and visited by priests. The nuns were very discreet in their sharing of what went on at the orphanage, but they couldn't help but talk about me. They saw lights and some small displays of power that brought the priests in to determine the likelihood between me being some kind of godly prophet or some kind of demon that they needed to dispose of with discretion." Antonio laughed to himself, as if his retelling of his potential religious sacrifice was amusing to him.

"Luckily," he continued. "Aurelius's contacts tipped him off about the infant with supernatural powers. That's how he came around to rescue me and raise me under more capable guidance."

"So Aurelius, Eastman, raised you?" I asked, not believing the hard lined boss man could be capable of giving a child as much attention as one needed, and generally stunned by the rest of his story. But then again, I wasn't sure if Aurelius was even the same person as he was when he was Eastman.

"He raised me as the best father I could have asked for," Antonio said. "Kana and Ikkyu helped. Zenda helped too. Everyone else kind of came and went as they progressed through the lives they lived in other places under different names. We all share the purpose of protecting and aiding the hunted. There are bad people out there," Antonio said, darkening his tone. "These bad people are just as strong as us, and sometimes they hunt us. We call them predators."

"Predators? They really hunt you guys?" I asked.

"They try to hunt the ones who don't know how to use their powers, because they're easiest to find," Antonio said. "But if one of us experienced immortals dropped their auric shields and broadcasted their auras like a Wi-Fi modem, a predator desperate and stupid enough would come around sooner or later to try their luck for their prize of an aura they could feast on for a long, long time. They wouldn't be able to resist the hunger that their unnatural immortality creates in them. Predators hunt to survive. That's their deal with the dark energy that lingers about this world."

"And that's why you're fewer in numbers? Because they

hunt you guys down and kill you?" I asked between spoon-fuls of broth, starting to taste the sweet tinge of magic in all of the food and drink that touched my tongue.

The more Antonio shared, the deeper I felt I had to drown myself with wine, as my understanding of life crumbled around me. I didn't understand why he was sharing so much on a first date with someone he didn't know, but I never felt the world open up to me in such a way as then. And with Eastman being involved, everything was starting to feel more connected than I was starting to feel comfortable with.

"Yeah, predators take a toll on our numbers, definitely. It's hard to find people to recruit with so many of them out there," Antonio said. "I was the first child actually raised by the group. They typically only invite adults, or teenagers if they are power-ful enough. We want people to experience life for the first time without the stain of immortality for as long as they can survive on their own that long. If we notice a soul with potential, we keep tabs and connect with them when they're older. Some-times the bad guys get there first. Sometimes something bad just happens before that. If we could save them all, we would, but parents deserve to raise their children and nurture them with love. That's important for a powerful soul. You didn't get that, though, which is curious," Antonio said, scanning the room above my head, as if checking to make sure someone wasn't there, reminding me of Joshua and the Bailey Bunch.

"Yeah, I didn't get that experience at all," I said. "I didn't spend much time with my parents growing up, honestly"

"You're strong, though," Antonio said, and I checked my arms to see if they grew.

"I was the weakest guy in the frat house," I said, defending my stature.

"Exactly, despite the frat house, despite your parents, you're still strong," Antonio said. "Your aura."

I couldn't help but be amused by Antonio's accusation. If I was capable of something like Kana and Ikkyu, I felt like I would have known about it already. I couldn't even see auras without holding Antonio's hand, and I couldn't walk around with my hand in his for the rest of our lives. Though, the thought of walking the world with him didn't sound too bad.

"So?" I said, betraying a hint of sarcasm. "Despite, what? My lack of love, and the hampering of living with homophobic straight guys as a closeted gay, I can still not do what you do?"

I watched Antonio take a second to assess his response, but I wasn't sorry for betraying some disbelief. I spent time learning about auras and meditating to activate chakras throughout my teenage years as I embraced solitude for the sake of sanity, but no amount of discipline opened me up to anything supernatural.

"You can do what you do well," Antonio said.

"What's that?" I asked, growing impatient for answers since the topic was on me now.

"You," Antonio said. "Are adept at viewing the past. It's a power that takes a great deal of mental and auric discipline. While living with your parents and at your private schools, your connection to your aura was somehow blocked. The auric power most likely turned inward and developed in the only direction it could go. Into the past. That's an incredible ability, even for us. Moving forward, we can teach you everything else you'll need to know."

Ikkyu's somber song turned into drawn out sorrowful breaths that reminded me of a bird flying on a long journey. Some of what Antonio said made sense. Sometimes I felt like I could slip into different years if I stepped on a crack on the sidewalk. I could see history so clearly when I read it or listened to stories. I was so good at seeing it in my mind, that I started to draw it, and then to design it. Then, Eastman noticed.

"That's how you found me?" I asked. "From my illustrations?"

"That's how Aurelius identified you as one of us," Antonio said. "We followed the one they call Joshua of the Bailey family, heir to the family fortune, and found you. Joshua tried keeping you closed off from your aura and hidden from other predators, which also kept you cloaked from us. Bailey's been around longer than I've been alive, but we don't know how, or even know for how long. I think he can change his age from the inside out, but all of us have our own opinions. Last time I saw him was twenty-three years ago, and he was an old man. Johnathan was Bailey's name back then. He was dangerous then, but he's more dangerous now, from what I feel."

"You can feel him?" I asked, starting to feel more worried about Joshua's incessant messages and dreaded over my own past dominated by him.

"Yes, big time," Antonio said. "He's definitely on the island. His aura reeks of burntness. It's been lingering everywhere, except for here."

"What keeps it out of here?" I asked, panic starting to build in my chest. "Can he feel my aura the same way you can feel his? He's looking for me, you know. Am I safe at home?"

"We've enchanted this building and every other building we own on the island," Antonio said. "So, first off, you're safe. We imbue spaces with our auras to cloak our energy frequencies, and we know he's looking for you. Once you arrived at Aurelius's bungalow, Joshua must have felt something was wrong after his connection to you was severed. I was surprised it took him so long to get down here, but I'll protect you. Nothing can happen to you as long as we're together."

"Now it makes sense why Joshua never mentioned his plan to come down here before I left," I said. "He must have not wanted me to know until it was too late."

"That could be the case," Antonio said. "We're not sure."

"Why can I only see auras and feel them with your help?" I asked, conscious of my waning awareness of the waves of auric energy around us, and looking for a reason to disbelieve Antonio.

"Only because you have a lot to learn," Antonio said, smiling at me in a matter of fact way that made him look the part of a cheeky philosophy student. "But that's one thing I can help you fix right here. I'll teach you how to control it a little," he said, holding out his hand.

I couldn't refuse. I grabbed his hand, eager to see more of what he experienced. For all I knew, I could have been dead if it weren't for Antonio and Aurelius. This was turning into a war, and I needed to learn everything I could to use against Joshua. I was tired of him always having the upper hand.

Antonio's azure aura came to life around our hands, binding them in a globe of humming cyan light that reminded me of the glow of a lightsaber. It hummed and vibrated just like one, and the intensity grew stronger at, I assumed, Antonio's will. Then Antonio closed his eyes, and his aura erupted around him, turning his body into the wick of an impressive azure blue flame. But around my body, I didn't see any change.

Focus, I heard Antonio say without moving his lips.

Close your eyes, he commanded, and I obeyed, realizing his voice was coming from inside my own head.

Focus on where our palms touch, he thought to me. I tried to focus on where his palm met flat against mine and on the way our fingers locked together.

Now visualize your aura flowing from your palm to mix

with my aura, he thought.

I followed his directions. I visualized my aura spilling out of my palm the way Ikkyu's aura poured out of his flute. It felt like minutes passed with the rush of energy filling my ears as I visualized my aura around our hands. This time felt different from every other time I tried to produce some kind of meditative magic in my bedroom. I didn't know if it was Antonio giving me a jump, or if things had changed within myself, but I pushed. I pushed as if I knew it would work, and I pushed as hard as I could until I felt something pop between my palms. My body flooded with warmth, and my hands, arms, and body glowed with electrically charged cobalt light that felt and gleamed like a buzzing external skin around my hand.

"There you go," Antonio said, pulling back his hand and returning to his ramen. "Your auric sight. Take a second to adjust to viewing the auric current. It takes some getting used to."

I was stunned into silence for not the first time of the night. The room made me dizzy as I looked around the restaurant at the rainbow of auric colors of all varieties, and when I wanted to focus on one, the others faded away around it until I wanted to see them all again. Ikkyu's aura was thick mint green smoke all over the stage and felt comforting and safe, as if his songs were charms, soothing us all into delight. While Kana's aura was a haze around the restaurant, surging around her like the bright strip in the core of a lightbulb.

The other auras in the room were more dull. A few had some luster, but none compared to the brilliance of Antonio's and his friends'. Antonio's aura was by far the brightest in the room and felt like looking at Caribbean waters on a sunny day, while my aura dazzled like a deep sapphire in the sun.

I wondered if it was a coincidence that both Antonio's aura

and my aura were both shades of blue. His on the lighter side, with mine on the darker, and what that meant, if anything. I wanted to see if they would entwine together if we went for a walk, or just blend into some in-between shade of blue that would look like it was a part of both of us.

You'll get stronger, Antonio thought as I watched him slurp noodles. *So, don't worry.*

Will I be as strong as you? I questioned inside my head.

"Maybe not as strong as me," Antonio said, assessing me with squinted eyes. "Joshua's influence did something to your aura. After dinner I'll take you to Zenda and Ikkyu's house. You can meet Zenda, and we can get a better sense of what's going on. Don't worry about Joshua. We'll keep you safe," he promised again. I trusted Antonio more than I did the average stranger, but his promise didn't make me feel any better about my childhood friend hunting me.

Antonio took his last mouthful of ramen by tilting the bowl into his mouth and savoring the broth with puffed out cheeks before swallowing. Despite his serious demeanor, his mannerisms were boyish. I wished I had the gift of seeing into the future to see if there was one for Antonio and I, but I couldn't help but feel that the answer was yes, anyway. There was no debating the reality of everything Antonio said about his world. After Kana's and Ikkyu's performance and Antonio helping me activate my aura, the proof of a future, more or less, together seemed destined and glistening around me in the cobalt light that hovered over my skin, like the warm pocket of air inside a hot air balloon.

"What is hunting for people like him?" I asked.

"If I'm not mistaken," Antonio said. "He probably wants your energy. Your aura is strong, so it makes sense. People become predators in various ways, but the main principle is that they need to hunt to perpetuate."

"So, they hunt to keep existing?" I said. "What do they do with their prey?"

"It's a complicated experience for prey," Antonio said. "Each situation is unique."

"Look," I said, growing weary as Antonio stumbled over his answers. "I respect your consideration for not wanting to overwhelm me with too much of the truth, but I need to know what I'm up against. I've been living around Joshua my whole life. The Baileys were always around me, and I was always around them. I was Joshua's friend before I could speak. Don't hold anything back, if you are. What does he want with me?"

"I'm honestly not sure," Antonio said, dropping his gaze in dejection. "They hunt to eat. Sometimes they have to kill their prey. Sometimes they have to feed off of their prey like a leech. Other times, they have to become their prey. It depends on how strong or weak they are. How they developed their power initially can impact how they keep it. There's a lot that goes into it."

"Joshua must be a leech," I said. "I felt the most drained over the last four years. I lived with him in boarding school too, but college was different. I thought I felt so drained from being around the guys and from closing myself off from everything out of fear of being outcast or targeted for being gay. I didn't think they were planning on killing me, but, even if I did, I'm not sure I would have thought this would be the way they'd do it."

"What predators like Joshua would do would be far worse than death," Antonio said. "What they would do to all of us, if they had the chance, would be a desecration of our souls. Energy stolen is always cursed and corrupted. Those are the kinds of consequences these people will accept by stealing from us. In most cases, they have no other alternative, but they're monsters for even becoming what they are. They see people as food or fodder for their pleasure and extortion. Don't get fooled by them now that you know better."

Ikkyu was still sitting center stage with his flute pressed against his lips, blowing in, then vibrating the room with the sound of distant rolling thunder. I closed my eyes and focused on activating my auric sight. When I opened them, Ikkyu's mint green aura was billowing over the side of the stage and snaking around the floor of the entire restaurant. Everyone walking was knee deep in thick mint smoke, while everyone sitting in the recessed booths was nearly submerged.

"How many predators have you fought?" I asked, wanting to know the capability of the hands I found myself in.

"Around a dozen," Antonio said. "Confronting Joshua was my first assignment twenty three years ago with Ikkyu, Zenda, Kana, and Aurelius. I'm like a toddler compared to everyone else, though."

"So are Ikkyu and Kana coming along with us?" I said. "Because it doesn't sound like a toddler can keep me safe."

"That's a fair point," Antonio said, looking over at the stage, perhaps sending a mental message to Ikkyu about leaving. I wasn't sure how to know if they were doing that or not, but it felt cool to imagine.

"I'm really not that helpless," Antonio continued. "But there's strength in numbers."

"Oh, yeah," I said, trying not to laugh. "I understand."

"This is no joke," Antonio said. "You're lucky Aurelius was tracking Joshua, otherwise we wouldn't've found you, you know. Aurelius was ready to give up his search. Joshua is great at covering up his power. He was great at shielding yours too."

"Okay," I said, trying to place my life into the context he laid out. "So when did Aurelius find me?"

"He was monitoring Joshua, and over the winter break Joshua went home for a week while you spent the week in the city," Antonio said. "You being so far from him allowed Aurelius to find you on your way back to your brownstone as he was scoping it out. Aurelius could feel his energy lingering inside you. Aurelius's job offer connection happened soon after."

"So where is Aurelius now?" I asked, relieved to have been noticed by the immortal.

"Right now, he's been in Spain meeting other immortals," Antonio said. "He'll be at Zenda's place, too, later. You ready to go?"

"I'm ready," I said, having finished the last of my soup, sushi, and tea, with not an ounce more of kanzake that I could stand.

As we got up to leave, the speakers around the room picked up where Ikkyu left off playing with surreal timing. Nobody else around the room seemed to notice the difference in the source of the music as far as I could see beneath the fog. When Antonio stood up, I got a chance to see his full aura and noticed how he wore it like armor, tight against his body, while mine was as thin as wisps, spiraling off my body like smoke. Ikkyu's mint aura looked as dense as crystal around him when he walked off the stage toward the front of the building. I played with the idea of auras growing over the years like the bark of a tree, expanding and hardening over through the changing conditions of each year, over and over again.

We met Ikkyu in the lobby area where Kana was waiting for us, now wearing a pair of brown pants and a red long-sleeved top, trading a sliver of her elegance for some edginess that I did not expect from her. Ikkyu was short of words, but respectful. I thanked him and Kana for such a great performance and for hosting me, and then we were out the door, back into the warm late-spring Ocean City air.

I followed the immortals down the front staircase of the restaurant, admiring the brilliant sky that stretched out past the bay. Ikkyu and Kana left Antonio and I so that they could take their own car over to Zenda's. Back alone, Antonio and I trekked through the parking lot.

Leaving the restaurant made me feel exposed, as I imagined Joshua sitting behind the wheel of every driver's seat we weaved past on our way through the rows of parked cars. Thankfully, as far as I could tell, Joshua wasn't anywhere I looked. I tried to feel with my aura the way Antonio said he could feel Joshua with his, but I had no idea how to tap into my aura to do it. I felt the waves of energy close up to Antonio, but anything farther away from me than a foot, I couldn't feel.

When we reached Antonio's car, Kana and Ikkyu pulled up behind us. Kana was behind the wheel of the Toyota SEV, while Ikkyu was hanging out the open window looking serious.

"We'll follow you," Ikkyu said, his voice low and deep.

Kana and Ikkyu followed behind us as Antonio pulled out of the parking lot and turned onto the main road. My eyes darted from mirror to window, on the lookout for Joshua anywhere he could be hiding. When I checked my phone, only the older messages from him were there, still left unread. I hadn't received a message or call since the hour before Antonio picked me up for dinner, and now it was half past seven.

"That's unsettling," I said, scrolling through the missed calls and unanswered messages. The sheer number of them were stark, but his messages asking where I was were the only thing I had telling me he didn't know where I was.

"What?" Antonio said, checking the mirrors and windows

as frequently as I did, making me feel that my fear was more justified than he was trying to let on.

"He stopped calling and messaging," I said. "He hadn't stopped since he said he was coming down."

"What do you think?" Antonio asked.

"Well, I think it's pretty obvious," I said, losing my cool. "He knows where I am."

"He might," Antonio said. "Or he's busy, which I feel that he probably is. Ikkyu and Kana felt it too."

"What do you mean?" I asked. "What's he doing? How can you feel him?"

"We're not sure what he's doing," Antonio said. "But it's beginning to feel like it did last time. It feels like he's gathering energy like a storm not too far from here."

"I thought he'd be weak without me," I said. "Isn't that why he needs me?"

"You said he's been around your whole life?" Antonio asked.

"He's a few months older than me, yes," I said, just above the drone of the car. He was really there the entire time.

"That's, what?" Antonio said. "Twenty three years of sequestered stolen energy? It's been festering inside of him, and now it's time to use it. That's what parasites like him do to stay alive."

"Why not just find another host?" I asked, not considering the severity of what an answer might include.

Antonio looked over at me with concern before turning back to the road.

"I don't want to lie to you," he said. "We all deserve the truth."

"I appreciate that," I said.

"This ends with the end of him, or the end of all of us," he said, and all hope left me like a body's warmth washing down the drain of a cold shower as I realized the true horror of my situation."Just hold tight. We're almost to Zenda's. Ikkyu and Kana are helping me keep you cloaked, so Joshua shouldn't be able to sense the slightest whiff of energy coming off you."

"Okay," I said, averse to the thought of continuing the evening. The threat on my life superseded the excitement of everything else. There was nothing I could do to help, either, and I hated being useless. I loved that Antonio trusted me enough to share his reality with me, but I understood fully that nothing would be back to normal until Joshua was gone.

I hadn't thought about the version of Joshua I knew compared to who he truly was until I took the opportunity to close my eyes and lean back against the passenger seat for a few moments of gray time before reaching Zenda's house. The Joshua I knew was always a cruel kid, even at young ages. He was a smart kid. A kid that nobody could ever say no to. Parents and peers alike. He was also the leader of the misogynist and womanizing antics of our other friends. Everywhere we went became Joshua's three ringed circus, where everything he ordered came to him. I thought the villainous character building he came to embody was the product of his spoiled upbringing. But I was starting to see the very real possibility that monsters were born, not built, to be their most destructive selves.

Zenda's house was a long, two-story, dark wooden mansion sized home with a vaulted roof that reminded me of the cliffside lake houses of upstate New York. It was down the Southern end of Ocean City where the main road became sidelined with the front yards of beachfront homes that faced the street but had backyards and balconies with views of the beach. The driveway of the home looked like it could comfortably fit six cars, without counting the garage.

Antonio made it seem rare that his group got together, but it looked like they were prepared for housing every one of their members if the occasion required.

As we pulled into the driveway, a woman in a dark emerald green silk robe opened the front, round topped door. She stood in the crack of the doorway watching us park. Her long dark hair fell to one side of her stunning face, reaching as far as her waist. I wouldn't have been surprised seeing her walking around DownTown Manhattan while fashion week dominated the landscape, showing off a new robe by a designer whose name I would probably never care to know unless modeled by a person of near perfection, such as her.

"Zenda?" I asked, not taking my eyes off the woman.

"Yup," Antonio said, cutting the engine. Zenda had a presence much more intense than the three immortals I had already met.

"She's strong," I said. "I feel it." I felt something, even if I wasn't sure it was her aura.

In the car's side mirror, Ikkyu and Kana pulled in behind us while Antonio opened his door to climb out. I let everyone survey the area before opening my door and getting myself out of the car. I checked the sky and up and down the street as I climbed out of my seat, making sure the coast was clear before closing the car door behind me. Ikkyu and Kana took the path up to the door, and I followed. Antonio took up the rear, until he came up beside me and grabbed hold of my hand. This time the only effect it had on me was the comfort of his touch, and that felt like everything I needed.

"For good measure," Antonio said, offering me a smile, which I was happy to return. I wasn't sure if the hand holding was the natural progression of a good first date or of a nightmare about to start, but I felt ready to see what would come next.

CHAPTER SEVEN

TIME WALKING

ZENDA STOOD ASIDE to let us through the wide door as we approached, and the four of us hurried in. Once inside, Ikkyu pulled Zenda over to him in the foyer for a hug and quiet word while Antonio led me into the great room of the house. The far wall of the room was made of large windows that displayed a brilliant view of the beach and sky as the highest clouds in the sky gleamed with sunlight. The room itself was large enough to fit an entire smaller house inside, with a round wooden coffee table at its center and four large dimpled antique styled leather couches that made a square for conversation. The furniture had the same dark brown color as the wood that made up the molding along the deep emerald walls. The second floor ringed the room like a horseshoe, its banister concealing the doors of the rooms above us. Ikkyu and Zenda stood in the threshold between the sitting room and front room, where the hall upstairs crossed above them and the staircase came down.

The emerald of Zenda's robe was present in many of the decorations displayed on the shelves on either side of the fireplace along the right wall, but nothing was as impressive as the fireplace itself, which looked to be made of emerald bricks that seemed to emanate light from their swirling green depths.

Antonio and I took a seat on the couch that faced the fireplace and Kana sat facing the back wall of windows. When Zenda and Ikkyu were finished with their hushed back and forth, they made their way over to join us on the couches. They took the one opposite Antonio and I, framing themselves within the fireplace before us. I didn't have to activate my auric sight to tell Zenda's aura was the same dark green that she incorporated into so much of what felt like her temple.

"Dylan, welcome to our sanctuary," Zenda said, calling the room's attention. The large house was quiet outside of the four couch square, making my words feel heavy in the presence of the four immortals.

"Thank you," I said, glancing at Antonio who looked between Zenda and I to see how we reacted to each other. "I'm grateful for your protection, all of you."

"I wish our meeting was under more pleasant circumstances," Zenda said. "But, there is someone trying to kill you who we should have found and destroyed long ago." Zenda spoke as if voicing an apology, making it sounds like she saw me as more of a sideline victim in the whole Joshua scandal rather than a central figure. I wasn't sure how to feel about that shift, but I wanted her to know I knew him better than I wanted to.

"His name is Joshua Bailey," I said. "I know him well."

Zenda leaned back into the pit of Ikkyu's arm as he pulled her to him. Kana kept her eyes glued on the horizon out through the back windows, and I activated my auric sight to see how the two green auras of Zenda and Ikkyu interacted with each other. Zenda's aura was as dense around her as the bricks of the fireplace, and instead of shining in a bright way, her aura absorbed the light around it to make the energy glow a deep emerald green as a matter of perspective that shifted from emerald to the shadow of black and back again in a second. It reminded me of a genuine emerald or dark, reflective tropical leaves, photosynthesizing in the dimness of a rainforest.

"We fought the man you know as Joshua Bailey a quarter century ago," Zenda said. "And we still do not know how he survived our battle. It's been a mystery to us for decades, but I believe your closeness to him and your abilities will show us how he escaped us. With that answer, I believe we'll be able to figure out how to defeat him once and for all."

"How can I help?" I asked, ready to offer what I knew. "I don't know how to do any of the things with my aura that you can do with yours," I said. "Antonio just taught me how to see them, and that's all I can do. I know Joshua well, so I can help you on the intelligence side of things, but my aura's weak."

"Tell me what you believe, Dylan," Zenda started. "What is life but what you will it to be?"

Zenda's question sounded a lot like Antonio's explanation of will from the restaurant, but I forgot the logical progression of Antonio's argument, leaving me without a good answer. Every time I thought of life and will I considered them to be separate beasts entirely. Life was life, will was what we wanted to do with life, but there had to be something more to the question's meaning than as simple an answer as that. Thinking of will being what you do with life reminded me of Buddhist philosophy and its concepts around the actions of a person being central to the roles of a person.

"I suppose, without a will to live, life ceases to resume," I said. It wasn't my finest response, but it got the group nodding their heads in agreement.

"So you understand, then. Life is submissive to will," Zenda said. "Life will bend to will, and our experience of life is therefore what we will it to be. Right now," Zenda said, lifting her arm to point out the window. "Joshua is out there gathering strength, drawing power to him. Willing it to him. The same way he willed the leeching of your aura into his for all these years. Will is the secret to the purpose of life, and it's the key to our continued existence on Earth. Will you help us find the answers we require?" Zenda finished, and the room was still and quiet.

"Show me how to will, and I can see if I can help," I said, and for a second I thought I heard the roar of the waves crashing on the shore in the distance outside against the silence. I didn't notice Kana walking over to the piano behind where Antonio and I sat, but her music filled the room as soon as she sat to play.

"Tonight," Zenda said. "I'm going to guide you through maneuvering yourself around the past using your aura. It's a power that is innate in you. We all are a little better at some things than others, and the same is true when it comes to aurics. Your inclination toward the past should allow you to view and browse through time at will, and we need answers on how Johnathan Bailey escaped us last time. This information will be crucial for us in our fight if we hope to end this cycle once and for all. But first, you deserve more proper introductions."

"I'll start," Ikkyu said, sitting up and leaning forward. "I have a rule not to lie to one of our own, and I lied to you by omission. Hate me, if you want. I would myself, if I were you back in my first life. These types of groups are not usually my thing, but out here, we're family. I come from feudal Japan. A time of invigorating adventure for me, but there were many things wrong with the world back then that are still wrong with the world now. My boyhood Zen Buddhist studies brought me my powers at a young age. Not as young as Antonio, but young enough for me to go on to find a path to Buddhist enlightenment. I spent the rest of my years making a point of my life to be a big pain in the ass for men who thought themselves better than the rest of us. My immortality made me bold, and bold enough to run away with Zenda after my full first life before hunkering down across southeast Asia, learning to fight with her, Kana, and other material arts masters of the time, broadening my auric abilities."

"I'll take over that part," Kana said, continuing her piano playing into a staccato rhythm of wind chimes hanging at the shore on a breezy day, relaxing the room under a mist of hazy auric pink clouds in the air above us, that complemented the blazing pink clouds streaking across the sky through the window outside. "I was born after Ikkyu, and in more secret than he was. We shared a mother and a father, unlike our father's other royal children. You see, our father was Emperor of Japan, and we, his bastard children. Our father sent our families' first born to live with the other bastard boys and the monks, but our mother was smarter with her second born. She hid me between the true love affair between herself and our father's most trusted spiritual advisor. The spiritual advisor had been tasked with helping the Emperor achieve immortality for longer than Ikkyu had been alive, but it seemed like our mother was the true magician. She told everyone around her a lie that she only told to save the life of her child, and that was a rumor that the Emperor was having a spiritual child through his divine power, using the vessels of his spiritual advisor and herself, our fathers' concubine. The Emperor had to act as if he knew of the plan when the matter was brought up, and I was born in a mountain retreat with only my mother, the advisor, who became my step-father, and the servants around us.

"Like Ikkyu, I was born immortal. Our father never knew, or suspected I was his true daughter. But after Ikkyu achieved enlightenment, our father had me trained in spiritual arts anyway. My true step-father trained me until our father, an emperor for life, and our mother died of age on the same night. Quickly after, our step-brother, heir to the throne, had sent for me to be assassinated. The man who raised me as his daughter and who I saw as my true father, escaped with me before they reached us, and the two of us set off on a journey across Asia until I was no longer a target. I held my existence from Ikkyu until I felt that he was ready to embrace the life I had found outside of Japan, and when I returned, it was clear that he had lived enough of the life that he had established for himself. Having reached such spiritual significance as he did. I found Zenda, and brought her back to Japan to meet Ikkyu, as she promised to help me rescue him from his fame and infamy. But not before my step-father fell in battle helping Zenda and I defeat a powerful predator."

"I'll start there, if you don't mind," Zenda said, prompting a laugh from Kana.

"I was about to pass it off," Kana said, sounding saddened by her memory. "Centuries of life and uncomfortable conversations teach the art of a great segway, more than anything else."

"I learned that in the jungles along the border between China and Vietnam, before lines were drawn so straight," Zenda said. "They sometimes call me the ancient one within our group, but I'm not one hundred percent sure I'm the oldest."

"You are," said Ikkyu. "Here especially, but globally, too."

"We could confirm that, if we knew how old I actually was," Zenda said. "But I was born in a time before calendars were shared beyond tribes, and when history was shared by memories. My people were a small but organized and spiritual jungle tribe, living off the land and at the service of surrounding tribes. My people were the guardians of the birthplace of tea, charged with protecting the most ancient gardens on Earth before other tribes started consuming the leaves. We were the ones tribes called on when their spiritual leaders failed to fend off the demons haunting and threatening their people. My tribe were the first and last people I knew to carry the strain of humanity able to access their auric energy without immortality. I traveled around the forests and mountains of Southeast Asia as a leader of my tribe, helping all who asked, until the shadow of history overshadowed my tribe with the brutality that befalls all of the civilizations worth preserving. After the destruction of my tribe, I lost so much of myself that I fell into a tortured and nightmarish state, where I was locked in a cycle of haunting the gardens we once tended to and worshipped. Then, Okuninushi no Mikoto, Kana's step-father and Kana herself found me and saved me from myself and the curse I'd fallen victim to. That's when the curse took him, and I vowed my life to helping Kana return her brother to her. We snuck into Japan and smuggled him out, and we started our lives as a small family that grew larger after meeting the famous Marcus Aurelius. I wish we had time for questions," Zenda continued. "But there will be time enough for them soon. We must start your training, or Aurelius himself will not be happy when he arrives. Come with me now."

And with a satisfied nod, Zenda rose off the couch, her thin emerald silk gown clinging to her figure like an emerald statue brought to life. And the staccato rhythm of Kana's music, relaxed me against the story of their struggle to build their family, neutralizing my fears for at least a moment. Her cherry blossom aura, filling the air too with the scent of sweet flowers.

"Antonio, come with us," Zenda said as she made her way out of the room and down a hall to the south side of the house. "And Kana, keep playing. I think it will help."

"I will, Zenda," Kana said, looking back at us without stopping. "Thank you, and good luck, Dylan. You're going to do great."

"Let's go," Antonio said, getting to his feet. He pulled me forward by the hand after I failed to move with him. My apprehension felt like glue making me want to sit on the sofa all night with the consoling sounds of the piano, watching Kana's aura chart across the vault of the ceiling like a powder pink night sky.

"Sure thing," I said, knowing that it was too late to decide to turn back and return to my old, quiet, lonely life. The action and adventure I was looking for was a lot less high stakes than a life and death battle, but no amount of bungalow tranquility, joints or baths would take care of Joshua. I had to get to my feet and follow Antonio across the room and down the hall after Zenda. Ikkyu and Kana stayed behind in linguistic silence, but I wondered if they were talking to each other through their minds, the way Antonio spoke with me at dinner.

The hallway was longer than I expected, with the kitchen opening up on the left and with a few doors lining the wall on our right as we passed. The kitchen had the same magnificent view through the back glass wall as the sitting room, with stone counters and a kitchen island between the ocean view and the hall. Beside the kitchen we passed a round wooden table that looked contoured and uneven that seemed challenging to use. Then there was the room at the end of the hall where Zenda had disappeared into.

Inside the room felt like slipping into another time period altogether. It was a rectangular room of bamboo mats and exposed beams with beige paper walls. Zenda sat on the floor in the middle of the room with her emerald gown spilling around her on the ground like the ripples of a pond. The light in the room was warm with the orange glow of old time bulbs, and beside Zenda was a small maroon pillow with embroidered golden calligraphy.

"Lay down here," Zenda said, waving a hand at the pillow. "Welcome to your first lesson."

I looked to Antonio for confirmation. I trusted Zenda, but the weight of her magnetism was intimidating. Antonio nodded, successfully receiving my plea. Before moving forward, Antonio slipped off his shoes, and I did the same. I walked over and lowered myself between them, resting my head on the pillow. As I laid back, I instinctually closed my eyes to the room, as if laying into the dentist chair. But it was my head and not my mouth that was about to be invaded.

Now, activate your auric sight, Zenda's voice came into my mind like the surfacing whisper of an old memory. *But keep your eyes closed. See our auras with your mind.*

I activated my auric sight as instructed. The light of all three of our auras popped into the blackness of my mind against the playing of the piano, which I could still hear from down the hall. The pink of Kana's aura was faint in the distant darkness, with pools of emerald and aqua blue nearby and all around me. My own dark blue aura was a glimmer of sapphire light that struggled to appear distinguished against the others, but I felt it alive around me more than before. Almost as if it was already getting stronger from use.

Now, Zenda thought, *I'm going to guide you through separating your auric form from your physical body.*

I didn't know exactly what Zenda meant by separating my

auric form from my body, but it sounded like a painful experience that I wasn't interested in having. However, my instinct to run, bury, or hide from my problems was a cycle I didn't have the luxury of enjoying anymore. Joshua wasn't a text message I could ignore. He was a monster with a motive to murder me in a way more painful than what Zenda would have me go through, so I set my jaw and determined myself to will the world to work for me, for once in my life.

Okay, I thought. *Let's do this.*

You're going to do great, Antonio's voice came through. *Zenda taught me how to peer into the past. The first step is the hardest, so focus on your energy.*

What Antonio says is true, came Zenda's thoughts. *Separating the auric form from the body is the most difficult achievement for a new student, but I believe you should find it easier than most. Your aura has gained considerable strength since leaving the influence of Joshua's corruption. I sense it's coming from a well of energy deep inside yourself. It feels completely clean, and somehow untouched by Joshua's feeding. That's the core of your auric form, and that's most likely what Joshua is after.*

That makes sense, I thought to the two immortals inside my mind. I wasn't sure what to do with my thoughts, the way I was never sure of what to do with my tongue while the dentist probed my mouth for every six month cleaning. But having Zenda and Antonio in my head felt far more invasive than a couple of fingers on my teeth. Instead of a cavity being the worst thing that Zenda and Antonio could find, they could find the fact that I didn't have what it took to save us all.

Now, visualize the room around you, Zenda thought. *Use your aura to outline the room in your auric sight, and will yourself up and out of your body. Think of it like getting up and out of bed in the morning. I'll try and give you a push. You're trying to connect with the Auric Plane.*

I did what Zenda said, one step at a time. Somehow I willed my senses to read the room with the energy of my aura. I could feel the energy shifts like the push and pull of a magnet, moving through the matter of my body and expanding around the room. I watched against the darkness a spray of my aura as it coated the room as if I 'threw some paint on the wall.' I leveled my breathing and tried to focus on seeing the energy with my mind. I didn't feel any help from Antonio, and I had a feeling Zenda was the type of teacher who enjoyed watching her students struggle hard before arriving at success all on their own. I hoped I'd be one of those success stories, but I still had doubts.

Despite how ready and willing I was to try to counter the Joshua threat, I felt the suffocation of being in wet denim on a steamy hot day, but I had nothing to do with my doubt except get rid of it so I could see what I needed to see. I focused on pushing through the doubt. I imagined wiping it away like grease off of a mirror. Wiping again and again until my auric sight started focusing in against the blur of my inexperience. Around me, the room became a mesmerizing representation of dark blue constellations against the darkness of my closed eyes, and I could see clearly all the way to the back of the room and beyond, as if in a place separate from the room full of my teachers' auras.

Perfect, Zenda thought. *Now, for step two. It's time to truly enter the Auric Plane, aside from just viewing it in your mind. You have to wake up out of your body as your auric form. As your auric energy itself, in fact. Do you get it?*

I understood what Zenda wanted me to do. It sounded a lot like astral projection, which I had tried before during my meditative middle school days. I failed to accomplish the feat on more sleepless nights than I could remember. Except, what Zenda described sounded much harder than simple projection. The thought of lifting my aura from my body seemed impossible. Though I wore my aura more like a beach shawl than as form fitting armor, my aura clung to the molecules of my body with a force that felt hard to shift. I imagined myself rolling out of my body as a wispy blue ghost of a person, but I couldn't push past what felt like a weighted blanket keeping everything intact.

Try falling out, Antonio thought. I was surprised by the proposition, but I wasn't sure why. It sounded like a very reasonable way of leaving the body. Outside of the physical realm, you should be able to pass through physical objects, I assumed, which would then put me right below the floor, if I achieved it.

I thought of falling into the pools of emerald and cyan below me, the spill over from the immortals' auras. I wanted to sink deep into their depths to soak up everything they could share. I relaxed my body and relaxed my mind. I imagined my auric form slipping out of my body, starting with my head. Leaning back. It took time, but eventually my neck let go and my head started to fall. I pushed myself down, away from my body, and into the floor. Harder and harder.

From the well of my stomach burst a cloud of cobalt light that spiraled out in shimmering glitter against the darkness of my mind, and my chest expelled everything in it, making me breathless. The force knocked me back. Down and into the ground, I fell. I was out of my body. My arms and legs were whispers of dark blue haze in the darkness. Their waning presence made me afraid that parts of myself might get blown away if I got caught in an auric breeze. I wasn't sure how all that worked, but I assumed that if you threw the word auric in front of a word, there was probably a comparable equivalence in the Auric Plane.

Come back, Zenda thought, and I wished I could. I felt immobile. I imagined myself standing beside my body, and in the second after, I was there. I was standing at the feet of my laying body in the room with the bamboo mats. Zenda and Antonio were shut-eyed, sitting beside me in meditative states, each holding onto one of my arms.

You did it, Antonio came through. *Are you getting used to thought messaging?* His cyan auric form appeared behind his body. Everything in the auric world seemed fuzzy to me, but his armor looked Roman in style, making me more curious about meeting Aurelius.

The what? I thought, and then, knowing he could hear me, I understood.

You get it, he thought. *You're doing great.*

Every step you take will be more difficult than the last, Zenda thought. Then her auric form appeared in the room behind her body. She appeared in her silk gown, with emerald hair and skin. I believed what she said about every step getting harder. I was surprised with my progress so far, but the focus it required was harder to maintain with every second that passed. But, despite the difficulty, I was ready for more of a challenge.

What's next? I thought, looking into the face of Zenda's emerald auric form. Her sharp angled features made her look like an emerald statue in the likeness of a goddess.

Browsing through time is like riding in the car, Zenda thought. *History plays the way the world passes by outside the window. Individual memories fly by like the trees lining a highway.*

So, I thought. *I'm trying to find a single tree along the highway of history?* The question didn't seem ridiculous until I heard it in my head, and at that point it was too late to think it back with Antonio and Zenda already there.

Along the highway of history, Antonio thought. *It's a long and dangerous road.*

How dangerous? I thought.

Not dangerous at all, Zenda thought next. *As long as you follow our laws.*

So this really is like driving? I thought, somewhat disappointed by the comparison.

Nothing like it, Zenda thought. *But to help direct you, I might use driving terms. Many terms are interchangeable. Now that you understand viewing history to be like passing it by from the backseat window of a car, you can imagine the timeline of it. You can hop on and ride the recent past, or you can will yourself to a moment that, with experience, would pop right into your vision while channeling into the Auric Plane. For now, you'll have to search. Once you find the moment you require, you can play around with selecting the second in which you wish to view.*

How do I start this carousel? I thought, eager to find the answer to Joshua's defeat. The focus required to keep myself engaged in my aura was growing more difficult to maintain. I wasn't sure if I was feeling Joshua's growing strength, but it was feeling more and more like we were already out of time. The stress of it all burrowed deep into the muscles between my shoulder blades and burned slower than the hot end of a cigarette.

Hold out your hand, Antonio thought. I felt more comfortable following his guidance, even though I had no reason to not trust Zenda. Antonio's guidance was more direct, and I appreciated that. So, I held my auric hand out in front of me with my palm up.

Now what? I thought.

Flick through the years, Antonio thought, as if he were telling me to flick through channels on the TV.

I waved my hand in the air with the focus of a lifelong monk, as the more I moved, the more difficult it grew to move again. I willed the room to show me what was behind my present curtain of time, so I could see what came before. As I pulled my hand through the air, my fingers caught what felt like pages in the air. I pulled on them to see what would happen, and as I flipped between them in the air, the invisible pages moved, sending a rippling across the plane. But nothing changed.

I pulled harder, hoping to see something change in my auric sight. My fingers inched through the air, making little progress for the amount of effort it required. Eventually, a cobalt tinged vision started to materialize like a live action rewind. In the vision, Antonio and I got to our feet and walked backwards to the door as Zenda followed after us, just as it happened earlier, but in reverse. When the door shut and the room was empty, the strain became too much. I couldn't keep the vision up anymore, and it fizzled from view.

Then my world went black, and I felt alone in my head. After what felt like a silent minute, the feeling of Antonio's hand grew hot in mine. While everything else didn't feel at all.

Eventually I could move my eyes and feel them rubbing the skin on the underside of my eyelids as I moved them. When I was finally able to open them, I was staring up at the ceiling of the paper walled room. Antonio was on my right, holding my hand to his chest. My hand was burning with the energy of his aura. I could feel my aura receiving the energy he was giving off, effectively charging every part of my body. Antonio's aura pulsed through the atoms of my arm like hot air through a tennis racket.

Zenda was on my left, staring back at me. Her eyes had become impenetrable emerald rings around her pupils, making her face look stony and rigid between the diamond cut angles of her cheek bones.

"What happened?" Zenda said, her eyes reverting to their natural dark brown.

"He needs to recharge," Antonio said, before I could think of an answer. My thoughts came to me as incomprehensible buzzing, but I knew he was right.

"He's growing stronger," Zenda said. "Every minute we wait makes defeating Joshua all the more difficult."

"I know," Antonio said. I could tell from the gravity of Zenda's tone that she was concerned about our ability to beat Joshua.

"Then let's go back under," Zenda said. "We can't stop until we know how to defeat him."

"That's not a good idea," Antonio said, looking down at me. "He's still too weak."

"Surely you remember your training, Antonio?" Zenda said, with a slight air of encouragement behind her words.

"I do," Antonio said. His furrowed brow told me he was more worried for me than anything else. I was glad that was the case. I felt spent. It didn't seem possible for me to do anything more just yet. I could hardly think, let alone ditch my body again.

"We were responsible for training you on thousands of years of self developed knowledge in a few decades," Zenda said, still talking to Antonio. "We can accomplish *this* at least by the end of the night. But," she said. "Sleep is good. Get some rest, Dylan, and we'll continue after."

With that, Zenda got up and left the room, and I was left staring up into the concerned face of Antonio. My mind was too numb for thoughts other than the one word Zenda said that I couldn't get out of my head, *sleep*.

Antonio helped me to my feet, despite their unwillingness to want to work. I felt like maybe my aura and body hadn't yet completely merged back together after the separation. I wasn't sure how all that worked, but I had no other explanation for how I walked out of the room with Antonio's help. I felt like a puppet, too dazed to move my limbs, but still stepping along.

"We can head up to my room," Antonio said, and I actually felt relief.

I walked with Antonio back to the foyer and up the staircase to the floor above. The hall was long in both directions with doors on both sides. Together with the decor, the sanctuary was becoming more reminiscent of the types of resort locations my parents would spend months in.

"That's the first thing to slip out of that mind of yours?" Antonio said, with a laugh. He had us turn right at the top of the steps, and we walked past a few doors before he said, "Here."

I couldn't think of a response.

The room behind the door was large and sparsely furnished, with long cerulean curtains teasing at a view from the windows lining the back wall. Antonio led me to the wood framed bed and laid me down on the dark gray comforter, propping up my head with a pillow.

"Sleep," Antonio said, rounding the bed before taking the spot beside me. "I'll be here, charging you up. Get some rest for now."

Seconds later, my eyes closed on the image of his face, and I drifted off into thoughtless sleep.

CHAPTER EIGHT

IMMORTAL METAPHYSICS

W HEN MY CONSCIOUSNESS returned, I didn't wake up in bed beside Antonio. I was back in the familiar black void of my mind. Thoughts of Joshua flooded me from all sides. Memories I shared with him spun around me like the horses of a carrousel, impossible to follow beyond a fraction of a second. The memories came in fast forwarded flashes, shot in first, second, and third person perspectives, all at the same time. It was a kaleidoscope of angles and viewpoints that were too much for me to process at once. As soon as I could catch an instance, it shifted into another time.

Joshua, the guys, and I moving into the brownstone flashed by. All of us on the football field for high school graduation. Despite my longing to walk far away from them and never return, I cheered them on as they walked up and took their diplomas. Me and Joshua and his date at our first middle school dance. All he ever did was complain about the girls he dated, before they came to understand they'd be better off alone or with some other guy. The other guys were on the dance floor with their dates, while we sat at the tables nursing bottles of cola with cold, dried up slices of pizza. I was always there for things like that, but I could never dance with the guys I wanted to dance with. I was only just starting to understand how to be myself years later. Seeing that memory made me swear to continue to make my life my own. I'd never sit at another table like that while everybody in the room had fun.

I let myself follow the memory train further down the ethereal tracks of my mind, and images of us as kids started popping up. Even as children, Joshua was cruel, but as a child his cruelty affected me less than the other guys. Nick, Walt, Carter, and Chris were Joshua's favorite targets of pranks, and they were all gullible enough to fall for his manipulation. He would alternate his physical and emotional attacks based on how he felt any given day, while having them carry out his most dangerous shenanigans. I suffered my share of attacks from him, but, even at a young age, he couldn't handle the logical nature at which I would break down his arguments and emotional overreactions.

Some of the memories that passed were unfamiliar to me. As I became more and more curious about Joshua in his younger years, the memories seemed to focus on him more. Many of the memories were of him in the small cave we used to play in as kids in the woods behind Joshua's house. I hadn't thought of the place since we were children, I realized, as I refamiliarized myself with the dark space.

The cave was a small hill that stuck out from the earth in a small clearing in the woods. The entrance was a thin crevice that was covered up by a larger rock that hid the cave mouth in a way that you would have to know where it is to find it. To get inside as kids, we would shimmy through the opening and into the twelve foot circle of the cave floor. A small amount of light filtered in during all the memories Joshua had there, where he sat alone, looking at the cave wall. It was hard to tell how long the memories were. I couldn't tell if I was watching minutes or seconds pass by. It felt like they could have been hour-long sessions, but they all made me feel more uncomfortable with every one that played. Aside from us boys, he brought only his young cousins to the cave. Never an adult. I wasn't even sure if any of the adults knew about the place, but all we would ever do in there was stare at the walls.

Staring at the walls of the cave was more entertaining than one would think at first. Despite no water being in the cave, the walls were always wet with a substance much thicker than water. It moved more like snot than anything else, but was as clear as glass. We would watch it slide down the rough and smooth surfaces like watching the ocean from the sky. The snot gleamed even in the darkness, glimmering all the way as it ran down into the dirt at a steady flow.

I never refused a trip to the cave. None of us did, but I always dreaded being in it once I was there. Even Joshua's memories inside of it brought back the cold feeling of dread that made my skin feel cold and wet. When I learned the word dread, my mind gave me the image of the snot dripping down cave walls, and they've been synonymous in my mind ever since. I feared the cave, but could never refuse it or the sorrow it evoked when there. And I didn't know what to make of that memory yet.

I was with Joshua so much of the time my whole life that for a long time I was even scared of my life without him. But we weren't always together, and I never knew what he did when I wasn't with him. The toxicity between us also made me never care to ask. Though, I knew he had very cruel relationships with his cousins to the point that his cousins would cry at the sight of him. I was surprised to see them follow him into the cave time after time as the memories shuffled through the past. As children, it was only in the cave when being around Joshua was bearable. That was perhaps the driving reason why we were all so willing to go along.

Whether with cousins or friends, Joshua and his guests would sit down or lay back and watch the slime. Just the same as he did. I wished Antonio or Zenda were with me to see what I was seeing. There was something I felt that I was missing from the memories of the cave that I hoped would be obvious to them. The strangeness of children sitting and staring at cave walls for hours was something I couldn't believe I hadn't thought of more in my recent past. As I thought back, it was only ever in the cave that I remembered thinking of the cave. As if the sticky snot was viscous enough to smother the memory of itself upon our leaving. That, or it had to be the work of none other than Joshua himself, covering up his crimes against us.

The years that went deeper into the past were beyond my ability to recall. They were from when we were small children. It was the age of playdates and supervision. Before we were old enough to go on our own and explore. Then, everything went black and I wasn't in a memory anymore. I felt like I was in another's mind. The blackness was impenetrable. My aura wouldn't light up the way it did when I was with Antonio and Zenda, but somehow I knew there was nothing to see.

Eventually, the darkness broke into the grayness of a cold and rainy night. I felt Joshua's familiar presence, but he was of a different mind. He was in a crueler state than I had ever experienced him in. His body was of an older man with the blond haired familial Bailey features, complete with the biological curse of a thinned lipped sneer for a mouth. He was sitting in the darkness of the cave, holding a few month old baby Joshua in his arms. I knew these things as a matter of fact by some means beyond my understanding.

The baby Joshua in the elder Johnathan's arms was the Joshua I never truly met, and I felt bad for the friend I was supposed to have known. His aura felt strong and bright for a baby. It was even stronger than mine, I guessed. The elder Johnathan knew of his grandson's gifts. He was envious of the baby's energy, and he wanted the baby's aura for his own. His grandson was everything he had been waiting for, I could sense, it was just too early for him to do what he was now forced to do.

As the older man held his baby grandson, he mourned the loss of the future his grandson had promised him if everything happened in its due time. The more Johnathan thought about his miss at true immortality, the weaker and angrier he became. He knelt in the shreds of his clothes in the dirt caked and wet desperation of his own making, but not a thought was on the loss of the grandson in his arms.

Raw blisters pocked Johnathan's arms and face with webs of emerald light sizzling beneath the wounds, and the slices around his body where he bled refused to stop bleeding. The disdain he had for himself in his current state made the cave feel like acid eating his skin. He looked down at baby Joshua, holding him over a duffel bag at his feet. Three basketball sized conch shells I had never seen in the cave before stuck out from inside the bag, two appearing crushed while the other glowed encased in copper light.

The older Joshua focused the last of his dried up auric reserves from the empty pit of his stomach and shined his ruby aura over baby Joshua's face. The copper aura of the conch in the bag beamed a ray of energy around the baby in Johnathan's arms, charging the energy he collected in his hand. In the span of the next few seconds, baby Joshua was encased in the blood red aura of his grandfather, as the copper aura growing bright below him suspended the child in the air, before Johnathan fell to the floor beside the duffel bag as the giant conch cracked in two halves. But before the light of the energy died, baby Joshua blinked out of the cave and into the cradle of his nursery room. Then everything returned to blackness again.

When darkness receded after a time, I was back at the shore. The world opened up to me as a bright and sunny seaside morning atop the docks of a marina pier, with seagulls calling overhead and the flop of the bay waves beneath the dock boards. I was on the outlet to an active channel, with the sun a few hours into its crisp morning ascent. These were the hours at the shore where time seemed to almost stand still. The perpetual salt breeze from the ocean side was cool and refreshing in a beautiful way that reflected the brisk intensity of the natural world.

An unbattered Johnathan was bent over, tying a boat to a bulwark in the body of his older self. This memory felt like it was exactly where I needed to be. Finally on the day Johnathan fought the Immortal Philosophers. I could feel it in him, even then as he started his day. A sense that he had missed something. That he was being watched, and that he didn't have the luxury of the time he thought he had to carry out the plan that he worked so hard on.

Johnathan moved fast for the age he portrayed. Once his boat was tied tight to the bulwark, he retrieved his duffle bag from the deck and took off down the dock under the shade of his faded black ball cap. He completed the decent old man look with a tucked-in thin sweater and blue jeans. Even the brown duffle bag under his arm failed to look out of place or ominous, though I figured it contained the three shells he had with him in the cave later that night.

I followed Johnathan in my auric form to the sea shell filled parking lot of the marina where he climbed into a cherry red 1960s Corvette that sat glimmering like a diamond in the sun. I never heard Joshua talk of the car, which would have been out of character for him if it meant anything to him. This car must have meant a ton to him, which made me feel like it wasn't going to make it to the end of this memory, as my ghostly self fizzled into the seat beside Johnathan. Even in the dream, I could feel the seat under me and the purr of the motor when Johnathan ignited the engine.

Johnathan took the Vette to the main road on the one road island and followed it for some time in silence. I tried to read his thoughts behind the grave look that turned his aging face into what felt like staring into a canyon, but I couldn't get in, even in the memory.

He looked to be in his seventies, but I had no way of knowing his true age. In this memory, I could only get hints of what he was thinking and where he was going. Aside from the movements of his eyes, which were fixed on the four sides of the car, he showed very few other signs of life. He was undistracted by traffic and passersby, following the straight road as if he were any other grandpa. It was me, him, the road, and the roar of the engine when he pushed down on the pedal.

As I rode with him, I wondered where we were. The island wasn't Ocean City. There weren't as many avenues as Ocean City had. This island was a strip, while Ocean City was a neighborhood. Despite the two islands' stark geographical differences, their streets were lined with similar shops and restaurants, mini-golf courses, and ice cream shops. We even passed an amusement park with a ferris wheel and roller coaster that reminded me of the ride pier on the Ocean City boardwalk. One of the shops we passed had mannequins standing along the sidewalk outfront, wearing LBI and Long Beach Island branded t-shirts and sweaters.

I heard of LBI back during SuperStorm Sandy. It was a one road in, one road out kind of town too, where the rich started taking over one street at a time. Destruction, construction, and reconstruction was everywhere a mansion wasn't. Here, most of the homes were empty for the majority of the year, so it was hard to see what really living here would be like through the manic summer state the island was enthralled in in the memory.

I noticed one of the few remaining bungalows along the main streets with a yard of trees and overgrown bushes. It was an oasis of cool days and comfortable nights. The memories around the shaded yard were full of children swinging in the afternoons on the wooden tree swing that hung from a branch by weathered ropes. On the other side of the tree was a hammock tethered to the trunk of another nearby tree. The hammock swayed in the morning breeze, heavy with memories of afternoon naps floating above the yard of green grass.

The summer memories were potent, but the house had memories of Christmases, birthdays, and family time all year. I hadn't had such a homey life since my elementary years, but even then, our family days weren't centered around having carefree, kid friendly fun. The memories of the LBI house were warmer than my memories of chastisement into a well disciplined, adult-acting, and obedient boy.

I was enthralled by the house. I wanted to spend time there and swing on the swing in the backyard all morning, waiting to be called in for lunch by a caring relative. The house was full of memories of catching lightning bugs after sunset in glass jars with metal lids poked with holes that you have to screw on before the bugs fly out, always taking the chance to catch another in the jar, knowing more might escape.

Johnathan didn't even notice the house. His mind was down at the end of the island, where the road and houses turned into trees, rocks, and a path to walk on. I could see in his mind the red and white toned lighthouse I felt like I had seen sometime before, in distant memory, maybe, but maybe not. His thoughts came as unexpected fumes that I had to catch and pull at to gather, but they were coming.

After a little more cruising, Johnathan turned into a diner parking lot. There was a blue sign in the window of the white brick building that read Island's Best Waffles. The font was the same color as the diner's inviting powder blue roof. My stomach got excited for something sweet before I remembered that my stomach wasn't even with me.

Johnathan took his time turning off the Vette and picking himself up from his seat. He was trying to act calm, but I could feel paranoia on the periphery of his awareness. Despite it, this stop felt personal and necessary for him.

When he entered the diner I noticed that the staff knew him. He was a regular. They greeted him with expectation and took him to his seat. A young girl around high school age and a tall middle aged woman were the ones who brought him over from the host stand. He smiled through the interaction, and delighted the women with his words.

"It's good to see you two," he said, holding up two fingers. He didn't yet have the ragged look he had in his memory of later that night, giving the ladies no reason to suspect the dangerous truth of who he really was.

"Good morning, Mr. Bailey. You rode in on the boat this morning?" the middle aged waitress asked. She had the North Jersey accent you get when your parents are from North Jersey but you grow up in South Jersey. Her dark black curls were hairsprayed high in the big-hair style I only remembered seeing in photos and on tv.

"Yes I did," Johnathan said. "The bay wasn't bad, but I think a storm will be here in a few hours."

"I heard something on the news today about it, but God, the ride over's gotta be beautiful first thing in the morning," the waitress said. Her powder blue shirt said her name was Kobo. I liked the name. I thought it fit her well, as she stood there with her hip thrust out at us and her arm bent with her hand clutching her waist. Her red lips and gum chewing were the cherry on top of the Jersey cliché, but Johnathan did love his clichés.

"Everything's a pain in the ass at my age, Kobo," Johnathan said in a candid way that had Kobo bent over laughing like a truck horn.

"You are too funny," Kobo said, slapping her leg. I wasn't sure if her act was a secret defense mechanism for keeping people away, or if it was a truly inheritable natural reaction. But I was impressed with Kobo's athleticism when it came to enjoying a good laugh. "I can't imagine. I don't know what I'm going to do when I get to be your age. I know boating will be waaay out of the realm of possibilities for me, God bless."

"Oh Kobo, you wouldn't ever want to get to my age," he said. "Life is most precious in brevity, unless otherwise prescribed. Let time take its toll without the bother of preservation. If you want to boat, then boat. The worst it could do is kill you."

"You know, Mr. Bailey," Kobo said. "All the riddles you speak really get me thinking about life sometimes. I don't know how far the thoughts are gonna go, but the way you sound, sounds so right. You'd love my church. My pastor is so charismatic and down to earth when you really talk to him. I still go out with my parents for Mass every Sunday. It's not as pretty as the boat ride, but maybe you're right. Maybe I'll take that boat ride before the summer's up this year. Ah, here she is. You take over, Clara."

"Oh, are you still a trainee, Clara?" Johnathan asked the younger waitress, who looked young enough for me to believe that this had to be her very first job. Clara's powder blue shirt was pinned with 'trainee' over where Kobo's shirt was embroidered with her name, so the answer was obvious, but Johnathan was playing a different game here.

"I am, yeah," Clara said, her smile big and bright with some of the straightest teeth I ever saw. She had a timid look behind her frizzy brown hair, but she seemed excited to be working in the world. "Today I'm leading, and tomorrow I'll be on my own."

"That's wonderful," Johnathan said. "That's an incredible accomplishment for a young person embracing work for the summer. Keep at it."

"Thank you, Mr. Bailey," Clara said. "Are you having your usual today?"

"Yes, I am," Johnathan said. "I had the same thing yesterday too." He laughed. "How was your day at the lake, yesterday?"

"Wow, was it pretty, Mr. Bailey," Clara said. "The water was clear all the way down to the bottom. And the fish! The fish were incredible. My dad and brothers caught a bunch, and then grilled them up for dinner. We had our supper right there on the lake. Then we swam out to the center and floated for a few hours. The lakes in the pine barrens are something else. We even saw a couple of bald eagles catching their own fish."

Johnathan was attentive to her story the whole time, as he was with Kobo, but with Clara there was something else as well. Something I recognized that he would do as Joshua, when it came to absorbing someone he was talking to.

"That's amazing, Clara," Johnathan said. "Those bald eagles catch snakes too. You've got to be careful. Once their claws get in something, there's no getting loose."

"Oh I didn't know about the snakes," Clara said. "Maybe next time I'll have to pay more attention."

"Well, it sounds like you had a nice time, don't think twice," Johnathan said. "It sounds like the days I had back up north in New York. As a boy, I used to swim in a lake that has since dried up behind our family house. I wanted to retire beside it, but life is always full of surprises," he said. "Even for old men like myself."

"Oh Mr. Bailey, everyday is a blessing, I always say," Clara said. "One day and one step at a time. But let's see, you're doing the waffles and black coffee. Does that sound right?" Clara asked. Kobo was nodding approvingly behind her with the smile of a proud mentor.

"That sounds delicious," Johnathan said.

"I'll get your coffee right away, sir," Clara said. "And did you want all three waffles this time?"

"Yes, I'll take the three," Johnathan answered, putting up three fingers and dropping them in her direction, before closing them into a fist. The motion pulled at her aura, vacuuming it away from hers, and feeding him through a crimson thread tethered around his finger. He wasn't feeding himself waffles. He was feeding off the waitstaff.

Clara's aura was crisp apple red, and with effort, I willed myself to see it from his perspective. Then, the memory shifted to my eyes in the sockets of the elder Johnathan Bailey. It was clear that Clara's aura was starting to grow too weak to siphon as she turned and went to get his coffee. Her aura was once dense, and the size of an apple in its core, but now the core was grape sized and fading. Most people have wispy auras with faint colors that are hard to make out, like Kobo's, and those were the literal bane of Johnathan's existence.

If energy was abundant in everyone, he would leech as he walked through the street, but that wasn't the case. He had to live like a scavenger, traveling and stumbling upon prey until someone like me came around, who he could leech off forever.

Johnathan felt limited by his body. His summers were successful along the Jersey Shore, but it had been a long time since he had been able to feed off a strong aura, with his own aura now starting to wane because of it. His dreams of retiring in the upstate New York home had been renewed by the birth of his grandson, but he would have to wait until the boy was older and stronger, having been born with a promising aura that needed time to strengthen in order for Johnathan to enjoy the boy's immortality after the transition of Johnathan into Joshua's body.

When Clara returned with his coffee, he thanked her before she retreated back to the kitchen to help finish his order. As she left the table, Johnathan waved his hand in the air, pulling at her aura again and causing wisps of energy to pull free from her at his command. He twirled the red band around his finger as it collected into a red spinning thread. Then Johnathan pointed his finger down, and into his coffee the red thread fell. It was caught by the surface of the water and held there for a second before sinking into the cup's inky black depths.

I watched him sip the steaming hot liquor with a grimace, knowing that my mouth would have been burned if I ever tried sipping anything at that temperature, but it wasn't clear whether or not Johnathan even registered the heat.

"Thank you, Clara," he said to himself, with a satisfying display of his thin maniacal Bailey smirk. The energy made him warm with the temporary delightful zing that comes with satisfying a sugar craving. He savored the sip and waited for the aura infused liquid to warm his gut before bringing the cup to his lips for another sip. I watched the swirling coffee through his eyes, wondering what it was he even wanted to live for. It seemed like the aura in the cup was all that drove him. It drove the deceit, the stealing, and all of the cruelty that he used to get his way. I always thought life was like a game for Joshua, and I was starting to see that it really must have been. It was a game to rob everyone around him of the most precious pieces of life itself.

I noticed that, while Johnathan waited between sips, a thin strand of red auric light ran from his cup and through the diner to where Clara was in the kitchen behind the swinging door, siphoning her as she moved about the restaurant, stealing a lot more than a few threads worth. When Clara came around with the three-stack of waffles, the auric transfer pulsed stronger, like from a vein, to an artery.

"Thank you," Johnathan said, looking down at the pillowy waffles dripping with syrupy cinnamon apples dusted with powdered sugar. "They look sweeter than an apple pie, I'll tell you. But not sweeter than the best apple I ever tasted," Johnathan said.

"That so?" Clara asked. "Was it a New York apple? I heard there's orchards up there from my cousins. They visit in the summers."

"It was a Jersey apple, Clara," Johnathan said, unfolding a napkin over his lap. "I love my New York, but Jersey has the best."

"I'll have to keep that in mind," Clara said. "I'm buying Jersey apples next time I bake a pie."

"Very good," Johnathan said.

"I'll let you dig into those then," Clara said. "Can I get you more coffee?"

"Absolutely," he answered, betraying his evil smirk. Clara didn't seem to notice the darkness in his grin, but I could feel it in the way his lips moved.

"I'll be right back with the pot then," Clara said, taking her leave back around to the diner counter where the coffee pots sat in their warmers. The red thread elongated as she moved away and retracted as she came near again. As she poured the coffee, her crimson aura flowed down from the pot in her hand at the suggestion of Johnathan's control.

"Mmm, mmm," Johnathan said. "Thank you, Clara."

"You got it," she said. "You enjoy the rest of your breakfast, now," she added, before leaving the table once more.

It was hard to keep myself from falling into the pull of her memories, so the sympathy I felt for the innocent girl was something I struggled with keeping out of my head. The shallows of her mind came to me like the tide ebbing in. I could see her last day of Junior year.

I saw her watch her younger brother graduate elementary school and the dinner they shared after watching a movie in their living room with their mother, the dark room and grainy tv. As I entertained the pull of her mind, the more I felt that I was slipping away from Johnathan's memories. I had to be present in Johnathan's mind to figure out how to get rid of Joshua. I had to pay attention and relearn everything I thought I knew about him.

Johnathan sipped from his coffee cup the sweetness of his success, but as the aura passed his lips, it might as well have evaporated before it even hit his tongue. It was a pinch compared to the energy he required to maintain his powers and life. I felt everything he felt. His mind didn't wander beyond the energy he was stealing.

After Johnathan finished his waffles and drained his coffee cup many times over, he wiped the soft crevices of his mouth with a folded paper napkin and brought a twenty dollar bill up to the register where he handed it to Kobo across the hostess counter.

"How was it?" Kobo asked, smiling for a response.

"It was the best yet," Johnathan said, straightening himself up.

Then Clara came from the kitchen. As they exchanged goodbyes, Johnathan shook hands with them in farewell, taking a last glove of Clara's energy with him out the door. The physical touch transfer was exhilarating for him. More so than the trickle of energy that transferred through space.

Outside in the parking lot, Johnathan made his way to the car. The sun was bearing down on him and the cherry red body of the old Corvette. But something made him pause. It was the kind of pause you make when you think you forgot your keys, or you notice a scratch on your door that wasn't there before. But nothing was visibly different with the car's body. He scanned the area for clues to what was wrong, but he couldn't shake the feeling that he was being watched again.

I caught sight of Clara in the window of the diner, cleaning the booth as Johnathan climbed into the car's driver seat. She wasn't the predator, that was for sure. She was a sweet girl who didn't deserve to be made prey by a creep, while Johnathan deserved every cold second of the feeling of violation that he subjected everyone else to. Although the anxiety he was starting to develop felt a lot like being an ant in a sun beam under a magnifying glass, I had no sympathy for him.

Back on the road, Johnathan seemed more focused on getting to the lighthouse. He didn't know who or what was watching him, and that worried him. I couldn't dip into

Johnathan's history the way I could with someone like Clara, but he knew that when he couldn't sense a strong aura, it was because the owner of it knew how to use it and conceal it.

Johnathan wasn't at the age or strength to do battle the way he expected he might have to in his effort to escape, and that worried him. I had to put Johnathan's paranoia to the side of my mind to focus on the world outside to get a sense of Johnathan's knowledge of it and test my abilities. It was beautiful being a little bit back in time. As we drove further down the island, the mansions started getting bigger rather than smaller, as if the people with real money wanted to be further away from the entrance of the island, which I could understand. It meant less traffic and reasons for people to be around, but it also meant a further drive to the mainland.

The cars were everything I used to see in the new and used car catalogs of my youth. I used to browse them beside the newspapers in the grocery store when my parents decided they needed to 'pick something up real quick.' I grew tired of chasing them around the store and getting lost with the wanderings of my mind. The catalogs kept me well occupied.

It didn't take us long to reach the end of the island where the lighthouse peaked out over the treetops of a small nature reserve, complete with a coastal gift shop selling Long Beach Island branded gifts next door to a Dairy Queen serving cones by the station-wagon full. The porta-potties lined up beside the DQ made me happy to be visiting in my sleep, with no chance of having to enter their always unsettling interiors.

Johnathan parked the Corvette under a shaded corner of the parking lot where the trees canopied the lot perimeter, providing a little relief from the punishing island sun. There were a decent amount of cars parked in scattered spaces around the lot, but nobody was around. As I figured he would, Johnathan retrieved the duffle bag from the trunk and swung it over his head to carry across his body before leaving the car. The brown canvas of the bag sank at his side with the weight of the shells as it bounced off his hip as he walked over to the trail entrance, where there were signs showing different paths that crossed the forest reserve.

He brought me through the forest lighthouse trail to where the path opened up to a crossroad where the paved path continued toward the lighthouse and a path of sand continued on the right. Here, I thought he was going to continue left, but he turned down the sandy path on the right. We followed along until the trees gave way to a wall of jetties that stuck up like a mountain range between the beach and the channel splashing against the other side of the jetty wall. A cement path ran atop the jetty that went all the way out past the beach and into the misty gray ocean haze.

Johnathan followed his own path beside the jetty wall, maneuvering around pools of water that washed in from the waves of the channel. Whole ecosystems were created from the back and forth flow, with small creatures of life tumbling into the pools with the motion of the tides. Small crabs, shellfish, and even some fish were swimming around in some of the bigger reservoirs, waiting to become food for the seagulls that sat in the seagrass nearby.

There was still a freshness to the day, with some people sitting to fish, while others were taking pictures with cameras around their necks, moving from one rock to the next. They all had a serenity that Johnathan had no way to notice or understand. Nothing broke through the paranoia of his mind.

Johnathan finally stopped when he reached a large dark

gray boulder that stuck out taller than the rest of the rocks that made up the jetty. It looked more weathered than the rest, as if it had been there long before the others. Maybe even back to when the entire island was a barrier forest.

When Johnathan placed his hand on the smooth face of the rock, a surge of energy pulsed through him, connecting him to it. The blood red color of his aura highlighted the outline of a door on the rockface, and a second later a handle emerged for him to press down on. He was more paranoid now than he was earlier, causing me a great deal of excitement. He didn't want to be watched, and though I wasn't the one he was afraid of, I felt closer to his secrets the more bothered he became. He knew something was wrong, but didn't have any other choice but to continue. And when he pushed on the door, it opened up to a wet, sea stinking cave.

Johnathan hurried in and sealed the door behind him with a pulse of his red energy shot at the entrance. For a moment, the cave was dark. Then Johnathan knelt down with the duffle bag in front of him and began meditating. Around him, the energy of his aura came alive in a haze. His bloody aura grew thick in the air as he hummed to the cave. His aura brought with it the smell of burntness. And as he meditated, the cave responded to the auric energy inside of its walls, pulling from him the energy he emanated into the cracks that ran deep into the stone.

The energy Johnathan pumped into the stone enjoined with the energy already locked within the cave walls. I couldn't follow the energy into the cracks, but I could feel the hungry response of the cave as it absorbed most of the energy he had stolen from the waitress at the diner. I felt so close to the answers I needed for Antonio, but it was hard to understand what was actually happening.

The cave's energy felt similar to Johnathan's own energy, but older and stronger. It felt ancient, to the point of prehistoric, while at the same time, it felt possessive of him. Johnathan's energy felt possessive of the cave's energy too. As did the humming that started in his throat and bounced off the walls before hitting his eardrums with the levels of echo that only caves can produce.

He was focused on setting the stage for what was to come, like a performer doing a mic check or a priest blessing napkins and bowls for bodily refreshments at an altar. After a few minutes of meditation, I noticed Johnathan's humming didn't dissipate the way sounds do in normal places. The echoes added to each other, like layers of sound being added one on top of the other in an audio track recording, giving the mind altering effect of floating in space and being lost in sound, unable to locate a start or end point of the source.

After a few more minutes, I wasn't sure if Johnathan was still humming to the cave, or if the cave was humming to him from the thousand cracks that pulled all of his aura out of his body to start forming a giant orb of dripping red auric light energy above him.

The energy swirled with the brilliance of an alien sun, bursting with thick tendrils that moved like red hot magma. My limited knowledge of energy and meditation from my time in the Buddhist club reminded me of how monks of mythological legend manipulated energy with sounds and music for levitation and enhanced mental and physical performance, and it looked like Johnathan was engaging in some kind of ceremony to achieve a similar effect.

He pulled the energy into his body through his nose and exhaled it through his mouth, while the cave breathed in his aura through its cracks and divots. They worked together, strengthening the light of his soulless body like the heart and lungs working together to shoot blood through a body.

Johnathan did this for some time, locked in the hum of meditation with the cave. It was obvious there was a large reservoir of energy somewhere deep within the rock. As I observed, Johnathan tried turning down the different avenues of energy to find a way past the locked layers of the cave. Some layers were put there by Johnathan himself, while some others were put there by people longer ago. Many of the layers deep within the core of the cave were behind walls of protection. Johnathan's aura was the fuel that started the engine of breaking down those walls and peeling back those layers to make the energy available for him to absorb into his own aura.

Johnathan struggled with the cave for what felt like the entirety of the hours of the afternoon before eventually unzipping the duffel bag in front of him when the blood red energy orb grew bigger than Johnathan was tall. He reached his hands into the darkness of the bag and grabbed hold of the first of the three shells.

He placed it on the sand between himself and the duffel bag, then set the other two shells on the sand beside it. I waited to see what the reaction would be from the cave, expecting some kind of immediate change or acknowledgement of the presence of the three conches, but nothing happened. Johnathan returned to his meditation, and the energy hanging in the room continued charging up and growing brighter, thicker, and denser.

After a few more hours of working through different energy barriers, Johnathan ignited his aura around the three massive conch shells, encasing them in his scarlet aura. The scarlet casings grew to an intense brightness as they started to vibrate the sand beneath them. As the sand shook, the shells sank down into the ground, and down into the cave.

As they were swallowed up by the darkness of the cave floor, it wasn't clear to me where the shells came from in the first place or what their purpose was. After a while more, the shaking ground went still. Johnathan's aura whirled around the air of the cave, suffocating everything with the stench of burntness and a furious heat that seared everything the energy touched.

While Johnathan meditated, everything seemed to be going according to his plan. He had silenced the panic in his mind about being hunted himself, and carried out what he needed to up until then. I tried once again to enter the parts of his memory relating to the shells, but I wasn't able to find anything about them. I could sense from the connection through his aura that the shells were old, but to them, Johnathan felt like a new acquaintance.

Johnathan's mind was a complex weave of thoughts as he manipulated his way through the layers of protection between himself and the cave's deepest energy reserves. He was sucking dry the thousands of years of energy stored within the rock.

By this time, Johnathan's aura was glowing more intense than I had seen an aura become. It was almost blinding to observe, even within a memory of the past. I was becoming nervous as I remembered Johnathan's impending battle. Antonio was never quite clear on how their first fight with Johnathan went all those years ago.

This night was at least two decades ago, and Johnathan was pretty beat up after. I wished Antonio had been more specific with his memory of events before having me walk into history with nothing but my own interpretations. He only said the fight didn't go in their favor, without mentioning how any of them walked away from the fight.

I couldn't imagine him stronger than after he finally maneuvered around the last wall of protection built into the cave's energy reserves, and after the cave flooded with a white hot energy that moved around the room like molten magma, building up pressure underground. The old man screamed with fury as every molecule in his body pulled apart by the force of pulling the energy through himself. His mind was the only thing holding him together. Everything that was going right a minute ago, was going wrong with the energy now.

All the energy he had already internalized control over, he lassoed around the parts of himself threatening to be pulled apart in order to keep himself intact long enough to fall back together again, if he could manage it without exploding.

Johnathan struggled to his feet, screaming in pain. His mind and body seared against the energy, sizzling with the intensity of a pan-fried pork chop on high flame. The pops and sizzles were deafening, but still Johnathan remained with his arms stretched out wide and high, absorbing what he could.

Then he lost control of his body and went airborne. His head snapped back, arms flailing, and he screamed with worst pain I had ever heard before. The pain was on a scale I had never felt before, which I never hoped to experience for real or in a memory again. But even the numbed memory of it was too much for me to bear.

But I couldn't feel sorry for him. I felt justice for his victims and for the lives they never got to live, even though I knew the pain would be fleeting for him. If pain was beauty, there was surely a lot of beauty involved in his pursuit of power.

When Johnathan's screaming didn't stop, I stepped back into his mind to see what his plan was, but there was no plan. The reaction from the cave was nothing he anticipated. He thought he was prepared to steal all the energy. He thought he had worked out all of the tricks of the cave, but he had never had such an issue with absorption before.

This time, the cave didn't want to give up what it had to him. This time, the energy in the room was trying to strangulate him by closing off his windpipe, crushing his rib cage, and gripping every molecule of his body to squeeze them into dust. The energy wasn't neutral anymore. The danger Johnathan was in wasn't the type you encounter when playing with fire, this was the danger of letting in something that wants to kill you.

Johnathan fought back with everything he had, pouring every ounce of power into taking over the energy of the room. I imagined it wasn't Johnathan's first time falling into a trap set by another, because he had come prepared. With a surge of energy thrust upward, the shells that had been buried in the sand earlier erupted from the floor and into the air, hovering around him. Each one glowed strong with his crimson aura and hummed loud, with more vigor than before.

In a mirage of red martian sunshine, Johnathan leveled his head against the force of the cave and shut his mouth despite his continued tight lipped cries. He reached out for one of the conches as they spun around him, commanding it across the air and into his hands. Where he held it against his chest and charged the shell with a torrent of energy sucked up from around the room, until the conch groaned with the hollow creaking of a tall rusty church door.

Then, he let the shell drift away to join the others. He carried out the same process with the other two shells, struggling against the violence of the cave's energy, until the power in the air started to thin. The shells spun around him, charged, and glowing a dangerous hazard red, but there was still a lot more energy for Johnathan to consume.

He lowered himself and the shells to the ground while the air buzzed. If the energy didn't kill him by force, he worried he would kill himself by overextending his own aura. He was exhausted, but he had one last plan to secure an escape with his life and body both intact.

At this point, the energy shifted to the bright orange of radioactive Martian clay, as it swirled around the cave in a sandstorm of sharp shards of fast moving particles that broke skin everywhere they sliced into Johnathan's skin. The energy moved with the full force of the cave's ancient command, closing Johnathan in with enough pressure for him to explode, but he fought it with everything he had stolen from all of his victims.

He swept the auric storm up into the air above his head, where it spun like a harvest moon, and brought it down nearer to himself. He commanded the energy onto his skin, and it smothered him like a million orange bumble bees, before erupting in another unending scream.

The radiating energy groaned against the pull of his command as he absorbed the energy and the curse that he knew he had unlocked and knew would kill him, if not in the moment, then by the end of the night. The energy burrowed into his veins, with trails of it snaking his skin as the boiling energy moved into every crack and crevice it could infect, blistering his skin as it did.

He had no choice but to absorb the poison to make it out alive. Eventually, his screaming stopped after his body collapsed on the ground over the conches. His aura glowed bright around him, red with an orange tinge from the cave's deepest reserves. His aura hummed with the charge of a jet engine, but he was too weak to even control his own body as he lay crumpled on the wet sandy cave floor. He was disoriented and dizzy, and struggled to lift his head for a while.

The poison of the energy inside of him made his body feel feverish and hot as he shook with cold chills. Blood ran from the wounds where the energy sliced into him, and he felt every droplet that leaked out of his wounds. He felt the cells touch the air and oxidize, grow cold, and die. He felt their cell walls start to break down and decompose. He felt the threadbare ends of the pain neurons along every line of the hundreds of cuts across his body and every millimeter of internal organ that the auric energy steam cooked inside of him.

For a while, Johnathan was writhing against the grating sand for control of his limbs. Little by little he was able to first get to his knees by holding himself up by his arms. After a while longer, he was able to pull himself into a seated, cross-legged position beside the shells. He struggled with the shells as he tried to move them into the duffle bag with waning control of his body. And by the time he got all three shells into the bag, the bag was half full of wet sand that there was nothing he could do to remove.

It took all of his remaining strength to lift himself and the bag up from the floor of the cave and cross to the exit door. He moved one leg at a time as his body worked through the molasses of the poisoned energy. When he reached the part of the cave wall where he had entered, he pressed his hand against it and waited for it to open. And he felt it fitting when the door never appeared.

Now, there was no doubt in his mind that someone was after him. If they weren't responsible for the cursed energy, they were responsible for the locked door. Someone didn't want him to leave the cave alive, and the fury of being trapped burned inside of him in the familiar way that Joshua would boil in stressful fits of rage and envy. As his fury expanded, the focus required of him to hold and control the energy he absorbed from the cave shattered, and he exploded with bright auric energy.

In the split second before the blast would have sent him

smack against the opposite wall of the cave, Johnathan directed the energy explosion to blow a way out. He forced the energy in the direction of the door, hoping it would be enough to free him. Then he heard the clap of thunder, felt the force of the explosion, and his heels dug into the sand from the backwards force, as the ancient cave wall exploded. The rock shattered like ceramic on a cement floor, sending chunks of cave flying into the cloudy sky outside.

Johnathan was relieved by the sight of the stormy night and the spinning light from the lighthouse shining through the rain. But he was weak again, and being back out in the open air made the feeling of being watched return to him. As he climbed out of the rubble of the cave, he tried to locate the watchful presence of his own predator, but all traces eluded him. He had a small portion of the energy he absorbed still within himself, and he pumped it into the armor he needed to keep himself upright, dry, and moving.

He ran for the car with the limping walk he could achieve, but he was afraid he wouldn't even make it there. He was in no shape for a fight. He was outmatched, without even seeing his hunters, but he was ready to use everything he could to survive. Dying, he was certain, was out of the question. He was going to make it to the end of the path, across the parking lot, and into his car. Once there, he figured he would be fine, but somehow the path that he took so many times before to bring himself back to the parking lot, had brought him instead in front of the lighthouse.

At the top, below the spinning light, he finally found the answer we had been waiting for. The five hunters hovered in their auric armor. The sky blue of Antonio, emerald green of Zenda, mint green of Ikkyu, Kana's cherry blossom pink, and an eggplant purple that I knew had to be Aurelius.

Johnathan was furious with them and even more furious with himself after walking into another one of their traps. His captors were stronger than he was, but he had gotten himself out of tough situations before. He knew he could get out alive, he just wasn't sure how much life he would have left afterwards.

"What do you want with me?" Johnathan shouted up from the tree line, disinterested in getting any closer to the lighthouse.

The rain fell hard, but it fizzled into steam as it approached his burning aura, evaporating into the humid air. The five immortals atop the lighthouse peered down at Johnathan without a word or motion of anything in acknowledgement of his inquiry. Johnathan needed to stall as he decided how to manage five against one.

"We offer you an opportunity to join us," boomed Aurelius's voice with the oppressive force of thunder. His purple auric armor, a thick bright robe of energy.

"Renounce your immortality and live out the rest of your days hunting vermin like yourself," Zenda spoke, offering a proposition I was never aware of.

I didn't understand how they could ask such a monster to join them. There was still so much I didn't know about the Immortal Philosophers, but their questions left me speechless. I watched and waited for Johnathan's answer, hoping he'd renounce them. Hoping they hadn't let him free to torture me. I needed answers from Antonio, and I needed to know if any of them had histories similar to Joshua's that I didn't know about.

"Or die now," Kana added.

"It's your choice," Ikkyu added. The group was much more intimidating from Johnathan's perspective than when I had met them as friends, but I wasn't sure what to believe about them anymore.

"I'm not interested in living life on anyone else's terms,"

Johnthan said. "Not for now, and definitely not forever."

"It's ironic the way you live then," Antonio called down, his voice warm in the cold rain, but to Johnathan it was comedy.

"I don't need a moral lesson," Johnathan said, now channeling his voice instead of shouting. "You can let me go, or do what you must. But I'm getting out of here alive."

"Life without living is not life at all," Aurelius said. "You've been dead for a long time already, but you can try to escape like the demon you are. Until we find you again."

And in a flash of blinding light, Aurelius blinked out of existence and reappeared in front of Johnathan, his grape aura blazing with heat and the scent of sour wine.

Aurelius swung a purple gloved fist at Johnathan's face and hit him square in the jaw. Johnathan's aura shattered where Aurelius hit. It took everything for Johnathan to remain standing, but he did. His aura repaired itself where it shattered, and he used his bloody armor like a force field, swiping up at Aurelius with his arms.

Johnathan's aura flowed out in an arc, smacking Aurelius with a wave of energy that sent the philosopher flying back. Aurelius's body bulleted across the clearing and cratered into the bottom white half of the lighthouse, but Johnathan didn't have a second to appreciate the blow he dealt.

In the next instant, the predator was surrounded. Antonio, Zenda, Ikkyu, and Kana each bombarded him with torrents of energy powerful enough to vaporize him to dust. In a flash, Johnathan channeled all of the energy he had in himself into a shield he held as he crouched over the duffle bag. The beams of blistering blues, pinks, and greens battered him as the immortals seared his defenses.

At the base of the lighthouse, Aurelius was still recovering from the impact and his fall, but he was coming to his feet. Johnathan knew if Aurelius joined the others in attack, it would be the end of him, so he needed to act fast.

Johnathan had had his run-ins with the odd gangs of inexperienced auric wielders, but these five were different. These five were professionals, like the groups he kept in touch with that hunted humans for immortality. He wasn't going to let immortals who didn't have to work for their immortality take his from him.

With seconds between life and death, fewer seconds than he had felt in his bodily memory, Johnathan pulled at the zipper of the duffle bag as hard as he could. The bag opened to reveal the three shells reserved as a last resort. They were glowing with the copper of the cave's core energy, already in sync with his purpose. He grabbed one of the shells and brought the conch to his lips, swallowing a deep breath as Aurelius shot up into the air. As Aurelius readied to aim a beam of purple energy down at the center of Johnathan's shield, Johnathan blew into the conch as hard as he could.

There was a loud hollow sound until the conch cracked, and from the crack came an explosion. The conch fell back into the bag, as everything around him blasted backwards. Even the rain. For an instance, everything was still and quiet in the gray night. His shield was gone, and the world around him was dust and smoke as everything fell from view. The lights of his attackers' auras faded out, and he couldn't sense them around himself anymore.

The only color against the gray came from the two remaining conch shells under him, still encased in his auric energy. Then, the space around us started filling in, and we were standing in the nursery over the crib of mortal, sleeping, baby Joshua. Before everything for me went dark.

CHAPTER NINE

SUNSET IN THE VALLEY OF NOW AND THEN

I DIDN'T KNOW HOW long I was asleep for. Everything was black for a long time, and I couldn't open my eyes even if I had wanted to. Laying there between consciousness and unconsciousness was all I could manage. My body felt more drained than it was before I fell asleep. I needed to exist in the gray of morning, just after the world wasn't dark anymore. I needed it to stretch on as long as it could and wrap around me in its soft folds while I warded off the harsh realities of what was most likely to come.

When I finally did awake, I was surprised to find myself in the arms of Antonio. He held my back to his chest, curled up against me. I was warm with the buzz of his aura charging mine where my back touched his front. The energy around my body felt like a breath of lavender, while Johnathan's had felt like pure terror. From the memories, I realized that the energy Joshua received was never of a calm or nurturing nature. It was always full of spite for having been bothered away from its core, but energy given in love flowed differently.

I didn't have to turn around or open my eyes to know that Antonio was still sleeping. In the grand scheme of everything that happened the night before, I ended up closer to Antonio than I thought was possible for a first date. Not only did I already have the opportunity to meet the family, but we would wake up together, too. But given the nightmare of my life's turn, I couldn't help but wish the night had ended in a simple kiss before he dropped me off at home.

As I absorbed his aura, that alternate reality played out in my dream fringed mind. I couldn't imagine being alone back at the bungalow after everything that happened since dinner. It felt so far away. My time asleep felt like days. Viewing the past felt like watching real time pass. I knew I desperately needed to tell Antonio what I saw, but all I could do was wait. Everyone would learn the information when I awoke, and they would or wouldn't know what to do to defeat him. Then we would win, or he would win. It all seemed so inevitable that time didn't seem to matter to me as much anymore.

Eventually my mind settled on the closeness of Antonio's body. He had one arm around my stomach and his other around the pillow at his head. The curve of his body against mine felt natural. As if he had laid with me every night and would lay with me every night more. And as I laid there, leaning back against him, I drifted between the clouds of my own mind with the butterflies in my stomach from his vibration.

It felt strange to think of Joshua as a man hundreds of years old, kept alive by the energy, time, and youth he stole from others, including the life of his grandchild. He was guilty of acts so beyond evil that I couldn't imagine a human carrying them out. I didn't know what other dark deeds Joshua was guilty of, but it was becoming more clear to me that there was nothing Joshua wouldn't do to survive. And after a while, I fell back to sleep.

Antonio was the one who woke me up next, with his movement behing me. This time, I was fully awake. The half conscious state I was floating between earlier felt like hours away, putting us somewhere into the future I couldn't pinpoint. My time asleep felt like days, but Antonio's room looked the same as it had before.

He was still curled against me, with his arm still around my stomach. He moved one of his legs, and I took the chance to slide my hand into his while I could. His fingers moved like an artist's wooden model hand as mine filled their gaps before he closed his fingers over the back of my hand, neither of us breaking the silence of the moment.

There was no good way to start the day we had ahead. The stakes were too high. Joshua was growing stronger, and while I uncovered how Joshua evaded his attackers last time, it didn't seem like there was any way to keep him from escaping a second time.

Don't worry, Antonio interjected between my thoughts. *We will find a way.*

I didn't want to think back. I wanted to speak back. I needed to take my mind off of our shadow war, and since Antonio was awake, I turned over to face him.

"Good morning," I said, as if nothing else in the world existed except us and the four corners of the bed around us. He watched me as I talked, looking as tired as I felt.

"You weren't asleep very long," Antonio said. "It's not morning. It's only sunset."

The time differentials between my time-walking and waking hours paralyzed my mind for a few seconds as I contemplated my grasp on my own memory. I felt like I had spent days digging through Joshua's memories, but it had only been just a few minutes.

"It's like we're taking refuge in a valley before a big battle," I said. "Like the Comanche natives. I heard a lot about them from my grandfather growing up. He was told all his life that he had a Comanche grandfather he had never met, who he revered all his life."

Antonio stared into my eyes, and I stared at him back, not

wanting to stop. But the story felt important to tell. So, I continued.

"My grandfather was so obsessed with this fact about himself that he had a room in his library dedicated to writings focused on or referencing the Comanche with all types of different artifacts he had purchased. A year before he passed, he even took a DNA test to find out the truth about his Comanche heritage. He was certain the blood was there, but how much of it was there was the question my grandfather wanted to know. It wouldn't have made a difference if it were a little or a lot, but it would have given him the ability to discover potential relatives while he was still alive. He wanted to know the family he descended from."

"Sunsets always remind me of the painting in his study above his desk of a Comanche campsite set up in a valley. What had been a peaceful scene of the tribe's camp life for had turned into an efficient display of preparing the horses to carry everything they had and every man, woman, and child. On the horizon, where the sun was setting, was an army charging to ambush them. My grandfather would always tell me that no matter how close the attackers thought they were to the Comanche, the Comanche would always be gone before the attackers would reach where their camp had been."

"I was shocked when the DNA results came back, and there was no Comanche blood to be found. But, this reaffirmed his conviction in his belief. It was exactly as he expected. The Comanche could not be found.

"We're in that valley now," I said. "*Sunset in the Valley of Now and Then*. The name of the painting. I'm there, and I feel how the Comanche must have felt. The fear of their attackers, but also the peace in knowing that if they did what they knew they could do, they would be okay. We can pull that off, too," I said. "We'll be okay."

"That's an incredible story," Antonio said. "Your grandfather sounds like a very interesting person, and you're right. We are in *Sunset in the Valley of Now and Then*."

The emotion of my memory melted my fears as the softness of Antonio's comforted me, and my eyes started to well with inexplicable tears.

"We'll be okay," Antonio confirmed, pulling me closer to him. I let myself be pulled, until my cheek was on his chest and he held my head against him. "I won't let anything happen to you."

I laid with Antonio like that for a minute or so, allowing my mind to return to the peace of the moment, and let the tears seep into his shirt.

"Thank you," I said, when I was finally calm.

"You're welcome," Antonio said. "None of us will let Joshua hurt you or steal from you anymore. I won't leave your side when it comes to whatever happens later. I've made that clear to Aurelius and Zenda. They know how I feel."

"How exactly do you feel?" I said, collecting myself, and taking Antonio by surprise. He wore the embarrassment of a child admitting to something he meant to keep secret and didn't know what to say.

"Sit up," Antonio said, pulling his legs up before bringing them over to his side of the bed.

"Okay," I said.

"Come sit next to me," he said, patting the bed beside him. I crawled over to the spot beside him and sat with my legs hanging over the edge too, facing the wall of curtained windows from which no light came through from outside.

"Sunset," Antonio said, and he waved his hand. The wall we were facing disappeared. The warm breeze came into the room, and I took in the sight of the pastel highlighter sunset. The sky was cotton candy pink and peach orange around the long fingers of clouds that glowed like wildfire where the wall used to be.

"All of us humans have lived with the same exquisite palette of the daily sky," Antonio said. "And all of its breathtaking colors and effects."

"I never thought of it like that," I said, feeling more connected to the people of the past just looking at the sky. "That's beautiful."

The sun bobbed just above the tree line, which was only a short time away from swallowing up the sun and leaving us staring at the brilliant streaks of shining sky above. There was no sunset like a sunset at the shore. I didn't want the opportunity to pass me by, so I eventually wrapped my arm around Antonio's shoulders and pulled him closer to me.

"Thank you. For everything," I said. The magic of the moment was an unforgettable experience. The missing wall was not missed at all. Bikers and joggers on the road passed us by, but they didn't even notice us sitting in the bedroom on his bed.

"You're welcome," Antonio said, looking down at his lap. "It's the least I can do."

"It's impressive," I said, curious about everything behind the thick curtain of secrecy the immortals lived behind and wondered why so much secrecy was necessary.

"What did the DNA results actually say for your grandfather?" Antonio asked. "What was he, if not Comanche?"

"Polish," I said. "One hundred percent. He went to plead his case to Comanche elders at the time, and they made him feel good about his beliefs. I don't know what they said exactly, but they didn't want to break the old man's heart. They let him believe his delusion and invited him into their tribe as an honorary elder. I don't think anything was official, but it was a dream made real for an old man, all the same."

"Did you ever see yourself or your dreams in that painting the way your grandfather saw himself?" Antonio asked.

"No, I never really felt like I was in the painting, or like my dreams were coming true the way he did. It's funny how some people dream, while others don't. I think now might be the first time I've considered dreaming freely. I still don't know what my dreams are exactly, though. I feel like I've barely gotten the chance to explore myself and what I want. I've just been focused on getting to the point of independence," I said, feeling more than thinking, as I spoke.

The glow of the darkening sky gave Antonio's skin an amber shine, and I moved myself closer to him. We were both intent on each other's lips and eyes before we inched closer and closed off the visual world before pressing our lips together. Feeling the doubt I had in him slipping away. When we kissed, every fiber of my body cheered me on with delight, and I didn't want it to stop. I played with his bottom lip with my tongue while he massaged my top lip with his. We did this until we moved our tongues between each other's mouths, losing track of everything except the places where our bodies touched. It felt like if I just did what I knew I could do, everything would be okay, and I couldn't have asked for a better way to feel as our fates awaited us on the other side of sunset.

Antonio pulled away from me after the last glow of light from the sun disappeared into darkness, when the stars finally became visible in the night sky. My body buzzed with excitement and the freshness of a mint bath.

Then we kissed again. We moved our lips and tongues as if we were writing the language we would be speaking together for the rest of our lives. It was a sunset burning with passion and lust, desperation, and, perhaps unwarranted, trust. I was on the brink of all that was known and unknown on that bed in the bedroom with the view of the sky where the wall should have been.

I didn't know what to say to Antonio after our period of intimate silence. My mind was at peace, staring into his caramel colored eyes with my arms around his neck. The air he breathed had the distinct scent of ocean spray. The smell was intoxicating to the point that I didn't want to turn away my head to breathe anything else. I didn't want to move forward from that moment or scare away the presence of what had just come to pass.

"I'm not letting him hurt you," Antonio said, his lips glistening as he spoke.

"You better not," I said. "Now that I have a lot more to look forward to."

"You know," Antonio said, looking unsure again, as I found he typically was. "Even if we weren't locked in a fight together with an evil predator, I still would have hoped to end my night with you."

"So all of the dating talk was real?" I asked, deciding to make a joke of the moment.

"All of it," he said. "I was hoping that was clear. I meant every word I said to you, and after we figure out the Joshua situation, I want to end my nights with you a little more."

"That all sounds nice," I said. "I want that too, but when do you think that will be?"

"Well, since you've figured out Joshua's secrets, it shouldn't take Aurelius long to come up with some kind of way for us to defeat him," Antonio said.

"Wait. How do you know I figured everything out?" I asked, knowing for certain I hadn't told him about my sleeping memory travels.

"I had to keep an eye on you in your sleep," Antonio said. "Your aura's been awakened. It's going to take some time for you to learn how to control it, even in your sleep. Now that Joshua isn't sapping every ounce of energy out of you, you're going to get stronger, and it's going to be more important that you can control your aura. You have an affinity for viewing and moving through the past. Soon, your aura will pull you into using it in other ways, and you want to make sure you won't hurt yourself or anyone else. Tonight, I wanted to make sure that you weren't freaking yourself out in your head or losing yourself in the past. You did a good job."

"Thank you," I said. "I don't know what I would do if you weren't here with me."

Antonio looked surprised.

"Really?" he said. "And here I am feeling the same way about you."

"Are you scared?" I asked, wondering what his answer would be. His team seemed capable of taking out Joshua back on the beach in the memory, if only Joshua hadn't escaped. They didn't seem like they had much to be scared about.

"This time will be different," Antonio said. "It's not going to be like our first encounter. Joshua didn't expect us then. We ambushed him, but he had a plan B. This time he's ready for us, but we'll just have to take away his plan B if he has one this time."

I shook my head to sink the rising memories of how it felt to be around Joshua. I didn't have time for the constrictions that trauma loops the mind around. I needed clarity of thought and a healthy sense of investigative objectivity. I needed to remember what I knew that would be useful in uncovering the mystery of Joshua's motives and weaknesses.

"Memories, like stories, take time to be absorbed and interpreted by the mind. Meditating on the memories will help you dig into all there is to remember. Knowledge and memory are auric entities. They're as real as the physical energy I can manifest into my palm."

Antonio held up his palm and pooled energy the color of Caribbean blue waters into the bowl of his big hand. "We just experience them in only a few of the many ways that knowledge and memory can be experienced," Antonio continued. "Aurics will start making more sense as you experience more of what life really has to offer. Aurelius is on his way. Zenda, Ikkyu, and Kana are meditating throughout the night on a solution. Aurelius is aware of recent developments. If Zenda doesn't have it figured out by morning, Aurelius will. We all play our parts on this team, and, when we do, we accomplish what we set out for. Now, we need you to rest so you're ready for whatever comes our way tomorrow. We'll all have a part to play. Here," Antonio said, holding up his hand, still full of auric energy, and said "Drink."

I drank the aura from his hand as he tilted it to my lips. It burned like vodka all the way down my throat, and into my stomach. When his blue met the well of my cobalt core, our auras mixed. A rush of energy raced to every part of my body in currents of azure particles, making even the hairs on my arms stand up in electric satisfaction, and making me feel more powerful than ever before.

"Whoa!" I said, unable to refuse my body's natural reaction to the prolonged presence of the pleasure of what felt like real power running through my body, all under my control. I surged the energy into the air around me the way I watched Joshua do in the cave. The energy evaporated off my skin and gathered into a thick cloud. The cloud glowed a bright sapphire that shone where it before was dull and transparent.

I gathered the vaporous spread of my aura close around my body and arms with my will, layering it until it hugged me the way Antonio's auric armor hugged him.

"There you go," Antonio said, pleased with my display of control. I felt like a car battery charged back to life by the jump from another.

"I can control it now," I said, looking around. My auric armor was as smooth as a latex glove filled with air, but it looked and felt as solid as a glass. Its blue form was transparent, so I could see my skin and clothes underneath the thin layer of warm, humming energy.

I held up my palm to see if I could form something with my aura the way Antonio did at dinner and closed my eyes. I visualized a spherical space above my palm, and visualized filling it with blue light. I pushed my aura out from my core, through my chest, and down my arm. I willed the energy into my hands and out through my fingers, and I felt the energy move as I directed. And watched the sphere fill with my energy.

"I've never seen someone be able to use their aura so naturally so soon after being awakened to it," Antonio said.

"Seriously?" I asked, impressed with myself, but sure Antonio had to be exaggerating.

"Yeah, seriously," he said. "And in all the memories I've seen. It takes years of meditation just for new learners to have enough control over their auras to do what you can do now."

"Maybe I'm a natural," I said, accepting my proficiency. It felt good to be good at something, and especially a magic something.

"Well," Antonio said. "I guess you never leave as the same person you were after a sunset in the valley of now and then."

"No," I said, remembering the bronze of his face in the setting sun. "To get out, you leave who you must become."

CHAPTER TEN

SPIRIT WARRIOR RITUALS

THE LONG NIGHT OF the dreamless sleep I was desperate for felt like it passed in the blink of an eye. My vision of Antonio's soft sleeping face fell away to the blackness of my sleeping mind. I imagined myself swinging on a hammock below deck, swaying with the slow back and forth of a sailing ship as I sank deeper into myself with the passing of the minutes. I wished I could have fallen forever at the easy pace of a feather. I had never been on a parachute, and I doubted the ride down from the clouds would feel so smooth. But I liked the pace where the world felt hours away, waiting to reach the ground so I could do it all over again.

Antonio was still in bed beside me when I awoke. The room was dark except for the sky blue light shining on the walls from Antonio's energy transferring to me. I was surprised he held the transfer throughout the night, but I felt great. My exhaustion from the night before was gone. Even my mind felt clear and ready. Above all, my aura felt like a weapon I could do a lot of damage with.

Antonio opened his eyes after a while. He looked more tired than I thought I did. His face was grayer and paler than it had been the day before. The radiant glow he seemed to capture from the sun and reflect through his skin was gone. I didn't realize using energy could have such physical effects on natural immortals too so quickly.

"You look exhausted," I told him. Then the auric link between us broke, plunging us into darkness. But instead of turning on a light, Antonio shot an orb of his aura from his fingertip at the lightbulb in the lamp at his bedside. In an instant the room returned to being the same cyan oasis it was before.

"I haven't been this tired in a long time," he said.

"Then stop using your aura," I said. "It's draining you."

"I know," he said. "It drains me, but it charges you. I'll be fine."

"Yeah, but you're going to be the one fighting," I said, feeling sorry for him. It felt like he was taking a risk, draining himself of strength before another battle with Joshua.

"I'm like a solar battery," Antonio said. "I have the strongest aura in the group. I charge the quickest, somehow. That's kind of my thing. It's from coming into my power so early in life, we think."

"You think?" I asked.

"Yeah," Antonio said. "We don't always exactly know things for sure when it comes to aurics, but we're the only authority on the subject. We can't go to the dictionary or a search engine for answers about why things are the way they are when it comes to our magic. We kind of have to make educated assumptions based on how we interpret energy and our observations. We try to apply our own scientific method. And maybe scientists will figure it all out one day, but our best guesses are all we've got right now."

"That's all fair," I said, laughing a little. The scientific method seemed so out of place for us to be discussing with the magic coursing through our bodies, but there seemed to be an underlying connectedness to everything, I was learning. It seemed maybe science and spirituality weren't as separate as Western culture seemed to conceptualize them to be.

"When will you recharge yourself?" I said, my mind returning to my concern for him. It wasn't quite yet love, obviously, but there was a kind of energy between us that felt familiar and comfortable.

"I'll charge at breakfast," Antonio said. "I'll eat and meditate. That's if Joshua doesn't show up and blow the house up before we get downstairs. That would just ruin everything," Antonio said, failing to be funny.

"Well," I said. "If he does, I'd rather it happen on a full stomach. I'm hungry too. I need to eat something soon," I said, trying not to think of the possibility of Joshua showing up unannounced. I saw the destruction he was capable of, and I knew his ruthlessness was limitless. "There's not a chance of him finding us, is there?"

"No, there's no chance," Antonio said. "I'm starving too. My body's had enough."

"Enough?" I asked. "So, there is a limit for you, then?"

"There's always a limit," Antonio said. "In everything, before it turns into something else, but especially with auric energy. We have to respect our limits, or else the flames that burn bright inside of us now will be extinguished by the errors of our ambitions. You have to be careful not to deplete your auric core. It could cause irreversible death. It's a serious game, playing with magic. It will take time for you to learn your limits, but along with exhaustion, hunger is one of the first signs of overextension."

"What else could help your auric core?" I said. "If you can't eat or sleep?"

"You meditate," Antonio said. "If you can. If you can't, then you just try to get by using the least amount of energy possible. Those are our immortal rules. Joshua's limitations might be more dire than ours, but, again, these powers don't come with instruction manuals. You have to tune into the vibrations of your body and follow the guidance of your internal compass. There are some stories of people channeling auric energy out of the auric current, but that's not something I've seen or know how to do."

"Okay, so with Joshua," I said. "Without energy, he just ages? Will that happen to you all?"

"No," Antonio said. "If we die from exhausting our auras, we pop like an expanding bubble blown too large for the amount of soapy water keeping it together, but that's the nature of overextension. It's a philosophical imperative that overextension carries with it undesirable consequences. There's no skirting that, even for us. You're one of us, though. That's a fact. Joshua would dry like a raisin without energy. He's like a gas car, we're like solar batteries. Time is our friend, but for Joshua it's a ticking clock."

"Okay," I said, making sense of it all. My status as an immortal. My reality as it was becoming. I felt out of place with so many unknowns, but the intimate way Antonio said 'us' made me feel included in something exclusive. I looked forward to seeing what life would look like beyond Joshua's reign over me. I wasn't sure how my dream of designing movie covers was going to fit into my new life, but I was open to holding off on that while I took care of the Joshua situation and adjusted to my new abilities.

"So, when was the last time you were up against someone like Joshua?" I asked.

"Well, after we ambushed Joshua," Antonio said, leaning back on his pillow. "Aurelius assigned us more active hunting jobs. Joshua blinked off our radars after he vanished that night, and we weren't sure if he even made it somewhere else alive. Aurelius wanted us ready for when he popped back up."

"Who was your last target?" I asked, curious to learn how immortals coped with different predators.

"It's gruesome," Antonio said. "More gruesome than most of the demented ones we've encountered."

"I think I can handle some gruesome truths after everything else I've learned," I said.

"We called her Mary," Antonio continued. "Because she reminded me of Typhoid Mary from the way she lored in her prey. She was a cook, like Mary, but instead of the sickness of her poor hygiene killing her victims, it was the victims she served up for herself that kept her alive."

"Ew," I said, as my stomach turned. "That's gross."

"You have no idea," Antonio said, turning to face the wall. "The memories aren't pretty. You wouldn't want to see them, but we had to save people. Mortals have no way of defending themselves against powers like ours. If we don't find and stop these groups and predators, like Joshua, they never stop and will always grow in numbers."

"How long ago was Typhoid Mary?" I asked.

"Two years ago," he said. "After Mary, the four of us took a break from pursuing predators. Every once in a while we have to settle down for a bit, re-establish our identities, and train with each other. Then Aurelius located Joshua and yourself about a year ago, so we all started putting our energy into helping him with your situation while maintaining our presence down here. We didn't know this would be the ultimate conclusion of events. We wanted to pull you away from him naturally and see if he would let go. The job offer, the bungalow. It was all made to offer you an easy way out, and it worked, mostly. We still didn't know how to beat him. The trap Aurelius had turned the cave into last time didn't work. Joshua is more knowledgeable than we expected. It looks like he's a master teleporter, if he can do it from here to New York. That's when he has the energy to achieve it."

"You make it sound like we still don't have a shot when you add everything up like that," I said, feeling hopeless against it all.

"We do have a shot," Antonio said. "We're some of the best immortals in our ranks."

"Do you think he knows I'm with you?" I asked, wondering if Joshua knew he might be in more danger than I was.

"He wouldn't be able to detect our powers," Antonio said. "And it would be hard for him to believe you found a group of us powerful enough to shield you or protect you. I could see him considering that maybe he's already too late. That maybe a group of, or a lone predator already got a hold of you after your powers started growing from being away from his influence."

"That seems the most reasonable thought, honestly," I said, agreeing with him. "You think he'll leave all on his own if we just wait it out?" I asked, hoping Antonio's answer might be the one I wanted to hear.

"I think he would leave eventually," Antonio said, taking in a breath that reached the bottom of his lungs and made his chest rise. "But we always have to think about the next victim. The targets we identify never stop unless we stop them. We can't forget that."

"I get that," I said. "I think I understand it better than anybody. So are we no longer prey? We're the predators on the hunt?"

"We're not required to, be" Antonio said. "Just obligated to, by our philosophy."

"That's a very roundabout way of saying we have to," I said.

"But I understand. I can do whatever you teach me to do to help defeat him and whoever we find in the future. I'm okay with that. How did you all wind up defeating Mary?"

"We…" Antonio said, looking troubled by the memory. "We had to poison her final victim," he said, pausing to assess my reaction. "It was a mess of a situation."

"It sounds like it," I said, surprised by what sounded like using someone as bait. "How did all that go down?"

"It wasn't the situation we wanted," he said. "But it was a situation worse than we could've imagined. South of here, down in Cape May, we tracked these three sisters who had to be as old as the Delaware River Basin itself. They ran a bed and breakfast off the coast. Most of their customers were a weird, human-fish hybrid type of creature, of which the sisters were too. We got reports of the unlucky guests who weren't such creatures disappearing as quickly as they arrived, and one night we found out why."

"The sisters would manipulate and drug their victims into being lured from the bed and breakfast to a deep and bottomless pool of water in the forest reserve at the end of the beach along the coast. Their victims would follow them to the inky pool where they would be manipulated to sink into the black depths before death would come from suffocation. Then the victims would be picked apart by tiny mouths and swallowed up by hundreds of aquatic predators."

"We knew that if we just took out the sisters, the hybrids would just replace the sisters with a few more charmers to carry out their circus charade, so we had to poison their last victim in order to make sure that every single one of them would be poisoned and taken care of. Nearly a thousand fish-like bodies floated to the surface of the deep pool within an hour of feeding. We scooped them out to make sure the pool was clean of them at every depth, and it was. There's no knowing how many victims they consumed over the centuries, but they're not doing it anymore."

"Now I'm the bait?" I asked in the still silence that followed. I couldn't think of anything else. It seemed like that was the logical conclusion to what Antonio was trying to conversationally avoid approaching. I couldn't forget the group's invitation to Johnathan to join their group, and I wanted answers about who they all actually were before I could really trust their movies.

"You're not the bait," Antonio answered, looking me straight in the eyes. "You're the hero of the story," he said, like he meant it. "This story is your story. We're just here to help you determine an outcome that works in your favor over Joshua's. Joshua's manipulation ends here, and I'm here because I had a feeling about you from the moment we met. I won't let you end up anywhere but next to me on our way to forget about all of this after we defeat him."

I heard everything he said, and I listened for the lie. But all I detected was the warm feelings that I had when I first met him in the café. Everything about him was different from everyone else, to the point that all I wanted to do was drink the image of him into my eyes and hope I'd get to look at him forever. He gave me a comforting feeling that I didn't have around anyone else that felt like the safety of a winter coat on a fall day. He made me feel like I had nothing to worry about or fear, even if the wind picked up.

"You're right," I said, determined to be on the other side of Joshua's demise. "I had a feeling about you too. After we turn Joshua into a memory I'll tell you what kind of feeling it was," I said, laughing and breaking the tension of the quiet room.

Antonio laughed with me. It was hard to reconcile the severity of the danger with my inexperience, while also trying to impress him, but it seemed like I was impressing him already.

"Do I have to worry about anyone on our side?" I said. "And what about the invitation for Johnathan to join the Immortal Philosophers?"

"There's no way for a predator to become one of us," Antonio said. "He would have expired by the end of the night from Aurelius's curse. It was the taking of his grandson's body that saved him. The invitation was trick for him to drp his guard. We are all dangerous, but we're all dedicated to you, so you don't have to worry. Are you ready to go see what Zenda's cooking up?" Antonio asked. "Aurelius arrived a little bit ago. He's waiting downstairs too."

"I'm ready," I said, relieved of my worries and more ready than ever to climb out of bed and feed my aching stomach. "I don't know if I've ever been this hungry before in my life."

"Probably not," Antonio said, getting up and making his way across the room. "Life's going to be very different for you from now on. It will be a lot more challenging and dangerous until we teach you to master your powers."

Instead of walking toward the door to lead us out, Antonio walked up to me, and stopped closer to me than I would've let anybody else get. I wasn't sure if there was even space between us for our auras to shine, making me notice how the smell of him was indistinguishable from the smell of me.

"I'm ready for all of it," I said, slipping my fingers into the palms of his hands and pulling him in for the kiss I had assumed he had come for. I leaned in. He followed. So, I leaned in more.

When we kissed, my lips tingled with an electric buzz that I only ever felt kissing him. I felt it the night before too. I thought it might have been the spark that people talked about finding with that one special person, the same one that people talk about losing just months later. I didn't want that to be the case, but there was something more to the feeling than just superstition around the sensation. This life actually felt like the one I was meant to be living.

The usual smells of breakfast were absent from the vast halls of the house as we left the bedroom. My nose searched for clues about the breakfast menu while I followed Antonio down the steps, through the foyer, and past the sitting room on our way to the kitchen. When we rounded the corner of the kitchen, Kana, Ikkyu, Zenda, and Aurelius were already seated around the circular wooden table before the back wall of windows. It was my first time seeing Aurelius in person, and he looked just like the webcam meeting version of himself from my interview. Curly black hair, almond shaped eyes, and a serious presence. He didn't look like he smelled something bad, but he looked ready to raise his nostril in a sneer at a moment's notice. His plain white tunic with white cloth crossing his chest was as I would have expected from a philosopher, but not from an emperor.

"Good morning," I said, unsure of what to say. They didn't exactly make cards for 'waking up to your doomsday' or 'your induction into a secret immortal society' day.

"Good morning," everyone said. Not in unison, but not in any special way either. It was dull. Even Kana seemed more serious than yesterday.

"It's good to see you, Aurelius," I said, grateful he was there.

"It's good to see you too," Aurelius said back. "Let's hope this is the last time you're the target of danger after this."

"I hope it will be, too," I said.

"What's all this?" Antonio asked, pointing at the table and directing his question at Ikkyu and Zenda, who sat with Kana on Ikkyu's right and Aurelius on Zenda's left.

"Have a seat," Ikkyu said, waving his arm over the table at the seats on our side of the room.

Up close, the table was the color of almond skin, with a smooth sanded top and grooves that ran like rivers around its center. Behind them, the morning sky was purple along the oceanic horizon, backlighting the orange glow of the dim kitchen. It was still early. Everyone looked only half rested and a little bothered, or worried. I couldn't tell the difference.

"I tried to make us a simple breakfast," Aurelius said, as we took our seats. "Oats on the stove top, but they wanted to do a ceremony."

"He'll need it," Ikkyu said.

Between himself and Zenda sat a teapot and one white porcelain tea cup for each of us beside a stack of clean emerald plates.

"What is the ceremony?" I asked.

"It's as old as I am," Zenda said. "We're going to carry out a tea ceremony from the forests of where the ancient plant originated. As I mentioned yesterday, the tribe I was born into were a group of spiritual warriors who harvested tea for its auric energy. Groups from all over south east Asia would send for us to help them cure their sick, wounded, and demented. We would hunt out demons, much like we do today, but things were different back then."

"The ceremony we will conduct today is the same we used to carry out in preparation for a hunt back then," Zenda said, as if she had explained the ceremony many times before. "We would sit around the fire of our camp, imbuing our energy into the leaves of our most sacred tea tree, awakening the sublunary energy deep inside the earth. Our tea trees were what are called auric wells, bountiful springs of energy, that made their tea one of the few vessels through which energy could be transferred to us from the energy cores within the ancient grounds. During this ceremony, we will receive some of this sublunary energy to help you access more of your auric potential. It will feed your auric core with power brought up from the core of the Earth itself. This is an honor few immortals experience so early in their training, but your aura has a will stronger than you give yourself credit for. This ceremony will help you unlock more of that truth."

"Thank you," I said, stunned and excited. "I'm ready."

"I can tell," Zenda said. "Your work last night was expert."

"With this ceremony, also," Aurelius said. "We induct you into the Immortal Philosophers. This is our offer to you. For training and support, and a life of helping others and protecting others the way that we are helping you now. Your autonomy would always be yours. You'd be free to do what you please at any moment, ever," Aurelius continued. "But when you're with us, you stick to the plan, and we'll teach you everything we know. We will protect you as our own."

"We will," Zenda said, bringing her hands to the table.

Ikkyu and Kana nodded their heads in agreement. Antonio watched me as I listened, as if trying to figure out what I was thinking. Even if he was listening to my mind, he wouldn't have gotten any clues to my thoughts. I didn't know what to say, but 'yes' was the only answer I could think of. If I wanted to walk, after defeating Joshua, I could, but I wasn't sure I'd be safe on my own if I chose to go that route. I wonder if Antonio got the same deal. If he was able to walk at any moment if he wanted. It would be good to know if that could be a plan B for us, if things just didn't feel right with everyone else, but I was invested in learning everything they knew and seeing how well I could master my abilities.

"Yes," I said. "I'm in. Help me, and I'll help you. It is an honor to take part in your ceremony and become an Immortal Philosopher. I may not be perfect all the time, but it doesn't seem like perfect exists in this world anyway. I'm in for it."

"Then allow us to carry out the Spirit Warrior Tea Ceremony," Aurelius said. "And anoint you into the lineage of the Immortal Philosophers."

"Now, we shall begin," Zenda said.

Aurelius held out his hands to his sides. One he held out for Zenda, and with the other, reached for Antonio. I reached my hand out to hold Antonio's hand and for Kana's hand on my left. Kana and Ikkyu were already connected to the chain before Kana and I completed the circle.

Then Zenda's emerald aura ignited in a blaze of green light that settled in the air in a ring around her, and everyone else's aura followed suit. When mine ignited around me, I felt it explode up and out of my auric core. My aura glowed brighter than I had ever seen it before, but nowhere close to as powerful as everyone else.

Antonio's azure aura was back to looking stronger than it had looked in the bedroom. I didn't think he could recharge that fast, but I was finding it hard to find something Antonio wasn't impressive at. Kana glowed from inside her pink cotton candy cloud of an aura that hugged her like a puffer coat, while Ikkyu's aura maintained the same mint green smoke effect that spilled out of his instrument on stage at the restaurant.

The vibration of the energy swirling around the room was so strong that it hovered somewhere between levitation and the atom splitting effect of standing in front of concert speakers for an entire show. I felt connected to the chain, and my body flooded with the immensity of the power coursing through it. Every molecule in my body was alive, and I could feel it. I could feel it, and I could control it, I felt, but dared not yet try to move it.

Zenda held up her green glowing arm with her palm facing out, and a flash of white energy beamed from her hand to the teapot, linking them together. I felt the strength of our collective energy surging into the teapot, lifting it into the air. I felt the lid lift off, and the dry tea leaves float out the top as I watched. The tea leaves spun around in the air, everything glowing with the pure white light that buzzed through us around the room.

The same way Johnathan had to work through the layers of energy trapped inside the cave, Zenda pried into the wells of energy stored within the tea. She peeled back the layers of the soft, infantile leaves of the tea buds, releasing the auric essence stored inside. The energy shined out with the rays of all the years of sunshine the tea tree had soaked up in its lifetime, and we were all bathed in golden sunlight.

The energy transferred to us through the light as it hit our bodies and entered the auric chain, turning the energy ring around the table a more rich, honey gold. The energy of the ring whipped around, through our bodies, forcing me to send with it everything I had that was mine, to hold all of everyone else's. At first, I wanted it to stop, but the power charging through me was thrilling.

"From this tea," Zenda said above the rush of power. "We draw on the power of the Earth, Sun, rain, and wind. For these are the building blocks of life."

As she spoke, the tea, teapot, and lid spun around in the air between us, the auric energy blinding around the tea.

"From this tea," Zenda continued. "We draw on the willful

power of the spirit. For this is the energy that brings life to matter. This is the energy of the auric core of our planet, the most nurturing spirit known."

Then the teapot settled onto the table. The tea leaves floated down into the pot, and, out of the thin air above, a steaming stream of hot water poured like a waterfall into the pot.

"With this water," Zenda said. "We make tea. With this water, we pull the particles and flavors that the tea tree selected from deep inside the soil and the rock. Here we extract the life-giving energy of the roots folded deep inside the veins of the leaves that the water refills with life before us. With this energy, we refill with life. With this energy, we preserve our lives and the lives of those with nobody else to protect them."

As Zenda spoke, I listened, mesmerized by her words and the energy feeding the auric vortex as the ritual progressed. As she spoke, I saw in my mind exactly what she meant. Memories of ancient tea trees as big as buildings standing on gray mountain days. Their roots that touch the plants of the forests that stretch all across the Earth, and the fuzzy growing buds along the outside of the trees that tickle the wind."

Once the small teapot was filled with water, the lid settled on top, and the vortex of auric energy flying around us condensed into the pot as it buzzed with a low hum. The bright white energy ran up the tendril of aura connecting to us, and the tea steeped. The cups that sat near Zenda all lifted, imbued with the glowing white energy, and settled in a circle under the hovering pot.

From the connection, I felt the liquid sucking the energy out of the leaves like the blood out of an artery. It slugged out with a vintage essence that felt older than any of us in the room. Even older than the energy trapped inside of Joshua's cave. Then, the auric infused tea liquor poured out of the pot and into each cup, filling the cups until all of the liquor was poured.

The room was fragrant with the scent of muscat grapes, rough granulated honey, and peaches still fruiting on an ancient, resinous branch. The leathered cedar notes wafted around the room as the lid settled to rest on the table. The cups slid slick across the tabletop to each of us from the center of the table, as if friction didn't exist. The liquor was as still as jelly across its surface as my cup stopped before me. The tea itself was a golden liquor, swirling with tiny shining hairs against the white aura that radiated from the tea.

"May this tea," Zenda said, lifting her cup, prompting us all to do the same. "Align our spirits with the ancient powers of this Earth. Align us with its ancient roots. Share with us the power of the cosmic and terrestrial energies of immortality, and nurture our auric light. Protect us from those who wish us harm, and fuel us in our fight. For we too are children of the Earth, though not planted with the bark of armor as strong and eternal as yours. We honor the tree from which you came and connect our souls with your mother plant. As we honor you, may you honor us.

"May we drink," Zenda said, and in unison we brought the cups to our lips and drank down the hot tea. The flavor was sweet and thick. Every taste bud on my tongue lit up with the jackpot of tingling delight. As the honey thick liquor slugged down my throat, the energy came over me like a wave of something akin to intoxication. Hints of medicinal herbs and the gills of fungus with an orchid like perfume took residence from my esophagus to my nasal cavity, making me feel boozy and woozy and fizzy in the mouth.

As the energy settled into the auric core of my stomach, there blossomed a white hot warmth that grew and emanated outward through my body. The energy from the tea was so hot that my organs and skin felt ready to pop into blisters. I let the energy go to work all on its own. It spread across my skin, solidifying like the immortals' auric armors. The armor filled in with detail and density as its cobalt color grew brighter. It was bold, and it was powerful. As I settled into the newfound feeling of my blazing aura, I let the energy fill me more.

Around the table, everyone's auras were blazing their respective colors. If anyone had been outside watching, they would have been nothing short of amazed by the ray of rainbow colors beaming out into the morning air. Aurelius's purple, Kana's pink, the greens of Zenda and Ikkyu, and the blues of Antonio and I. Making me feel like we could do it. We could win.

"Welcome, Dylan," Aurelius said from across the table after our energies died down. "Welcome to the Immortal Philosophers."

"Thank you," I said, feeling more like one of them in my power.

"You're welcome," Aurelius said, taking the lead as Zenda gathered the tea instruments from the center of the table.

"I wish the circumstances around our meeting were better," Aurelius said. "But they could very well be worse. It's good we found you in time to intervene."

"Thank you for that," I said. "I'd probably be dead by now if it weren't for your protection. Do you know what he wants with me, exactly?"

Aurelius's expression dropped into dejection as he considered the question in his mind.

"From your findings," Aurelius said. "It's clear he needs either your body or your auric core. Either way, he won't get either. In the grandness of life and its possibilities, having him around in the past most likely kept more dangerous predators at bay. But look at you now, you're ten times stronger than you were just days ago. Joshua's a feeder, apparently, with a long history of familial sacrifice. All so he can preserve his demonic existence. However, his plans will not come to pass as he intends. In the next twelve hours, we will be on the other side of this mess, and we'll be looking to train you up so you won't have to worry about him for the rest of your forever. Now, tell me your thoughts on last night before I take you in the training room for a lesson on how to kick auric ass," Aurelius said, lifting his bushy eyebrows.

"Well," I said. "The most shocking part was Johnathan stealing the body of his grandson."

"And what a tragedy that history is," Aurelius said. "It shames me all over again to have seen the impacts of my failures, but what a special experience it was to be able to have witnessed it from Johnathan's own eyes. It's not often that we get such an up close and personal perspective on someone we hunt. What you did is no easy feat to accomplish, and I am grateful to you. Without your unique power and connection with Joshua, it would have been an impossible feat. You are quite the time walker."

"Thank you," I said. "Do you have a plan to defeat him?" I asked.

"Not yet," Aurelius said. "We all needed to sit together to figure this out. Your input will be crucial in figuring out what will work. We only have one shot."

"Okay," I said, leaning back in my chair to get ready to plan. Antonio and the other immortals watched us from their seats around the table. "Let's figure this out."

"I prepared rice for everyone, for after the ceremony," Zenda said, snapping her fingers. Emerald smoke popped onto the table in front of each of us, leaving bowls of pearly white rice with chopsticks and side dishes of golden syrup. "We can eat and discuss."

"Ah, Zenda. Thank you," Aurelius said, picking up his chopsticks and taking a bite.

"Thank you," I said, and Zenda nodded to me with sympathy in her eyes.

"After such a powerful tea," Zenda said. "This rice is one of the best things for you."

Everyone dipped clumps of rice into their syrup and chewed it down. The maple flavor of the sticky rice was exactly what I needed. If the magic infused tea was like the ichor that brings power to mortals, the rice was like the body of a god melting over my tongue as it filled my stomach. The satisfaction from the combination left me hungry with the feeling of revenge.

"So," Aurelius said, pointing his rice clump filled chopsticks at me. "Let's plan."

"Gladly," I said. "I have a few thoughts to start us off."

"Bold boy," Ikkyu said. "I like it."

"Let's hear these ideas," Aurelius said.

"Yeah," Antonio said from his seat beside me, seeming surprised that I spoke up first. "Let's hear them."

"Well," I said. "We have to get Joshua in front of a crowd. He hates crowds. He hated them in my time with him and as his older self. Something about being around a lot of people bothers him."

"Alright," Aurelius said, with the Eastman vigor I remembered. "Let's take that thought and break it down a little bit."

"It's probably difficult for him to focus," Zenda said. "I'm the same way, having been raised in a small tribe when the numbers of humans on Earth were not measured in billions, but I've come to adapt over the last few hundred years. If he's like I was, we might have an advantage in a crowd."

"Let's get him in a place with as many people as possible, then," Aurelius said.

"Does that put anyone else in danger?" I asked.

"It could," Antonio said.

"Nobody else is going to get hurt," Kana promised between clumps of maple rice.

"Maybe that's what Ikkyu and I should focus on then," Zenda said. "We'll keep Joshua from hurting anybody."

"I'm up for that," Ikkyu said, smiling over at me. "I told you I had your back."

"Thank you," I said.

"That would be excellent," Aurelius said.

"I'll protect Dylan," Antonio said.

"Don't leave his side," Aurelius said, as he ate his rice dry of syrup. "Kana and I will handle the takedown." As long as Dylan and the public are safe, I think we'll be alright. Zenda, Ikkyu. You'll need to confuse him and his senses."

"I agree," Ikkyu said, dipping his chopsticks into the syrup before sucking the syrup off the wood in his mouth, followed by a clump of rice on his sweet maple coated tongue.

"We can do that," Zenda said, dipping her rice into the syrup and eating it the way I ate mine.

"Where's the best place to do this?" I asked, feeling good about what we established so far. Nobody answered until Antonio leaned forward, pulling everyone in.

"We have to go to Atlantic City," he said, as if it were the only option that made sense.

The group sat on the thought for a moment before appearing to come around to the idea.

"It's the nearest place with the most people," Antonio said. "And he'll follow us there. It's not far at all."

"Excellent," Aurelius said. "Atlantic City it is. Plenty of people. Plenty of indoor spaces, and it will be difficult for him to escape. I think we have a winner."

"I like it," I said, looking at Antonio.

"I've been thinking about it all morning," Antonio said.

"We have to go to the Trop. It's the best option."

"That sounds reasonable," Aurelius said.

"What makes you say that?" Kana said.

"Kana's a fan of Bogadda," Antonio told me. "She only likes going to that casino for some reason."

"Their noodle bar is the best," Kana said, nudging my arm with her elbow. "I'll take you, don't worry."

"Thanks," I said, letting out an uncomfortable laugh. "But I've never been to Trop either. Why there?" I asked Antonio.

"There's a dining quarter with a fountain ringed with restaurants, bars, and all kinds of clubs. There's a second story balcony that overlooks the quarter where we would all be able to see Joshua coming, and around six o'clock it'll be the most crowded space in the city."

"I like it," I said, visualizing the plan unfolding in my mind. "I just wish I was better equipped to at least protect myself."

"I'm glad you said that," Aurelius said. "Because that's where I come in."

"You're really going to teach him now?" Antonio asked.

"Some things," Aurelius said. "There's no better day for a first lesson than the day of induction, afterall. We'll make our way to the tatami room after we wash up. Is that okay with you, Dylan?"

"I can't refuse a lesson from a master," I said, containing my excitement behind a smirkish smile.

CHAPTER ELEVEN

AURIC BATTLE CLASS

After breakfast Antonio and I returned to his room where we took turns showering in his bathroom. I needed the time under the hot water to reflect on the events of the last twenty-four hours. I expected more emotional flux the deeper I stepped into the world of the Immortal Philosophers, but my mind was getting more used to focusing on my aura and energy. Every minute I spent with the immortals brought me more into focus with the way I needed to operate in the world if I wanted to have control over my life, and I wanted to take full advantage of that.

I was one of them now, and that fact felt so true to me as Antonio and I made our way down stairs to the tatami mat room to meet up with Aurelius. I had a mission, and nothing was going to keep me from completing it.

The tatami mat room was as empty as the day before. Now that I knew that they used the room for training, the emptiness of it made sense. The buoyant floor mats, bare walls, and exposed wooden beams of the room transported me into the pictures in the books about the Buddhist Japanese tea ceremony that we shared around the Buddhist club meetings at NYU. I never imagined I'd be part of a tea ceremony myself, especially one that pre-dated the Zen influenced tea ceremony of Japan that we studied.

Aurelius was sitting in the center of the room when we entered, legs crossed and eyes closed. His black curls were stark against the paleness of the room, but his skin was a golden olive color that reminded me that Antonio had said Aurelius was just in Spain. I had to remember to ask him where in Spain, because I had always dreamed of going.

Aurelius had changed out of his gray robe and into a pair of tan colored pants that fit tight but looked flexible enough to wear while fighting. His shirt was of the same color, with a deep V that exposed the black hairs bushing out of the top of his martial arts fighter chest. Antonio had a change of dark blue shorts with a gray t-shirt that I was able to change into, since all my clothes were still at the bungalow. While Antonio threw on a pair of black joggers and black tee.

"Are we learning how to meditate?" Antonio asked, his sarcasm dripping. He and Aurelius seemed to have a more playful relationship with each other than either of them seemed to have with the others.

After a second of thought, Aurelius popped one eye open, finally acknowledging us.

"I'm sure you've both had a good deal of sitting around in your lives," Aurelius said. "Meditation is just one step between boredom and sleep. Now is the time to act. Antonio, come with me, and Dylan, you stand at the back end of the room. In front of the tatami wall, in case you fly back. I don't want you to hurt your head before our big fight."

"You're not serious, right?" Antonio said.

"About the directions, I am," Aurelius said. "About the potential for injury, I'm more or less not serious. Take your positions."

Aurelius got to his feet and made his way to the left side of the room. While I walked over to the opposite side alone to faced the two of them, determined to show them, and myself, what I could do.

"Are you ready?" Aurelius asked, with a warning in the way he raised his eyebrows.

"Yes," I said, feeling light, ready, and free of doubt. I had been waiting to learn something new all morning, and my aura was primed for use. "I'm ready."

"Magnificent," Aurelius said, pumping his fist at me in encouragement. "Get low," he said, spreading his knees and crouching down to a lower, more stable stance than standing straight up. I followed his direction, spreading my feet and bending my knees like a surfer. I could feel the pool of my energy sloshing around inside my gut as the position activated something inside me.

"Whoa," I said, feeling my aura come more under my control from taking the stance. The energy reserves I had to tap into were more powerful than before, and I didn't want to take too much at once for fear of losing my grip on it and hurting myself, if that was possible.

"Welcome to lesson one," Aurelius said. "Control. Just like there are positions for a body that offer more or less stability and power than others provide, there too are stances that help us balance our energies and offer us more control over our aura. This is one of the many stances that we have discovered and use on a regular basis for all sorts of reasons."

"I definitely feel the difference in control," I said, feeling the weight of my full aura around me.

"Do something with it," Aurelius said. "Defend yourself from me."

"What?" I asked. "Defend myself? My energy feels so heavy."

"You don't have to move it all," Aurelius said. "Move a little. Move as much as you can, if you can. You don't have to move it from around yourself. You could simply will it to protect you. Get creative, and think outside the box. Aurics is an art of spiritual expression, even in combat."

"Okay, I think I get it," I said. "I think I can do it."

"I know you can," Aurelius said.

"Aurelius always believes his students are holding out on him and know more of what to do than what they admit to him," Antonio said.

"That's right," Aurelius said, squaring himself up against me. "A push off the cliff is the fastest way to reach the bottom. Ready or not, here I come."

Let's go, I thought, ready for anything.

I locked my knees and wrists, watching Aurelius throw a punch at me from across the room. As his fist drove through the air, a small flame sparked around one of his knuckles, white hot and sizzling. In the next second, the lighter sized flame erupted around Aurelius's full fist, and when the punch swung level with my chest, the flame shot in my direction. A thrill of awareness washed over me that was new, but the anxiety of it fed me with exactly what I needed. I readied my aura around my hands with gloves of cobalt light and prepared to strike the fireball out of the air. I hadn't yet tried to transform auric energy into anything else, and I wanted to try that skill against the fire.

There were a lot of options to use against an attack from fire, but the one that came first was to use ice. As the fireball shot through the air between us, time felt like it slowed down, but I had to work fast. As the fireball reached half way, I held up my arms, reaching the outer perimeter of my aura that hung dispersed around me. Instead of collecting the energy tighter, I pumped some more power into it, hoping to create a shield like the one Joshua used against the immortals at the lighthouse.

As soon as I could picture the sheet of ice spreading out where my aura was, I willed it into existence. My focus strained against the mental demand of using my will for this new attempt. The energy layered itself into the perimeter of my aura, solidifying into a thick sheet of ice in an instant, like a bubble blown in freezing temperatures. I pushed more energy into it, and it grew thicker until it felt thick enough to withstand Aurelius's attack.

I watched the fireball through the sheet of ice as it made contact with the shield, willing my defenses to work and hold firm as I held my stance. When the flame made contact with my ice shield, the fireball grew in size, intensity, and brightness. It smothered my ice shield from top to bottom, causing me to almost let slip the control I had over my aura. It took all of the focus I had to fuel my ice shield with more energy. I wasn't sure how long I was holding out or how much longer I'd last as the ice melted and the fire continued to burn. I couldn't let in the attack, and I couldn't think of a different solution. My aura was only trickling out of my palms in thin streams, while Aurelius's aura had to be unlimited in strength compared to mine.

I couldn't yet feel the heat of the fire through the thick shield of ice, but I was starting to sweat from the strain of keeping the shield up. I had an idea to better my defense, but I was running out of time. I tried to channel the spirit of 'the best defense is a great offense' strategy and feed the aura below my feet. I let the ice build under me until I was standing on a thick circle of ice that made me feel like I was on the inside of a snowglobe, but my plan didn't end there. Once the sheet of ice was thick enough, I slid it out from under the ice shield and kicked it in Aurelius's direction.

In less than the time it took for the ice puck to reach Aurelius, the inferno around my auric shield dissipated. I merged the ice shield back into the light energy of my aura and pulled it all back to me.

"Great thinking!" Antonio cheered from across the room. I felt amazing.

"Excellent use of your mind," Aurelius added, tapping his temple with his forefinger. "You're a natural. You can counter, as you did, with natural barriers, or you can use pure aura as a defensive wall. All ways of defense work well, you just have to be smart about it. Don't try to use a wall of fire to keep a bullet from hitting you in the same way you wouldn't use a sword against a boulder. It's not complicated, but whether it works or not is mostly based on power. The stronger you are, the more powerful you will be when stretching your will. Which means the more of a threat you will be, but your wit is going to give you an edge if you can so quickly pull off counter attacks like that in the heat of a real battle. Repetition is the principle of success, even with aurics, so understand what you are getting into. The last thing that really determines strength and can turn a battle, is emotion. The purity of an emotion can change everything. Be careful with it."

"I get it," I said. "It helps to know how everything really works."

"Aurics is a complicated study," Aurelius said. "Much like our natural sciences, we have only scratched the surface of the possibilities of what we might be capable of, but with every training of a new philosopher we learn a little bit more about the whole of what aurics is truly capable of."

"Are you ready for lesson two?" Aurelius asked. As he talked, so many questions came to mind, but I didn't want to break my focus or distract him from teaching me more. I actually felt like I could reform the ice shield at any time if I needed to. Like it was a tool I had used before and could never forget how to use again.

"I'm ready," I said, feeling more ready for the second lesson after surprising myself with how well I did on the first.

"Each of these lessons may be the difference between life and death for you tonight, if the worst case scenarios come to pass," Aurelius said. "Each scenario is going to help you gain a different skill. This one might eventually develop into enabling you to fly, but for now we can only hope that it will keep you from breaking your legs, or worse, if you fall."

"Oh, flight?" I said, more excited than Lois Lane. "I'm definitely ready for that. How do I do it?"

"Flight, if you can manage it. There are a number of ways," Aurelius said. "It's up to your preference, but your adept use of your aura might offer you an upper hand by achieving flight that way. Activate your auric armor, and lift yourself up as you would any other object your aura may enchant."

"Is my auric armor also strong enough to stop a flame?" I asked, wondering if the ice wall was the best option.

"Your auric armor may be one of the most useful tools in your toolbelt," Aurelius said. "Eventually you'll have the ability to change the elemental structure of your armor the same way you did with that ice wall. You can turn it into steel, rock, ice, or water for a few example. It's incredibly useful, but everything takes time to master. Moving a whole body suit of a heavy material is no easy feat either, even for us. But, now, flight! Are you ready?"

"Yes," I said, keeping my stance and igniting my auric

armor in a blaze of cobalt light. It was solid around me and warm to the touch. It didn't yet have the detail that the other immortals had, but it felt more protective than it had before the tea ceremony. "I'm ready," I said.

"Focus on it," Aurelius said, his purple aura blazing around him in eggplant flames. The light then solidified into a sleek robe that reached all the way down to Aurelius's ankles and swayed as if there were a breeze blowing through the room. "Grab hold of your armor with your mind and pick it up like you would anything else."

"Are you afraid of heights?" Antonio asked, igniting his own sky blue auric armor around himself, and pumping a fist straight up into the air like Superman, lifting himself a few inches into the air, where he folded his arms across his chest.

Aurelius kept his wide stance and lifted up into the air to join Antonio without moving any part of his body. I watched on, excited by the lesson.

"I can manage heights if I have to," I said. "I can handle this."

I closed my eyes to focus on the feeling of my aura around my body. I felt it press against my skin with a pressure I hoped I could use. I focused on that force, but, as I willed it upward with all of the might of my mind, I didn't feel myself lift up off the ground at all. I thought maybe if I jumped up into the air I could have my aura catch me underfoot. It seemed like a cheap alternative for flying, but I couldn't will my body up.

To give my version of flight a try, I jumped up, lifting my knees as high as my chest, making me feel like I was in the gym, jumping for height. But I struggled to keep my balance as my feet hit the floor with my back fully extended. I lost my balance, and splayed out on the tatami mat floor.

"Well that's not the first time I've seen that," Aurelius said, looking over at Antonio. "As a child Antonio would do that same thing. Again and again. He was amusing, to say the least, but it didn't take him long to figure it out. Try again, but until you learn to control your aura with your mind, your body will only make using your aura more difficult. Keep that in mind."

"Try lifting one foot at a time," Antonio said. "If you can at least get the aura under your feet lifting you up, you can balance on them and figure out how to keep your whole body up."

"Okay, okay," I said, getting back to my feet and bending my knees for stability. "I'll try it that way now."

I refocused my energy and centered my attention on the aura beneath my feet. The space was smaller than trying to move my entire body, and this strategy made it much easier to focus. I felt control over the area, but I still had the struggle of lifting my entire weight with my mind. Focusing mostly on my heels and toes, I imagined the space between my feet and the floor growing and widening, as if the floor was lowering itself without me, but I didn't feel anything change. I opened my eyes to check, and I was still on the floor.

On my next try, I focused on the same areas of my feet, but instead of imagining the space, I made it my goal to lift each foot with pure will. I focused, and imagined my mind lifting, lifting, lifting up my feet into the air. I channeled the feeling of thrill that I imagined would accompany achieving flight, and for a second I felt my right foot lifting, being pulled up from the heel and toes, like a marionette having its strings pulled. My right foot left the ground, and lifted about six inches off the floor. Aurelius and Antonio were a foot off the floor at least, hovering below the ceiling.

I kept my right foot steady, and lifted my left off the ground myself to balance on my right. Even with only air below my left foot, I couldn't get my aura to firm up beneath it. I refocused on my form and crouched over myself as a surfer would on his board and got an idea. Instead of focusing on each foot individually, it occurred that it might be easier to focus only on one spot, and to spread that spot until it reached my other foot. So, I melted the auric armor around my right shin and let it bleed out into a disk that started spreading between my feet until it reached my left foot and fused with the aura that was there already.

The control I had over my right side immediately transferred over to my left and over every inch of the snowboard shape the energy took when it finally stopped spreading. It was steady to the point that I felt like I might as well have been standing on the ground, but the board was still responsive to my mind in the air. I lifted the right end of it up, and up it went before I balanced out with solid footing.

"Whoa!" Antonio cheered. "Look at you getting fancy with it!"

"Yeah," I said, unable to keep myself from smiling like a Rockette on Thanksgiving. It took all my concentration to keep control over the board and my balance, and I was only still about six inches off the ground. I didn't want to talk. I was having too much fun, but I wanted to go higher and really feel weightless.

Instead of feeling the power and the aura and the board, I decided that it might be better to work to not feel anything at all. To effectively feel weightless. So, I leaned back my head and kept arching back, like a slow motion diver diving backwards into the pool, but I was weightless. I was weightless. I was weightless, and when I leaned back past where I would have fallen, I knew I was weightless.

I didn't feel anything around me. My auric armor was still there, and the air, the room, Aurelius and Antonio too. But I felt like an astronaut floating in zero gravity. I moved my arms and legs in the air, and simply floated in place. With my mind, I pushed myself around in spurts as if I were using thrusters in space.

"Now that's impressive," Aurelius said, floating over to me.

"Wow," Antonio added, moving with him.

"After one ritual and one timewalking lesson," Aurelius said, looking me over with concern in his eyes. "At full power, you're going to be something I'm not even sure I would want to go up against. Great power can be incredibly dangerous."

"Well if his power didn't actually go dormant," Antonio said. "And it just developed in different ways, like with time-walking and constant regeneration from constant leeching, wouldn't it be the case that his aura has mostly developed? Now it should only be a matter of how powerful it will be as it reaches its natural potential. Now that Joshua isn't around."

All I could do was listen, as if I were in a cloud, unable to focus enough on their conversation to respond. Any distraction from my focus on being weightless would send me face down to the tatami mat, and I wanted to stay weightless for as long as I could.

"I think your conclusion there could be correct," Aurelius said. "It's not as if his aura is untrained and just learning discipline. He has developed his mind and aura to have the discipline our skills require. In the same way that Joshua's presence in his life had kept him hidden from other predators, Joshua had demanded a constant level of torturous training that not even I can imagine."

"I don't envy the power for the road that got him here," Antonio said. "To live like that is..."

"It shows his resolve," Aurelius said, cutting his flight off and falling to his feet. "You can save yourself from a fall. Big whoop. Lesson three starts after you let yourself down."

"What's lesson three?" Antonio asked, still in the air as he followed Aurelius back to the other end of the room.

"He's going to need a way to keep Joshua out of his mind," Aurelius said. "This will be the most crucial key to our plan. If one of us gets compromised, we're all compromised, and we can't guarantee we can protect his mind at all times. He has to be able to do it himself. We know Joshua is old enough to have figured out a lot of dark aurics, so we have to prepare for the worst."

'The worst' sounded like nothing I wanted to experience. The mention of it broke my concentration, and I fell from the air. My auric mind reflex shocked me with a reaction quick enough to stop my body from hitting the ground by suspending me an inch from the floor, before I got onto my hands and knees and then to my feet.

"And look at that reaction," Aurelius said.

"Yeah, it looks like he could use more of a challenge," Antonio said, lowering himself down onto the tatami mat floor to join us.

"For this one, we can have a seat," Aurelius said, lowering himself crossed legged on the ground. I did the same, feeling great about my skills after achieving flight, but worried about whether or not I'd be able to accomplish lesson three. If Joshua was in my head for the last twenty odd years, I wasn't sure if I would even be able to block him out at all on my own.

"How much was he in my mind before?" I asked, looking for an idea of what I was up against.

Antonio looked over to Aurelius in the uncertain way he does when, I've noticed, the truth is uncomfortable for him to speak.

"For the purpose of simple understanding, his footprints are all over your mind," Aurelius said. "Like muddy boots on white carpet."

Aurelius's explanation was clear, and I appreciated it, but

there was no greater sense of violation I had ever felt before. Joshua must have known everything about me, even the parts I thought I kept so hidden. Which cast every homophobic slur and awful joke Joshua made against me in an even more sinister light. He didn't say them for himself and his own demented mind, he said each one so that I would feel pain and more alone and stuck in the nightmare situation he made me feel there was no way out of.

"It won't happen again," I said, simmering with desire for revenge, and making me more determined than ever to keep Joshua out for good. "I'm ready. Try to get in my head now."

I'm already here, Aurelius thought inside my head.

It was incredible. I had no idea. I had no sense of him at all. No sense that I wasn't alone. I scanned my consciousness for any presence other than my own, and I couldn't sense him. I considered, maybe, he was jumping in and out without me noticing, bouncing between where I could and couldn't locate him.

"Where are you?" I asked. "How do I find you?"

"Ah," Aurelius said. "That's exactly the reason you cannot. You're searching too hard."

"You have to listen," Antonio said. "Slow down and listen, to locate."

"And then what do I do when I find him?" I asked.

"Kicking someone out of your mind is like uprooting potato fruit stuck between thick webs of tree roots," Antonio said. "Brute force is fully required."

"However," Aurelius said, looking like he had something more important to add. "Kicking someone out is harder than defending against someone getting in."

"That's true, too," Antonio agreed.

"So where should I start?" I asked, feeling more confused than assisted.

Silence your mind, and locate me inside, Aurelius thought. *Start with that.*

Will do, I thought back.

To silence my mind, I closed my eyes and sank deep into the silence of my mind with each breath I drew in and blew out. I felt myself descending, sinking into dark oceanic depths. But instead of growing cold, I grew warm as my aura pulsed with the beat of my heart.

I didn't try to listen or breathe or do anything at all. I just took in the rhythm of my own existence. I had no pain. No fear. No unsettled thoughts. I was at peace, and like that I sank deeper and deeper into the well of my being.

After a while of existing in that altered level of consciousness, I started to distinguish something inside myself that I didn't feel belonged to me. It was a part I had no control of to silence or do anything else to. It was a part that my mind, it seemed, would have been happy to ignore. Yet, Aurelius was there.

That realization scared me. It felt like he was burrowed in a hole that any inquiring soul could slip right into and get away with residing in without detection for as long as they desired. I felt paralyzed from doing anything about it. If I tried to think about a way to remove him, I would lose him, and it took time to locate him again.

You're doing well, Aurelius thought, after I rediscovered him for the fourth time. I couldn't think back at him without losing him, so I drifted along the currents of my mind. I floated in one direction, and then in another direction, always keeping the burrow in my mental periphery.

Then, I started drifting towards the burrow at the will of my mind taking control. I thought maybe I could dislodge

Aurelius from the burrow and drag him out of my mind as I moved around inside. It sounded like a doomed plan, but it was really the only plan I could conceive of while holding my focus. I wasn't sure how long I had been meditating for, but I knew with every passing second we were closer to our inevitable encounter with Joshua.

As I inched closer to the invisible mental sensation that was the mental intruder Aurelius, I felt his presence grow more intense, like the blazing of the sun in the darkness of space. I had no way of knowing what would happen when I reached him, but I kept moving in his direction. When I came upon him, I knew it, and I wrapped myself around him in a way I cannot explain but that resulted in him being tugged along with me. Then, I directed the two of us to drift further into the outside periphery of my mind.

However, instead of drifting out into the unknown, as you would if you were to drift out into the ocean, it felt as though we were drifting towards a more familiar environment. It was as if we were approaching the physical room and leaving the cosmos of my mind as we went. I tugged him along, concealing him inside the orb of my consciousness and cutting off his control. We kept on until we were in the physical room as two glowing orbs with a complete view of the room as I would have been able to see it with my physical eyes. Aurelius's purple orb still hovered within my cobalt energy, completely under my control, before I loosened my hold and he floated out, free. He made his way over to his body, and I hovered beside my head until I saw his purple orb meld into his face before opening his eyes.

I thought about returning to my mind afterwards, but then thought better of it. I wanted to see if I could accomplish part two of this lesson without having to start all over again, so I expanded my orb enough for me to cover my head. Then moved around it, encasing my mind with the same protection that I used to keep Aurelius from escaping the hold I had contained him in.

From this position, I felt the hole in my mind where Aurelius had burrowed. It felt like an old dig. I did what I could to seal it up with layers of energy that would hopefully at least alert me if someone were to find it, before turning my attention back to the immortals across from me.

Try to get in, I thought into the room, hoping the thought would reach Aurelius and Antonio.

Then their auras both sent out tendrils of energy that spiraled my way. Their energies plumed through the air as they got closer, until they were right on me, but they couldn't penetrate the globe around my mind. As their energy flowed, it pooled around the sides of my protective orb. At first, I didn't think I would have to worry about the gathering energy. I thought I figured out how to keep them from getting in, but then the pressure from their assault started building.

All around the globe felt like needles pricking into my defenses, trying to break it apart, and threatening to pierce through to my skull. Even from the visual perspective of the orb I could still feel and move my body if I wanted to. I could also move my energy, and it was the energy that I needed. With as much focus as I could spare, I pulled energy up from the auric core in my gut.

The energy fed the protective glassy orb, hardening it and pushing out the purple and cyan needles that had managed to puncture their way in. I pulled from all the energy reserves I felt inside myself, and the energy that flowed came with a force that seemed like something was releasing from somewhere I hadn't felt in a long time. And it came to me with the same flavor as the tea from earlier.

I kept the energy flowing, until my orb expanded around my body and my body was sitting in the middle of my cobalt auric orb. I pushed their energies further from me and back out into the room as my control grew. But as I pushed, they both pushed back, and as the energy that they countered me with grew stronger, I tapped a little more into my reserves, not feeling a bottom to its limits.

As the energy flowed, my focus was tested. My body was shaking down to the bone with the micro vibrations that buzzed from the power surging through the auric energy. The intensity of countering two masters was intimidating. It didn't make sense that I would be any match for them, but I set my mind to it, and as they pushed against my energy, I pushed against theirs until I heard the thought of Antonio from outside my head, telling me to, *Let us in.*

I decided to take the new direction as my next challenge. I didn't want to return to my body or break down all of my defenses just yet. I wanted to see if I could allow them in exclusively, while still keeping everyone else out, figuring that if I were able to accomplish that, it would help me out later that night. I wasn't really sure where to start with allowing them access, but I started by trying to channel their energy into my orb with two canals that pulled their orbs in and sealed back up after they were inside.

Love what you did with the place, Dylan, Aurelius thought, now a floating purple orb inside my own cobalt orb that encompassed my body, half the room, and the orbs of my two teachers. *I have never had a student quite like you at all.*

In a good way, I hope? I don't want to have to find another master, I thought, not knowing where I would start if I had to find one. Of course, Antonio would be my teacher even if

Aurelius wouldn't or couldn't.

There's no way I'd pass on the opportunity to have you as my student, Aurelius thought. *You have now managed a good number of feats that I was skeptical we'd be able to ever have you achieve. You'll be a fine student, and will teach us new things everyday, I anticipate. Though there are some things we might have to have other experts teach you. I'm thinking Leibniz, Antonio, how about you?*

That's an absolute yes, Antonio thought. *But for now it's going to be harder going up against someone like Joshua compared to us. You have some basic skills, but in a fight there's no time for thinking of how to protect yourself if you don't already have a set way. Much like in a fist fight, you have to meet your opponent with everything you have at all times, or else you risk them hitting you harder than your defenses can manage. You have to meet every blow with as much as you can counter with. The energy you have is getting stronger, but it's going to be virtually nothing compared to Joshua's energy. We need to make that clear to you. We're holding back big time.*

I agree, Aurelius thought, adding to the warning. *You can't take him on your own. You can't defend against him yourself.*

But you have to counter his attacks with as much energy as you can wield at one time, Antonio continued. *I'll be there to cast my own protections over you. I'm going to hit Joshua with everything I have, but there's no guarantee that my energy will work alone. We failed against him once already, and that can't happen again. There's too much at stake for you, the public, and for us.*

We might be immortal, but we're not invincible, Aurelius chimed in.

I understand, I thought. If anyone knew the severity of the situation, it was me. I had been under Joshua's control my entire life, and I witnessed how he worked with his aura first hand.

Is anyone else in the group coming to help us out with Joshua? I thought.

I'm afraid they can't, Aurelius thought, and his orb dissipated.

Then Antonio's did the same. I broke the connection that I had to the orb to return to my bodily consciousness, and I was back looking through my eyes at Aurelius and Antonio looking back at me. The room was still bright with energy, so I pulled all of mine that I could back to myself and layered it into my auric armor. It didn't feel like I had lost any energy, but my mind was foggy from the exhaustion of using it.

"So we're on our own?" I said, starting to feel the weight of the danger of seeing Joshua again as the high of auric training started wearing off.

"We are," Aurelius said. "Everyone of us Immortal Philosophers is on assignment, at all times, if we're available. Sometimes the lives we live are too dangerous to leave from. Our absences from them compromise our covers, and, in turn, our own survival. This is one of those times that we're all too much involved, unfortunately. It was even trouble for me to make it out here, but I couldn't miss this opportunity after so many years and all of the planning we had already done as I worked you into my cover as a book publisher."

"It's a great cover," Antonio said.

"How many Immortal Philosophers are out there?" I asked Aurelius, wanting to know the size of our group.

"We're all around the world," Aurelius said, looking at the ground and then back up at me. "We're a multitude of members, and I understand your question. But what's more important is that I'm connected to them all right now. To every single one of them. Everyone of them who is now, who has been, and

I believe that you have the ability to connect with all of those who will become one of us, too. That is why tonight is more important to us than anything else. If we can train you right, we might be able to save every single immortal born on Earth. You will be the savior of an innumerable number of immortals just like us, as they are just starting out their lives. Your connection to and affinity towards time is a gift that none of us have ever seen, and there isn't a lot that we collectively haven't seen."

"Your abilities impress us, and your adaptability with the way you pick up these skills so fast is a testament to how far you can go. Our impression was that your aura was underdeveloped, but it appears like it holds much more potential right now than we thought. It isn't weak in the way an untrained aura more often is, and it is controllable, which means it's under control. That feat alone often takes years of meditation to accomplish for beginners. Don't underestimate the power in that by any stretch of the imagination. You are one of us. You are an Immortal Philosopher. Do not underestimate your power."

"You think I can help find all of the immortals?" I asked in disbelief. As I listened to Aurelius, I was drawn into his words like a hypnotist. Everything made sense as he talked. The way my aura worked and had worked in the past. My affinity for time and the past. The one thing I was unsure of was what Aurelius had said about me viewing the future.

"I'm more sure of it every time you use your powers," Aurelius said. "The doubts I have concern only how far you can push your powers."

"So this really is just the beginning?" I asked, as the disbelief wore off. Everything about my mind and body felt more different than it did my whole life, telling me something had changed. "Thank you," I said, feeling grateful for their guidance into my new life.

"It's our pleasure," Aurelius said with a smile that made me feel like I belonged.

"I think we'll be leaving soon," Antonio said. "Zenda and Ikkyu are in the garage preparing the car."

"Why don't you two get some last minute refreshments before we head out then," Aurelius said. "I will see if our friends need help. Meet us in the garage when you're ready."

CHAPTER TWELVE

TREPIDATION ON TROP

THE KITCHEN WAS EMPTY when Antonio and I entered. Aurelius continued down the hall and past the living room to the garage. In the kitchen, Antonio went for the cabinets against the back glass wall to get us some mochi to snack on. Neither of us were hungry for anything too heavy, but mochi sounded good. The digital clock on the stovetop of the dark walnut island read 04:25, and I couldn't believe how fast the time had passed while we trained. With the time being so near 04:20, I thought back to the night I spent on the futon, smoking just enough to lay down and drift into the depths of relaxation that comes with a joint. That night felt so far away, and the dreams that I had for my life that night felt even further behind me. I didn't know what I would want at the end of the night, but I knew everything I could have wouldn't come unless I made it through.

"What are you thinking about?" Antonio asked as he pulled out the familiar looking plastic package that mochi seemed to always come in. I was surprised he didn't have a dedicated cabinet for gourmet mochi the way they had gourmet coffee and tea.

"Those are the same ones I used to buy back in Manhattan," I said. "I'd pick up a few packages to stock up in my room from Chinatown."

I wondered if the other guys ever knew anything about Joshua's secret past, but I doubted he was honest with any of us. The more I thought about it, the more I understood how Joshua used them to create the worst environment possible for me by poisoning them with the beliefs he wanted them to adopt.

"Oh yeah?" Antonio said, standing in the corner of the kitchen where the last kitchen cabinet met the glass back wall of the house. "These are the best I've tried. Kana orders them as house snacks. I usually eat most of them. They're the perfect amount of red bean and green tea sweetness. What's really on your mind?"

"There's a lot on my mind," I said, leaning with straight arms on the island, looking across the kitchen at him.

"You can share with me," he said, walking over and setting the pack of mochi on the dark wood counter. He had a sensitive look in his eyes. I knew he cared, but I hated sharing feelings before I fully understood how I felt about them.

"I'm just thinking about how I'll adjust to all this," I said, walking around the island to lean back and stare out the back window. Antonio joined me at my side with the mochi pack.

"I can understand that," he said, holding out the pack to me. I took one of the powdered pillowy delicacies and took a bite. The rice flour and red bean paste blended between bites in the beautiful way I remembered.

"It's impressive," I said. "What Aurelius said about me in there. That I might be able to see the future and find future immortals. That's powerful. That would be transformational."

I took another mochi as Antonio listened while I made my point. Outside, the ocean stretched out past the beach, below a sky that was gray and dark enough to foretell an approaching storm.

"It feels like if I go that route, I'm ending up kind of back in the same situation I just left," I said. "In a way, I'd be back living my life to maneuver around the lives of others, and I've only just started living on my terms."

"Nobody can fault you for feeling that way," Antonio said. "There are a lot of freedoms I have, even when it comes to working for our cause. You're free to be off on your own if you need time. We don't expect you to be a superhero. We just want to be here to help you until you can protect yourself out there. Whatever you want after is up to you, no matter what Aurelius says. I'll handle him if it comes to it, and, as for me, I won't leave you until you're ready to protect yourself. Unless you want me to disappear sooner, after all of this blows over?"

"No," I said. "It's not like that. I'm not scared of you or Aurelius or anyone else. You all seem so put together in your own ways, and I'm just not that. I've always tried to build myself up by doing things. Like busying myself by sticking to a routine, regimenting my life with things that would take me out of myself so that I could exist within the neutral zone of everyday life, where things aren't really enjoyed but at least satisfy away from something worse. I just don't want to go down a road where I don't know how the story ends."

Antonio looked at me with the warmth of a heartened parent and smiled before taking a bite out of another mochi. I watched his white powdered lips chew while he thought, feeling better after making sense of my situation aloud.

"Not knowing how the story ends is part of the beauty of life," Antonio said. "And you'll have a long life. And most importantly, life for you will be what you will it, regardless of what's destined in the eyes of others."

"That sounds good, but sometimes life doesn't feel as simple as lines of philosophy," I said.

"You're right about that," Antonio said. "But you can't read a book without reading each of its chapters. And every chapter opens up the possibilities of the next chapter."

"Like tonight?" I asked.

"Like tonight," Antonio said, again offering me a go at the pack of mochi. Only one piece remained, so I took it and popped it in my mouth as the fact settled that nothing else mattered if I didn't make it through the night.

"Having to see him again makes me nervous," I said. "Being around him makes me feel like I'm wearing a cold, wet blanket over my shoulders. What if he drains me or takes over my body the way he did his grandson's?"

"I won't let that happen," Antonio said. "It won't be like how it was before. He's powerful, but we'll take him. He won't expect us or what we have planned for him. He also won't expect you to know so much about aurics. We have an advantage. You have an advantage. He's underestimated you your entire life, and that mistake is coming back to him. You've made great progress. The biggest question left is, are you ready to put it to use?"

"Yes," I said. "I'm ready for this chapter to be behind us already, and I hope you're right. Let's go."

Antonio led me through the kitchen and past the sitting area with the grand fireplace. We continued down the hall until we came to a door that opened up to a large garage with two empty spaces and an all black, tinted 4Runner SUV in a space at the other end of the garage. Zenda sat in the open door of the back seat wearing jeans and a maroon blouse talking with Ikkyu who stood outside the car wearing black pants and a black v-neck. Aurelius stood beside Ikkyu in a purple t-shirt with jeans. He noticed us when we walked in and waved us over from across the garage.

"We're all set," Aurelius shouted.

Kana came around the back of the SUV, wearing what looked like a black romper that cinched at her knees, where long black socks took over and covered the rest of the way down her legs. I wasn't sure what inspired such an outfit choice, but nothing could soften her serious demeanor.

"We're all set too," I shouted back, eager to impress and feel as ready as I could. Aurelius looked pleased.

"Maybe you can help me sense Joshua's aura while we're on our way to Trop. It could help me out later," I asked Antonio as we crossed the garage.

"Yeah," Antonio said. "We could try. We should sit in the third row together. It looks like Zenda and Ikkyu are going to take the middle row. Aurelius will drive. Kana will probably sit next to him."

"Aurelius really takes charge while he's here," I said, trying to catch Antonio's eye, but his attention was on the SUV.

"Yeah he does," Antonio said, sounding pleased. "These are his missions. Like I said, we've kinda been on hiatus since the Cape May mission two years ago. We're always ready to help, but it's still not exactly fun having to run into battle and risk being killed. You learn to treat it almost like a meditation after some time."

Antonio stopped walking and faced me, before he continued, "On nights like these my own mortality surfaces to the top of my mind, and all I can do is live in the moment. There's no tomorrow or thoughts of ten days ago or even the future. My world zooms in around me and the objective of the mission, and everything else becomes background noise. That quiet instinct of making it through everything alive comes back to control me, and it sometimes becomes difficult to tamp down. As philosophers, we meditate on overcoming the attachment, but I'm still so young that my mortal emotions still hit me hard."

"It sounds like doing this takes a toll on all of you," I said, as we continued walking the second half of the garage.

"You haven't seen anything yet," Antonio said, and I couldn't argue with that.

"All aboard?" Aurelius asked, smiling brighter than the moment required.

"Ay, ay," I said, ready to climb into the SUV. Kana came around the back to lean against the side, with her arms crossed.

"I'll let you in," Zenda said to Antonio and I, hopping off her seat and moving Ikkyu from his place inside the door.

"We all know the basics of the plan," Aurelius said. "We all know what we're responsible for, and this isn't our first clash with this Bailey. Let's all make it back here safely. I don't want any other outcome. We all have important roles to play moving forward, so let's take care of business tonight, and tomorrow will be a new day."

When Aurelius stopped, he made his way over to the driver's seat.

"Dylan and I are taking the third row," Antonio said. "I have to teach him one last thing on our way."

"Beautiful," Zenda said. "Such an eager student you are, Dylan."

"Nothing's more encouraging to a student than certain death," I explained.

"Well, I wouldn't call our deaths so certain, but you're not wrong," Zenda said, moving aside for Antonio and I to climb into the third row seats.

I climbed in frist. After Antonio was in his seat, Ikkyu slid the second row seat back into position, and he and Zenda climbed into the row in front of us. Kana climbed in last, as Aurelius started the SUV.

Over the bay side of the island, clouds started rolling in, tugging along with them what looked like another late spring thunderstorm. It seemed to match the danger of the evening, but I was more focused on Antonio's hand in mine as I watched him stare out the window at the road as we drove.

Okay, I feel him now, Antonio thought. *Let's try something. Are you ready?*

Yeah, I thought, focusing on the energy that blended in a cobalt and azure swirl of blue light around our hands until I felt the control he had over his energy start to move.

Try to feel everything I can feel, he thought. *I'm letting you in. Feel my energy.*

I'll try, I thought. It sounded difficult, but as my energy mingled with his around our hands, I could feel the rivers that his power used to run throughout his body, but I couldn't feel anything else.

I feel you, Antonio thought. *You must be feeling me too.*

I think I am, but I'm not sure, I thought. *I don't feel Joshua, that's for sure.*

Not yet, Antonio thought. *But I do. Let me think.*

While Antonio figured that out, I looked out the window. We were coming to the middle of the island, where the avenues filtered traffic onto the main bridge back to the mainland. I was surprised when Aurelius passed it. I saw the road rise into the bridge in the distance a few intersections away until it dipped out of view. Shops and townhomes with rental signs zip-tied to their balconies blew past. I had no idea where we were going. Joshua could have been staying in any one of the homes we passed, and we had no way of knowing.

Do you know where he is? I thought, thinking maybe I could use Antonio's frequency to help me locate Joshua as long as I was tethered to him.

It's not that I know where he is, Antonio thought. *It's more like I can feel his strength. I could tell if we were getting closer or if he were getting closer, but I think we're actually moving further away from him. Focus on feeling his energy behind us. Follow the auric current.*

I closed my eyes, relieved to be moving away from Joshua, and I focused on the space behind us, waiting for the feeling that I had known so well for so long to make its way back to me as I beckoned it. After a minute, I didn't feel a thing.

I listened for the energy like I was listening for birds, and then I heard something buzzing. It wasn't the familiar hum that our auras made. It was more like the sound of a wasp, thumping its wings faster than humans can see them move. The sound wasn't familiar, but the fear associated with a wasp around my ear felt reminiscent of being inside our brownstone in the Village, with Joshua hiding around every corner.

I think I did it, I thought. *I hear him buzzing.*

That's not it, Antonio warned, but I wasn't sure what he meant.

When I did understand, I wished I hadn't tried to feel Joshua's energy at all. The buzzing grew louder and louder. I couldn't think of anything else. His energy came in a wave of power that seized me like a nightmare-triggered sleep paralysis as I sat there in my seat. My body started to shake as I struggled against my inability to control the way I moved. The fear made it feel like I was in the state for minutes, but in seconds Antonio cupped my cheek with his free hand. His energy warmed my face and melted away my connection with the currents of auric energy. When I came back under my own control, Antonio was looking at me with a horrified expression while I recovered in my seat, unsure of what really happened.

We're not doing that again, Antonio thought, putting his arm around my shoulder. *Are you okay?*

I think so, I thought, fingering my ear where I still felt the shadow of buzzing hovering around.

I think he almost found you, Antonio thought. *Your reaching out must have been like a beacon. We need to keep you closed off from him. You can't connect to the auric current until he's taken care of.*

It felt awful, I thought, grateful for Antonio's quick action.

Let's hope that's the closest he gets to you, Antonio thought.

Does he know where we are? I thought, surprised by his calm reaction to my near connection with Joshua.

I doubt it, Antonio thought.

Either way, I thought. *We're about to find out.*

For the rest of the ride, Antonio and I were silent. I felt safe with my hand in his, and I appreciated the privacy of the third row. I pushed away the thoughts of fear and death and decided to just enjoy what could be my last peaceful moments with Antonio. It felt silly that after a week I was starting to develop close feelings towards him. It could have been our situations bringing us together, but our connection felt like something more substantial than coincidence or Aurelius's planning. I couldn't explain how, but I knew I didn't want to take for granted a second of it.

When we came to the Northern end of Ocean City, Aurelius continued onto a bridge that brought us to the shores of a much smaller island that looked to be inhabited for the purposes of the marina nestled in one of its two coves and for the roads and bridges that connected Ocean City to Longport, Margate, Ventnor, and Atlantic City. As we crossed over the first bridge, I got a view of the busy channel between the ocean and the bay. The boats were coming into the marina for safety as the bayside storm approached. There were a few people on the beach in rain jackets with umbrellas. A few had binoculars, but I couldn't make out what they were looking at as we passed them.

In less than a minute, we were off the island and crossing over into Longport. Longport looked like a typical shore town, with modest row homes and the urban feel of bustling working life. As we crossed into Margate, a giant elephant named Lucy welcomed us as she drank water with her trunk from a barrel the size of our car. She was nearly double the size of the mint green house that she stood next to, and she looked ready to offer visitors a view from her back, as her saddle came complete with its own giant lookout pagoda. I wondered what we looked like through the windows inside her brown eyes, and if she could tell we were different from the other people that passed her. Or if she just considered us all the same.

The more we got into the heart of Margate, the homes started turning into modest mansions. It was an incredible location, with the backdrop of the Atlantic City skyscraper casinos in the background, offering the leisure-riche a powerful view from their widow's peak windows. Heading north along the traffic lit blocks, we entered Ventnor, where the homes were a mix of options between those of Longport and Margate. Then we came upon Atlantic City proper, with the iconic street stores and bodegas typical of American cities popping up with neon signs, glowing off the umbrellas of the people walking past as the rain trickled from the sky that had grown dark with gray clouds.

Atlantic Avenue brought us all the way from Longport to Atlantic City. We came to an intersection where Stockton University's academic campus dominated the surrounding blocks with cartoon osprey logos and streetlight banners featuring arts events and plays. From Atlantic Avenue, we split onto Pacific Avenue. I knew these streets only from the Monopoly board game, but even that connection was enough to make me feel like I had known these streets my whole life.

The buildings along Pacific Avenue were taller than those in Margate. The streets were lined with apartment buildings, condominiums, and hotels. Trop was the first casino that we came to. I knew because 'Trop' swept across the top of the new bronze glass tower in fancy scarlet LED font. The older parts of the casino below gleamed with chromatic bronze paint that made the tropical architecture of the casino gleam with twenty-first century glamor.

Aurelius pulled under the port-cochere, where he parked before the front entrance of the casino and signaled the valet. The front doors of the casino were all glass, offering a view of palm trees and fountains inside the hotel lobby. I inspected the inside for signs of Joshua, but only saw vacationers ready to gamble and staff ready to head home. I envied them all for living their lives.

As we waited, Antonio tightened his hand around mine. His skin was softer than mine, and we had sat so long with our hands together that a moisture had developed between them that made me not want to let his hand go. The valet approached Aurelius's window, and a flash of purple light came from the driver's seat. The valet nodded to Aurelius's silent commands and stepped aside for Aurelius to open his door, and Kana opened her door too.

"Here we go," Antonio said as we waited for Zenda and

Ikkyu to exit out Zenda's side. I followed them out after they popped the second row seat forward for us, and Antonio came out behind me. We waited as a group while Aurelius watched the valet pull the SUV up and park it in front of the valet stand before turning off the car and rolling down the window, as if he was to wait like that for our return.

"He's watching the car for us," Aurelius said, turning to us as the casino crowd buzzed in and out of the building around us. A good amount of people were out front smoking. Some were walking around, talking on the phone. Most just seemed to be a little obnoxious from the sounds of their conversations.

"Let's get into position, then," Aurelius said, directing us inside the building.

Inside Trop, the gloomy day disappeared, giving us blue skies to look up at behind the Spanish style facades of Avenida de Fiesta on the other side of the hotel lobby. Instead of building beautiful architecture outside on the city streets, to add to the actual city's beauty and culture, they put a small tropical city in a box and attached a parking garage to it to keep the city out. It felt typical for a resort location, but it was a shame that public infrastructure came second to private infrastructure in too many places with similar histories.

"Antonio," Aurelius said. "Take us to where you said we should set up. Let's scope out the area before we uncloak Dylan. There's no telling how fast he'll get here after we remove our protections, and I'd rather be ready before he arrives. This should be a smooth operation."

"Okay, smooth operator," Antonio said. "Follow me." Then he took the lead.

He led us down the boulevard, where the casino floor opened up around us. On our left was an endless sea of all different shaped and sized slot machines with bells, whis-tles, and LED touch screens. It looked more like the arcades of my childhood, rather than a traditional casino floor with pull levers and spinning cylinders behind glass win-dows. On our right, were separate areas for card games, roulette, and craps tables. The atmosphere was bright and sunny, with palm trees growing in large pots throughout the casino floor, while waitresses and waiters in tropical skirts and shirts shimmied their way through the crowds. The drinks on their trays were adorned with umbrellas skew-ering fresh fruit, and I wished we were visiting for fun.

We followed the marble tiled avenue through the ca-sino floor, passing stores and ice cream shops behind glass windows on our right, with the casino floor on our left, until we came to a split. The casino floor continued on the left, while straight ahead opened up to a wider boulevard lined with the designer apparel and accessory stores, creating a real outside appearing shopping district, complete with a café where the street came to a bend.

The fenced in patio outside the café served to wrought iron tables on the boulevard under the palm trees and blue sky behind the decorative third stories of the shops. Everyone walking the strip was walking in the direction we were going, and I soon understood why.

I smelled the restaurants before they came into view, and everything smelled delicious. At the end of the hall we came to a massive fountain, ringed by a dozen restaurants of all types and flavors. Some were upstairs on the second floor, and some circled the first floor fountain. Groups of people gathered around the front entrances of the restaurants, wait-ing for hosts and hostesses to seat them. People were lined up for movies upstairs, and above the fountain the ceiling was transformed into a cosmic display of the moon and dazzling stars against a dark off purple sky in the dome of the ceiling. The music pumping into the plaza was the cherry on top of the cacophony of distractions to overwhelm Joshua. Antonio had picked the perfect place.

"Good work, Antonio," Aurelius said. "This reminds me of one time in Malagá. I'll tell you about it later. I want Dylan at the edge of the fountain. For now Antonio, you'll stay with him."

Aurelius looked at Antonio for a few more moments before directing his attention to Ikkyu and Zenda, making me believe he had thought something over to him he didn't want the rest of us to hear.

"Kana," Aurelius said aloud. "I want you with me. We'll take position on opposite sides of the second floor. I'll take the top of the spiral staircase behind me, and I want you above the Italian restaurant."

Kana nodded her head, already scoping out where she would be perched up behind where I was standing. Aurelius would be in front of where I would be, in the top balcony of the spiral stone staircase that looked ready for a classic prom staircase photo, making it seem appropriate for a former Roman emperor to perch himself inside of.

"Now, you two," Aurelius told Zenda and Ikkyu. "I'm confident in you both. Keep Joshua under control. I don't want any of the mortals hurt, and we need to keep his mind confused. The more distracted he is, the better it is for us. He's going to have to come through the whole casino, so hopefully we can get the jump on him before he gets the jump on us."

"Yes sir," Ikkyu said, accepting the challenge, nodding his head like he already knew how to ace the test. I was hopeful that he had something good up his sleeve.

"We won't disappoint," Zenda said, with a slight bow. "Every demon meets their end. I'll post up in the back of the plaza. I have a few ideas to resurrect for this fight. Round two calls for the use of ancient magic."

"Ancient magic sounds serious," I told Zenda. "Thank you."

"It's my pleasure," Zenda said, reaching for Ikkyu's hand. "This is the obligation of the Immortal Spirit Warrior. This is how we repay the balance of the universe for the blessing of immortality. This is our duty," she said.

"Stay focused, and you'll do great," Ikkyu said to me.

"I will," I said. "I'm ready to end this."

Ikkyu and Zenda both stared at me for a minute the way I saw other parents look at their kids. It was a mixture of pride and concern that felt foreign to my life for longer than I could remember. Then they turned and started their way to the back of the plaza, leaving only Aurelius and Kana with Antonio and I.

"Alright," Aurelius said. "This is where we part for now, Dylan. Kana and I will get in position upstairs, but before that, we may as well lift our protections from you. Keep an eye out for Joshua, but we should be able to give warning when he gets close."

"I'm ready," I said, swallowing the hesitation in my throat.

"Antonio," Aurelius said. "Keep him safe, and this should be over quickly. May the current flow at our backs."

Then Aurelius and Kana departed for the spiral staircase to get into position.

"Three, two, one," Antonio said, counting down for some reason I wasn't sure about. "And now you're exposed."

"Wonderful," I said. "How long before he gets here?"

"I'm not sure," he said.

Now that everyone had left us standing beside the fountain facing the spiral staircase, I was starting to feel a little more vulnerable, but I didn't want to focus on those thoughts. I decided to lean against a dry space along the edge of the fountain while, beside me, Antonio scanned the faces in the crowd.

"It will probably be around twenty minutes before he gets here," he said, not taking his eyes off the crowd in reconnaissance. "It shouldn't be too long."

I recognize we haven't had much time to talk since I arrived, Aurelius thought, and somehow I knew it was a message only for me. *While we have a few minutes, I think I owe you more than a few answers. So, if you can think of a question, I'll have an answer.*

Thank you, I thought, surprised by the immortal. But before I could consider a question, one slipped into my mind. *Who are you?*

That's a fair question, Aurelius thought, before I had the chance to correct myself. *I was an emperor, a warrior, and a philosopher. I've been called a philosopher king, and at the same time I was only just a vessel. I felt many of the same things you've felt over the years, but, most importantly and ever since his adoption, I've been Antonio's father. And right now, I'm helping the person he cares about. And I won't let him down. But we all know this night depends on you. You are Joshua's burden, as much as he is yours.*

Then Aurelius left my head as fast as he came, and my mind melded into the music coming from the plaza speakers as it echoed around the court, floating in and out of my awareness. Until a wave of focus washed over me, and I activated my energy to prepare for what was to come.

"I feel him more now," Antonio said. "He's getting closer."

"I'm ready to end this," I said, again.

CHAPTER THIRTEEN

A BAILEY BUNCH BONANZA

WE ALL SEARCHED THE FACES of the crowd from our vantage points around the quarter. Antonio stood beside me, taut jawed and focused on his search as we leaned against the gushing fountain, waiting for the moment to strike. Aurelius's words spiraled around my own thoughts of seeing Joshua for the last time. When I left Manhattan, I never imagined not seeing him ever again. I wasn't at the age where I considered a last time for anything, even though every time I had been around him I had wished it were the last time.

He's near, Zenda thought.

I think you're right, Aurelius thought back.

Anyone see him? Kana thought. She was perched atop the second floor balcony behind me. If anyone had the best view, it was her. So I figured she had the best shot at being the first to see him.

No, Antonio thought. *He feels like he's in the building though. I can feel his aura, but I can't see him or his energy.*

Be ready, Aurelius thought.

No... Antonio thought back, but it came as a whisper.

Joshua's energy hit me in a wave of scaring, explosive pain that made my bones burn like white hot charcoal, sizzling my flesh from the inside out.

I feel him, I cried out in my mind, as my body blistered. *Shut him off!*

I was under attack. It felt like what I feared would happen if his energy reached me in the car. My teeth clenched with a vice grip so tight my jaw muscles strained with the threat of popping. I tried my hardest to shut off Joshua's control, but I was frozen, staring into the wild looking face of who once had been the true baby Joshua Bailey.

Joshua was far down the hall in the back of the crowd, but my vision blurred everything that wasn't the electrified look of his strawberry blonde hair and pale, blue veined skin that cracked with bloody red patches of raw flesh on his cheeks, brow, and lips. Then my heart dropped when the faces of his eight cousins emerged behind him, all with his same tortured blood red eyes.

In the next moment, Antonio jumped between us, auric armor ablaze around him in sky blue plate armor, bright with charged energy. But my body was already consumed in a flame of blood red auric fire that flickered off every inch of me.

Antonio stomped the ground and punched up in the air at the same time, creating a sky blue auric wall in front of us that burst out of the floor and severed the connection that Joshua had with me. When his attack cut off, I fell to the ground. The pain inside my body throbbed with tender rage around every bone and joint, and I wasn't sure my body was as ready as my mind was to continue the fight. While my body adjusted, I listened to the sounds of Antonio launching auric orbs down the Avenida de Fiesta, while Aurelius and Kana loosed a flurry of auric arrows from bows they formed with their auric light energy. I couldn't look up yet to see Joshua, but when mint smoke started creeping across the cobbled floor and emerald pixie dust fell, collecting like snow,

I knew the immortals had everything under control.

I pumped everything into my auric armor and solidified my mental defenses for another attack from Joshua before my body came back under my control and I was able to look up and see the battle. Antonio's auric barrier had solidified into an azure tinted glass, buzzing with charged electrical volts.

What are we doing about his attacks, Ikkyu? came Aurelius's thoughts, just as all nine of the Baileys started charging through the crowd of people up the Avenida. As if on command, the crowds around the room blinked out of existence under the low hum of a flute note that crescendoed into a high flutter.

Ikkyu's music filled the hall from wall to wall and into the domed ceiling. The palm leaf fans spinning along the middle of the hall started circulating thick mint colored auric smoke that cascaded down in fluorescent tendrils until it dispersed over the hall in a near turquoise mist.

Through the auric wall, I watched the Baileys fire lava hot globs of blazing red auric energy in every direction of an immortal. The staircase and upper floor balcony melted the stone where the globs landed, disintegrating the staircase tower with Aurelius inside.

The terracotta-shingle roofs where Zenda and Ikkyu were positioned were targets too, but Joshua couldn't reach them. Zenda was cast in jade armor, standing on the roof, and casting her aura into the hall, while Ikkyu floated cross legged on a cloud of mint smoke with his flute between his lips nearby, both dodging attacks that got close.

He's controlling the others, Zenda thought, as Joshua charged up a basketball sized orb of energy.

My auric armor solidified around me into charged cobalt crystal hardness.

We need to slow them down, Kana thought, and her pink aura flashed across the boulevard like the flash support lights for a photo shoot, releasing a locust swarm of razor sharp pink auric cherry blossom petals in the direction of Joshua and his cousins.

I knew his cousins. They were as innocent as I was in everything, and I didn't want to see them hurt.

Don't hurt the others, I thought, crying out as I watched the flower petals approach impact. But the cousins all lifted their hands in unison and spilled forth a web of red aura that caught the flowers like flies and sent them launching back at the walls of the hall, where they stuck into the stone.

Joshua sneered and shot his basketball sized attack up the hall, straight for Antonio and I.

The orb of energy smashed against Antonio's defenses, shattering the block of glass into an explosion of blue and red powder as a crack of lightning struck the center of the dome above Antonio and I. The dome held, but Joshua had a clear shot at us.

We're going to have to try a little harder if we're going to win this, Kana thought.

Ground assault, Aurelius thought, as the staircase fell from the wall and crashed to the quarter floor behind the fountain. He jumped before impact, pulling at the air around him as he floated to the floor in his auric robe. As he landed, a purple auric curtain swept across the quarter where the quarter opened up to the hall, creating another barrier before Aurelius pulled out from his sleeve a purple auric gladius.

Then, Ikkyu's music took a darker tone. He sunk us deep into the depths of the sad notes of despair. He played them long and drawn out, so that their hollow howls echoed against the walls and reverberated into each other, creating visible waves of sound up and down the hall so that the stone walls of the boulevard started shaking. The vibrations stopped Joshua in his tracks as he clamped his hands down around his ears and solidified his aura around his head into what looked like a knight's helmet.

I'll separate the others from him, Zenda thought, and emerald energy sparkled through the air in powdery pixie dust sparkles that gathered on the ground in front of the curtain as Aurelius burst through to Joshua's side for the ground assault. Kana jumped from the second floor behind us, conjuring a suit of Japanese samurai style auric armor as she fell, and cracking the ground where she landed before running after Aurelius.

Zenda's pixie dust magic collected into what appeared to be about a dozen bright glowing orange legs that looked feline in nature, as auric beasts materialized from the toes up. In seconds the legs grew bright orange and emerald striped bodies, a head, tail, and big white teeth that were unnaturally long for our current evolution of the tiger. The six ancient tigers then flexed their jaws in roars and set their eyes on Joshua before sprinting down the hall in his direction with Aurelius and Kana on their heels.

Two of the tigers approached Joshua, crouching low as if to pounce as he struggled against the force of Ikkyu's sonar waves threatening to pull him apart. I knew the strength of Ikkyu's music, and I couldn't imagine how it would feel as an attack. The other four tigers circled behind Joshua and made their way to his cousins, causing their zombied selves to turn their attention to the long-fanged beasts.

"It's all of you again, isn't it?" Joshua screamed, crying in pain. I had never seen him in such a state before, even in his memory. This feeling seemed new to him. I could feel his agony. A tender trace of the feeling pulsed around my bones as if it took root in my body too, but the more time it spent with me, the more it calmed down. I was afraid it would wind up turning me into one of his minions, but I had more of an effect on it than it had on me.

"Nobody can get away from us forever," Aurelius's voice boomed around the plaza, echoing down the hall as he and Kana approached the tigers squaring up with Joshua.

Then the two tigers lunged with needle sharp claws and fangs out and ready to plunge into Joshua's body. Behind him, the tigers circling his cousins pounced too. The nine of them were seconds away from being shredded into confetti, and my heart dropped in horror. But I couldn't look away.

Kana drew one of her katanas and held it at her shoulder while Aurelius readied his gladius. Then, before the tigers met their targets, Joshua threw up his arms, pulling all the blood red energy around him to his hands. It caked around him like mud up to his elbows. The movement ripped out all of the sequestered energy from his cousins' bodies, shredding their backs into paper cut thin slits before they fell to the ground in limp puddles of blood.

Joshua roared in rage from the burn of the excess energy, and blasted it at the tigers. The green energy of the tigers burst into a shower of the shimmering reds and greens of Christmas lights, and somehow I could feel the energy inside of Joshua as if it were my own. I felt the energy struggle under his will in a way I hadn't felt before. He was afraid of the power. He had split it up between bodies because it was too much to hold at once without it killing him, and I remembered Aurelius saying I was as much a burden on Joshua as he was on me.

Kana and Aurelius burst through the jade dust of the magic tigers with flashing sword strikes, which Joshua blocked behind an auric knight's sword and long shield he conjured with the pulsing, atomic energy around him.

Ikkyu, get in there, Zenda thought. *I can hold the phase over the mortal shroud.*

A second later, Ikkyu dropped from the sky in mint green layers of auric samurai armor. He crouched, leaning back and forth as he assessed the flurry of parries between Aurelius, Kana, and Joshua. Pulses from energy blasts flashed between their armor as they shot energy at one another between blows. Some blasts missed and shot into the walls and ceiling of the hall as they moved faster than it was possible to keep track, creating explosions of rock and glass where the blasts landed.

Ikkyu pulled his flute back to his lips, but the notes he played were silent. They conjured mint smoke around Joshua's legs, eating away at the ground beneath his feet.

"The more you struggle, the faster you fall," Ikkyu said, and Joshua struggled against the pull of the syrup like auric slime that started eating his feet as he defended attacks from Aurelius and Kana.

"Your tricks won't get me this time," Joshua bellowed before the red energy around him gathered to his lower body, elevating him out of Ikkyu's auric pit on a column of red energy. From his position in the sky, Joshua raised his arms, channeling more stolen energy into a giant auric orb he lifted above his head, aiming for me. "You're mine!" he shouted.

No way... I thought, turning to Antonio. He looked at me, without a glint of fear in his eyes, causing me to panic more. Joshua launched the orb down the hall, and it sailed through the air. Ropes of pink, purple, and green aura lassoed around it, but disintegrated as they tightened. Everything else was still aside from Antonio, who bent over into a sprint ready lean. Fearing the worst, I channeled everything into my auric defenses, creating a thick armor around myself. When the orb reached halfway down the hall, Antonio launched himself into the air, taking flight with his gladius raised and readied like a baseball batter readying to swing.

The events that followed happened in quick succession and almost too fast to take in. Antonio swung, making impact with Joshua's attack orb, but the orb didn't stop. The slice he created separated the energy into two halves, sending one flying into the mouth of the Italian restaurant, shattering everything it hit, and exploding in a blast of shattered rock, clanging metal, and dust. The dining area erupted into the flames and smoke of a warzone, and the walls snaked with cracks throughout the quarter. The other half of the orb diverted off course with a self propelled momentum that told me Joshua still had control of it, but instead of directing it at me, he sent it up into the dome of the ceiling above me. Down the hall, Antonio had landed on Joshua's podium and started battling with him. I watched Antonio fuse an auric gloved hand to the face of Joshua's shield and rip it from his grip, leaving them sparring with only their swords on the tight space of the auric pillar that sunk into Ikkyu's energy pit with every second of battle, bringing them closer to Aurelius and Kana below. Then Antonio got the better of Joshua, shoving him off the pillar, and sending him flailing into the air behind him.

Dylan! Zenda cried as the second half of the orb made contact with the dome, crashing into the stone with the flash of a thunderstrike shaking the building, and the dome cracked above me. I held up my arms, willing for my aura to keep me safe as the stone of the dome shattered into SUV sized chunks and fell, revealing the sky outside and exposing us to the rain.

Before impact, a flash of Antonio's aura streaked across the hall, but I knew he was too far away to reach me in time to help. I pushed everything I had into the defenses of my aura, blazing in a fire of cobalt auric light around me.

I felt the mental wall I recognized as the well of self doubt I had lugged around my life, and I didn't see any use for it anymore. I let it too flow out of me, and up through my body. I turned it into a beacon of cobalt light that shined up through the skylit dome. The blocks of stones falling above me disintegrated into sand and slid out from my protective light, pushing the stones set to fall nearby a little further away from me until they landed with explosions that threw everyone back, even Antonio.

My defenses broke after the force of the multiple explosions bombarded me, and I flew back from the force in the direction of the shattered fountain. But then, something in me shifted as my aura caught the air. The concussive forces of the explosions faded my consciousness, moving me between my body and my aura seamlessly, until I was weightless. My aura slowed me down as I gained control over my flight. It wasn't easy to maintain the focus on staying weightless, but I maintained myself in the air as dust and fog filled the hall and the room buzzed with shock.

I couldn't see any of the immortals, but I felt Antonio's aura not far from me. But something wasn't right with him. I searched where I thought I saw him flying toward me, but there was only a pile of huge stones and sand, now stained with wetness. The tile floor was slick around the mound from the fountain and rain. Then, through the dust, I saw his auric booted foot sticking out of the rubble.

I didn't know where the rest of the immortals were, or

where Joshua was exactly, but the corners of the hall were silent. The dust still swirled in the wind blowing in from the blasted out skylight, and I needed to use its cover to get Antonio out of his trap before Joshua found me.

I guided myself to the ground and landed before the pile of sand and stone above Antonio's auric boot. Sand was directly above him, but a chunk of the dome rested atop of it.

"Antonio," I said between a crack in the stone from where his auric light shined through. I waited for a response, but could only hear the buzz of his aura.

Antonio, I thought.

Still, nothing. I placed my hands atop the stone and moved all of the aura I had under my control to my hands. I breathed deep into my belly, channeling the energy of my auric core as my heart surged with the warmth of love, and I willed my aura to shake out the stone tomb around Antonio. I focused my mind, blocked everything out except myself and the stone, and as I pulled the energy from my gut, I felt the tug of what felt like a string that connected all the way to Joshua's reserves of energy.

Through the connection, I discovered Joshua's agonizing auric reserves to be more loyal to me than to him, and I felt more confident in what I had to do. I wasn't sure if energy had a will, but the energy Joshua had stolen from me had no allegiance to him at all. It boiled his bones like a curse worse than it did mine when it first hit me in his attack.

I tugged hard at the thread of our auric connection, and the energy gushed more steady down the line. The stones vibrated under my palms, and I pulled at the energy harder. It flowed to me in thicker torrents than Joshua was able to pull from his waitresses and his caves. What took Joshua hours of intense layering of energy within himself, I did in seconds as

I took back from him what belonged to me.

The energy worked for me, happy to be back under my control. After a few seconds, I had the stone quaking against the ground until it reached the soundless state of bursting into sand that fell in piles around Antonio. I dug down into the sand, pushing away piles to pull Antonio up and out, hoping he was okay. When I saw his face inside his helmet, I tried to sit him up as best I could and pulled him from under his arms to the top of the sand pile.

I gathered him in my arms, happy to feel the warmth of his aura and hear the soft whistle of his steady breathing. I placed my palm against the flat angle of his cheek and brought my fingers around his ears. I wiped what could have been a tear streaking through the dirt under his eye with my thumb, and spoke his name, hoping he would hear me. But he didn't move.

I beat back the wet fear building in my own eyes, and clung to the feeling of love I had for him, as I nudged him and tapped his cheek with my palm to stir him awake.

"Antonio, wake up," I said. "I need you."

I felt my words permeate his head and linger around for a moment, laced with aura. I waited as the energy moved through him and found its way to the front of his mind, stimulating his motor functions and, to my desperate relief, stirring him awake.

"Hey," I said, watching with relief as he opened his brown crystal eyes. "You're okay. I'm with you."

I pulled him close, and the look on his face was panicked. He looked me up and down the way I did him, making sure every part of me was okay.

"How… are you?" he said, grimacing in pain as he spoke.

"I'm okay, too," I said. "Better, now."

Antonio smiled with the dreary look of someone half conscious.

"Here," he said, holding his hand to my chest. His auric reserves transferred over to me in an instant, lighting up every part of my body with electric shock. "I'll be right behind you, but only you can take him down. It feels like he's down for the moment now. Find him and finish him."

"Stay safe," I said. "I got this."

I rested Antonio's head down on the pile of sand, determined to end the fight before somebody else got hurt. Since I had it in me to siphon back some of Joshua's energy, I was determined to take it all.

I stood and took reconnaissance of the battlefield through the dust. The hall burned with the purple, pink, orange, and red light of sunset as the fire of the battle's destruction emanated with the spent and fresh glow of auric energy. The immortals and Joshua were scattered around the room, unmoving from where the haze of their auras burned through the fog.

I held up my hands to prepare phase one of my attack. Instead of receiving little bits of aura at a time through a connective thread, I needed to take back the majority of my energy at once to prevent Joshua from cinching the siphon. So, I set about treating him like my own battery cave.

I felt the air for all my energy that wasn't under my control, and it lit up red, raging around Joshua's still body like a solar flare trying to escape the sun's gravity while he was unconscious on the rubble. The feral energy stung with the memory veins of pain it had entangled around him for decades. He always knew it had been too much for him to handle, and since I had left, the strength of my energy turned against him, ravaging his insides like poison. It hungered for me and to be near to its core, driving him mad in a way no other auric energy ever had.

The truth of his plan came to me as I set about freeing my power. He split the energy into his eight cousins to use them as batteries while he tried to capture my spirit inside his mind like a prisoner, where I would have generated the energy he needed until the end of time, while offering him the ability to take over the consciousnesses of his eight cousins. He would have had nine sets of eyes to look out of and control at any given moment and all at the same time. Without me, though, the energy was a terminal sickness making him sicker, and now it was time to set him free.

As I maneuvered around his energy reserves with my auric senses, I made it to the barrier around his auric core where his energy met mine. I peeled the barriers apart from each other, one section at a time, like trying to peel a sticker off in one piece. I worked in this way for a few minutes while the immortals stirred. Then Joshua stirred all the same, making my time to pull this off even more limited.

When Joshua woke, I knew right away. He clamped down hard on the energy, but as I separated it all from the mental grip of his aura, the control he had over my energy evaporated.

"No!" Joshua shouted, exploding into the air by the power of the dull haze of only his own auric power, as the last of my energy ripped apart from him and slugged toward me. Then Aurelius, Kana, Zenda, and Ikkyu shot into the air, all aiming for him in a fresh and final aerial assault.

Joshua spotted me as the last of my energy reached me. When he saw me, he blinked away into thin air, then popped back up in front of me. His face was a tortured nightmare of what he looked like before. His aura, or my aura, had blistered his face so bad that every spot of skin was a bloody wound around his frantic, auric shot eyes. Before I could think, he grabbed my arm, grunting at me, and the Trop Quarter disappeared.

In the next second, we were out in the wind of the storm with the waves crashing hard against the shore and washing far up the beach. Lightning cracked, lighting up the sky between the clouds above, while buckets of rain poured on the city and sea off into the horizon.

"Get off!" I said, pushing Joshua off of me. The ocean water foamed around where I landed on my back on the flooded beach. Joshua was face down in the water, limp, and disoriented next to me with the last of his energy spent.

Before he could, I got to my feet. The strength of my aura surging around me with tendrils of thick, cobalt power.

The energy left inside of him didn't feel like enough for him to survive much longer, and he knew it. I never imagined him as the psychopath, filicidal serial killer he was, but he was a monster of his own design. He was a threat to the innocent people he brought into this world and a threat to everybody he encountered without the ability to defend against his predation. He would use the last of his energy on keeping himself alive through the torment of others, which made him more of a demon than a man.

"I see what you liked about feeling powerful," I said, looking down at him as he lifted himself onto his hands.

"No...," he said, drawn out and raspy. The redness in his eyes had disappeared, but the blackness of his eye sockets were as thick as the residue of a candle's burnt wick.

"I'll kill you," Joshua said, finding the energy to lift himself onto his knees. He stared up at me with nothing but hatred. "I'll kill you, and we'll both go down. You're nothing but poison!"

Joshua gritted his teeth, and blood dribbled from the corners of his mouth. He was bruised and scraped from his battle with Aurelius, Kana, and Antonio, making me understand how close to losing the battle he really was before his final attack.

"You should have never been so dependent on me in the first place," I said, channeling my energy to my palms. His life force was fading, but he didn't deserve a chance to escape. I willed my energy to expand around us, and my aura was nimble to my command as the adrenaline of battle still rushed through my veins.

I focused in around Joshua, throwing auric bands around his wrists and ankles, chaining him to the ground. He didn't have the energy to fight back anymore, and without turning around, I heard the soft pops of the immortals teleporting onto the beach behind me. I hoped Antonio was among them, or somewhere else, as long as he was safe. I wanted to be over this and back with him.

"You won't do it," Joshua said. "You can't kill me."

"I could," I said. "If I wanted to."

"You're too much of a fucking faggot," he said, widening a sneer that looked joyful for him even in his pain, proving in so many ways that the depravity of humanity was as dark as our imaginations could bring us.

"I wish you find love in your heart in maybe the last moment of your life," I said to him, sinking us both into the blackness of his mind. Even in the Auric Plane, he was bound by the will of my energy now, unable to escape. "And may the souls that you desecrated in your time on Earth take comfort in your torture after death."

Joshua cackled with rage looking up at me, proving there was no getting through to him or in getting him to a place where he could be anything but a monster.

"You're a fool," Joshua strained to say, reaching his neck as high as he could to see me from his hands and knees. "You're going to die in this world faster than you think, acting like a wuss. If you had any balls you'd take me out yourself instead of letting me waste! I could see the patheticism in you ever since I laid eyes on you the night your parents brought you to my home to meet my grandson. This arrangement was always the product of your greedy family. Your grandfather had instilled something in your mother that had driven her and your father mad every day of their lives, to the point that they gave you to me for as long as I needed or wanted in so long as I was using your energy to figure out how to share my powers with them, you see. You were conceived for that very reason alone. You were always mine, even before you were born."

"You're a liar!" I said, holding back the cold hand of the paralyzing shock that reached up from the roots of my raw childhood terror.

"I'm not," Joshua said, smiling through blood. "Let me die. But if you want justice for your lifelong torture, you'll have to run home to your father and mother."

Memories as old as I was started flooding my mind from the times when I was small, appearing as though they might confirm the reality of what Joshua was talking about, but I didn't want to sink into them. The waves down the beach were growing more mountainous and severe looking than they were before, and the sky was static with electricity as my energy grew atomic in intensity. The faces of his victims from present times and long swirled around my mind, coming to me with memories that were foreign to me, but full of the emotion of the victims involved.

With a shot of blasted energy around his feet, I solidified my aura into blocks of molten metal that fused with his flesh as they hardened. Joshua screamed in pain, but I couldn't hear him over the workings of my own mind. With the auric blocks around his feet under my control, I thrust him backwards along the beach, sending him flying back down the beach. I pushed him all the way to where he split the waves like a glacier and entered the ocean. I pushed him back, further and further. I pushed his body and split the ocean like a demigod flexing his powers, and down Joshua went. The block of metal dragged against the ocean floor as he let out the last breath his aura could offer him, and the ocean crashed down over him, as I crumbled to the waterlogged beach from the overexertion of power.

"Dylan," Antonio called out behind me, and then he was at my side, wrapping my arm around his shoulder to hold me up out of the water. I looked up at his face flickering in the lightning flashes and felt the last breath Joshua's life force dissipate into the auric current that ran through all matter and time, as an indistinguishable part of the consecutive storm of energy we experience as life.

"You okay?" I asked, looking Antonio over once again, more concerned about him than I was about myself. Our clothes were drenched, but sand still clung to his cheeks from the rubble I had left him in.

"You did it," Kana said, standing behind us.

"Yes he did," Aurelius confirmed, standing on the side of me opposite Antonio, arms crossed and looking down at me. "It's an honor to have you with us. Not just for that," he said, pointing to where I split the water. "But for your mind and for the steps you took to be you and do things your way. You should be proud of yourself."

"Alright, Aurelius," Antonio said. "He's had a hard enough night already. Let's not subject him to the struggles of one of your lectures."

"He's a good man," Aurelius said. "What can I say?

You're lucky I found him for you." If I hadn't been so relieved, I would have been more embarrassed than ever in my life with all of the compliments and romantic teasing, but all I could do was laugh, grimace against my tired body, and smile.

Antonio and I were hunched over ourselves in too much pain to stand straight. He held his side. I was still processing everything Joshua had told me, and I knew everyone had heard him too. I didn't want to think about any of it now. I wanted to feel good, and I did feel good. Joshua was a memory. Zenda, Aurelius, and Kana stood around Antonio and I, and I was grateful for them too.

"Where's Ikkyu?" I asked, scanning the beach for him, but he was nowhere around.

"He's back at the house," Antonio said. "He and I were the reason we took so long getting to you after Joshua teleported the two of you. Ikkyu was hit badly. But it's a physical injury. He should recover, eventually."

"Ikkyu will be fine," Zenda confirmed when I looked at her.

"And Joshua's cousins? Did they make it at all?" I said.

Everyone looked grave at the mention of them. I didn't want to think of so much loss of life, but I had to know for sure.

"They were torn to shreds when Joshua ripped their souls from their bodies," Aurelius said. "That's evil, barbaric aurics that I hope we never see again. Let's get out of this rain and check on Ikkyu. We've taken care of everything back at the Trop."

"I'm ready," I said, holding Antonio tighter to myself, grateful to have survived the night, but still in shock over my family's history.

Aurelius conjured us a swirling tyrian purple portal and moved aside for Zenda and the rest of us to step in. Then we all disappeared into the sitting room of the immortals' seaside mansion.

CHAPTER FOURTEEN

BUNGALOWS, BOARDWALKS, BURIALS

I KKYU WAS LYING ON the couch where he sat when I first came to the house. Zenda sparked the fireplace to life behind him with traffic cone sized emerald flames as she made her way to Ikkyu's side and knelt beside him. I moved with Antonio out of the way of Aurelius and Kana coming into the room behind us, and we made our way to the couch opposite Ikkyu. Zenda ran an emerald glowing hand up and down his body, something I hadn't yet seen before.

Ikkyu's body wasn't bloody or maimed in any way. He looked at peace and unharmed in his sleep, which worried me more than if there had been a cut or something visible. On the beach, Antonio said Ikkyu's injury was physical, so I wondered if it was perhaps mental, like a concussion or even something with his spine. I didn't yet want to know how immortals died, and for some reason I knew it was different than the way Joshua had.

"This is nothing I can't fix," Zenda said, squeezing onto the couch beside Ikkyu. "He's in a dreamy state from hitting his head. It's nothing he can't be woken out of. I think Joshua surprised us all with his... displays. We've been away from the action a little too long, I suppose."

"I'll agree with that," Kana said, making her way behind the couch where Ikkyu laid. "This is unacceptable."

"We all know the risks, Kana," Aurelius said. "This isn't our first injury this century."

"I know," Kana said. "It's still unacceptable. For our squad, at least. We should have had someone else with us for back up."

"We can spin around with the possibilities of the past, or we can make ourselves stronger," Zenda said. "We need to help Ikkyu heal. That's our priority."

Zenda now used both hands to work on Ikkyu. Kana joined by holding her hands above Ikkyu and casting a pink light that shined down on him with glittering healing energy.

Ikkyu is a great teacher. I hope he recovers fast, Antonio thought. *He knows more fighting styles than any of us other immortals. It could take lifetimes for him to teach them to a single student, and another few lifetimes for the student to master them all. You're going to have a lot to learn with us.*

I'm not sure I'm ready to settle down and learn quite yet, I thought. *I'm going to have some things to take care of in the next coming weeks.*

I know, Antonio thought. *And I want to be there with you. I want to help you through everything.*

I don't know my plan yet, I thought. *It's going to be a while before I decide anything for sure, but I have until the funerals.*

What funerals? Antonio thought.

The funerals for the Bailey cousins, and the one for Joshua himself, I thought. *It will be important for me to be there. I'll see my parents there. I don't know what I'm going to do with them either.*

Whatever you decide, I'll help you out, Antonio thought back. *I'm sorry about all that. You deserved a better life than they gave you.*

I came to terms with how they treated me a long time ago, I thought. *That part isn't new to me. Now I know the reasons why they are how they are, and honestly I'm just happy to live my life free from them.*

I turned to look out at the gray world through the windows along the back side of the house. The patio was wet with the rain from the storm, and the wind was howling in every direction it blew, causing the house to groan and creak where the wood beams connected to one another.

"Dylan," Aurelius called from behind Ikkyu's couch. Emerald fire danced behind him while Kana and Zenda worked. "Why don't you go lay down. Your body has gone through a lot today, and I'm sure your mind would appreciate a break."

"You're right," I said. "I could use a break, too. You're sure there's nothing more I can do to help?" The adrenaline of the fight was starting to wear off, and my body felt the wounds and weight of the use and abuse of battle.

"We will nurse Ikkyu back to us," Aurelius said. "But your time to help us will come again, at the proper time. For now, go rest."

"Could you take me back to Sixtieth Street?" I asked Antonio, patting his leg with my hand. "It already feels like a home to me."

"Of course," Antonio said. "Let me get my keys."

Antonio followed me into the bungalow after driving me home. I didn't have a plan for the evening. I barely had the desire to decide on anything except crawling into bed and letting the night cover us with the dark hours of the moon. I knew we'd probably have to eat something, but I wasn't interested in cooking or thinking about feeding myself.

The bungalow had the quiet of a church after everyone left from a midnight mass. There was something holy to the peace in the air, and being back in the house started to remind me of the activities of life. The bath and shower felt like nice places to numb the bodily pains of battle.

"You did good," Antonio said, leaning against the door with his back. I was a few steps away by the coffee table. It seemed superficial to be so engrossed in the presence of Antonio's body, but all I could think of was holding him by the waist and kissing his lips. I craved the feeling of the comfort I found in his arms the night before, and I felt like he felt it too.

"Thank you," I said, grateful to still be alive, but I didn't want to think about that. So, I took a step forward, deciding that Antonio's direction was probably the best direction I could go in.

"Do you want me to leave?" he asked, taking a peek out the bay window at the sky. "I can come back in the morning and give you some time alone."

"Please," I said, unsure of how to respond. "Stay the night with me."

Antonio's eyebrows raised in surprise. The look was starting to become one of my favorites, and it made me smile as I took another step closer, narrowing out the room around us and making it so his eyes had little space to break away from staying on mine.

"I don't have to leave until you tell me to," Antonio said, relaxing against the door as I got closer.

"Good," I said, reaching out. I wrapped my hands around his waist, staring into his eyes. I closed my eyes as my body pushed up against his, and I leaned in for a kiss. He leaned back into me, and we kissed.

Where his lips pressed into, my lips folded between. I let him take control, as I melted into the smell of his skin, the taste of his tongue, and the ecstatic sensation he massaged into my mouth with the muscles of his lips.

He wrapped me in his arms, but we fumbled on the edge of frantic arousal. I stumbled back, and he stumbled forward. And in a few breaths, we reached the bedroom. I felt the bed behind me as endorphins flooded my mind and my blood pumped like a bass drum, faster and faster. After I laid down on the bed, he broke the seal between our mouths to tongue play with the skin of my neck.

My skin erupted in chills that made me shiver everywhere. I opened my eyes as the cold of his hands touched the bare skin of my stomach as he reached under my shirt, and I saw the four little sun pictures hung over the bed where they had been when I moved in. I only focused on the one depicting the sunset, feeling some connection with the dreamer inside my grandfather's delusions as I felt the dreams I had held onto just beginning to come true.

The next morning was a bright blue skied day with a wetness that held heat against our skin under the bed sheet we held over our heads after we woke up, before we broke the silence of dawn. Against the glow of the sunlit sheet, I traced Antonio's cheekbones and brow, while he drew circles with his finger on my side. I dozed in and out with the rhythm of his breathing against the crash of the waves that made its way into the room on the windless morning.

Each time I woke up, I found Antonio's crystalline chestnut brown eyes, encrusted along the fractals with azure blue auric energy. I didn't know how he did that with his aura reflecting in his eyes, or if it was even something he was doing on purpose, but it made laying there with him the most magical morning of my life. It felt like I had grown up, and the man I had fallen for was proof that all of my childish dreams for my life would come true. Together, there was nothing beyond what we could do.

I like the idea of that, Antonio thought whispered into my mind.

It's true, I thought. *After all of that, I think maybe we should focus on getting to know each other better before getting deeper into the auric arts. I want to get to know you before I have to start calling you master and doing everything you say.*

You're really funny, Antonio thought, laughing at me with a smile I couldn't help but kiss. *We'll go at your pace. I care about you in a way deeper than I've ever cared about anyone else in my life. It might sound crazy, but it must make sense, because you feel it too. And you'll never have to call me master if you don't want to. We're close enough in age, and if we're together, then that custom doesn't apply. Make sure you do say master when talking to others though, especially once you start training with us and meeting other Immortal Philosophers.*

It feels unreal to be here right now. Just a decision away from living that life, I thought.

It's not a bad life, Antonio thought.

I know, I thought. *It's more than I ever dreamed of. I always wanted to design movie covers because I loved movies so much. I loved heroes, and to be one with so much power is unreal to me. I'm just not excited about the danger of it all.* Antonio looked concerned. *And my parents. The last time I'm going to see them will be at the funeral. I don't want anything to do with them after this. There's no redemption for people who could plot against their own son the way they did. They're just as bad as Joshua. Our families had been friendly for generations. There's no telling what kind of horrors they've all been involved in. Half of me wants to lock them in that cave on the Bailey grounds and seal it up for good, but the other half just wants to live my own life and forget them once and for all.*

I almost know how you feel, Antonio thought. *For a long time half of myself wanted to know my parents and chase some kind of connection that I might have had with them that I couldn't have with anyone else. As a kid, I harbored feelings deep and for many years. It has a lot to do with how I advanced in my abilities so quickly and why my aura is so strong. I used that desire to find that connection to push myself, while the other half of me would run to my bed at night, on occasions, and cry myself to sleep, wishing to forget that the two people that brought me into the world once* existed at all. *Our minds are impossible to control sometimes. Aurelius even brought me to live with my family in Puerto Rico after rescuing me from the orphanage. He wanted to make sure the family that had lost so much knew the youngest of their line. I grew up with my cousins there with Aurelius as my father. Zenda was with us most of the time, while Kana and Ikkyu came in and out.*

With the immortals' help, our family farm that had gone unused for generations was brought back to life as the coffee source for my café. But, I didn't find in my cousins any stronger connection than what I had with Aurelius, Ikkyu, Zenda, or Kana. I've felt more of a connection with some of the other Immortal Philosophers who I hardly see for years at a time, which is a long answer for me to tell you that you never lose the ability to make meaningful connections with the people who come into your life. That's also how I learned that sometimes the desire for a more extreme and emotional outcome is misguided.

I didn't know those things about your parents and family though, I thought. *I'm sorry they passed before you met them.*

Everyone has their own life stories, Antonio thought. *I don't hide from mine, and I'm not ashamed at all. Along the lines of the words of the great Gottfried Wilhelm Leibniz, everything is a reflection of the universe that reflects the complexities of everything that is.*

Don't tell me he's one of your immortals, I thought, remembering the mysticism with which one philosophy professor spoke of his work. *What's he like?*

He's the maddest man you'll ever meet, Antonio thought. *He doesn't leave Europe much. He's in Malaga now, but he's a character and a half. He'd have you peering into different galaxies if he ever got hold of you. He's still trying to figure out the secrets of the universe, and he'd tell you he's not far off from figuring them all out.*

I'm sure, I thought. *That's what most philosophers say. Is everyone in the group a real philosopher?*

No, not all, Antonio thought. *I'm prime example number one, but you'll meet some you'll recognize and some you won't. We've walked all types of different lives. Some of us have lived in the spotlight many times, while some of us never dare. It's really a personal preference despite the times where we've had no other choice. Although, you might have better luck uncovering more of our history than probably I even know of.*

You make me sound like an enigma, I thought.

You are, he thought back. *You're my enigma.* Then he closed his eyes and kissed my lips. I kissed him back, rolling into him until his back gave way and I was laying on top of him. When our mouths parted, we were out from under the sheet, and I had a view of the window from where I rested my head on Antonio's chest.

"I wish this day wouldn't end," I said, feeling for the first time in my long term memory that there wasn't anything I'd like to change about my present.

"I wouldn't mind that either," Antonio agreed. "Maybe now I could get that second date?" he asked.

I looked up at him and started laughing. After everything we had been through the night before, the thought of a date seemed so superficial, but I couldn't think of anything that sounded better.

"Of course," I said. "I'd love that. Do you have any ideas?"

"Just one," he said, looking down at me. "Let's take a stroll on the boardwalk. I want to show you this Korean place that serves some great japchae. We can get lunch and some water ice. It'll be a good time."

"That sounds perfect," I said, eager to fall into anything that Antonio proposed. "But I don't want to get ready just yet. I'll just lay here for a little longer."

"That's fine," he said. "Take as long as you need. I won't go anywhere."

When we finally got out of bed, it was closer to noon than sunrise, and we both needed a good wash up before hitting the boardwalk. I steeped us both some tea while we got ready in the bathroom. I missed my tub, shower, and the view I had of the backyard out the bathroom window. The feeling of joy in being near those things again made me feel so at home. I didn't feel like this was a place I wanted to escape or leave from for very long, and having Antonio with me made me feel like everything I wanted had fallen into place. It felt like such a long time had passed since I walked up to Antonio the first time at his café. I couldn't believe it had only been a few days.

If I had chosen a different spot to relocate to, or had closed myself off from people in general, things would have played out a lot differently. If I had never pursued Antonio, I might not have been able to learn what I needed in time to defeat Joshua. All of us could have fallen to him if that were the case, and he'd have been the one celebrating life instead of us.

Antonio wasn't shy of himself and didn't leave room for me to be shy with myself either as we got ready in the bathroom. In the essence of time, he insisted on climbing into the shower with me. It was the first time I showered with another man who was interested in me, having had to shower with my classes and sports team in our boarding school locker room showers. This was a much nicer experience for me. Antonio was amusing and took the time to clean my body with his soapy hands the way a potter molds his clay for a masterpiece. I didn't know how much I would enjoy the intimacy of the experience, but I enjoyed it so much that I paid it back in turn.

After showering, I got a change of clothes together for Antonio to get into for our date. It was amusing to me, seeing him wearing my clothes. I hated when the guys would use my stuff at the brownstone and in high school. It was mostly because they were gross and would return things reeking of their poor hygiene, if not completely ruined, but Antonio was different. I found an old Captain America designed shirt that I had printed for my coursework at NYU. It had the stars and stripes running down the front of the shirt, and I couldn't think of a better option for the day. I gave it to him with a fresh pair of underwear, socks, and a pair of gray athletic shorts. Everything fit him nice and tight against his muscles, and we were both happy with our looks for the day.

"Which superhero are you?" Antonio asked as we looked ourselves over in the bathroom mirror. I was wearing a white t-shirt that read 'BEACH REBEL' in blue lettering across the chest and a pair of blue shorts.

"I'm me," I said, smiling at him through the mirror.

"Does this shirt come in the Captain Puerto Rico version? With one star and the blue of my aura?" he asked.

"Unfortunately not," I said, thinking about the combination. "But I could design one for you. I can picture it in my head already."

"Yeah, that'd be cool," Antonio said, looking down at his shirt. "I'd wear it more often than you think." And we both laughed.

Before hitting the road, we took a minute to walk up the sand dune with our mugs of tea to get a look at the beach and the ocean. The day was getting warm as noon came around. The beach was dotted with groups of people congregating around umbrellas and coolers the way people circle around campfires.

"I love the beach," I said, between the sound of the crashing waves.

"Then I can't wait to take you to Puerto Rico," Antonio

said. "You're going to love it there. I'll show you some of the most beautiful beaches in the world. We'll eat fresh coconut flesh and drink piña coladas in the sun. It's something close to heaven, certain places down there."

"I'm ready to go when you are," I said, sipping my tea. The feeling of the day was so new to me. The flavor from the tea was stronger. The way the sun felt on my skin was warmer, and even the way the sounds of the birds and seagulls came to me had changed. Life with Antonio and my restored control over my power was starting to seem so much more sweet and littered with endless possibilities.

The Ocean City boardwalk was another spectacle of the island. While the beach by the bungalow was sparsely populated, the beach along the boardwalk was packed. It seemed like everyone within fifty miles had nothing to do except sit on the sand or dip in the waves. The boardwalk itself was a long stretch of shops, hotels, and eateries that burst onto the boardwalk with music, signs, and samples for all of the families to enjoy. We started our walk along the south end of the boardwalk, where the shops started to the north and houses ran south. A live performer was singing Sinatra to the tune of the piano he laid across the arms of his folding yard chair.

"This is really nice," I said, walking up the boardwalk, impressed with the small town beach culture.

"It's a little slice of something special, I like to say," Antonio said. "See the ferris wheel?" he asked, pointing up the boardwalk and to the left. Behind the row of buildings the top of a ferris wheel poked out with a view that had to be impressive. Beside it were the cherry red rails of a roller coaster track about to drop a cart full of people on the edge of thrill.

"I do," I said. "It looks fun. There's a whole amusement park here, right?" I asked.

"Yeah," Antonio confirmed. "There are a couple, actually. It's great for kids and families mostly, but we immortals enjoy the pace of things here."

"I think I do too," I said, learning more about myself the more I learned about Antonio.

We walked about half way up the boardwalk when Antonio pulled me over to the Korean chicken place he mentioned earlier. I got us one of the few tables outside on the boardwalk, while he ordered our meals at the counter inside.

We ate our poke bowls filled with japchae noodles, tofu, and other cut and cooked vegetables. Everything was delicious, and the hearty portion of pickled ginger left my mouth tingly even after we finished. For the next part of our walk, Antonio brought me over to the booth selling Polish water ice. I wasn't sure what the difference was between Polish water ice and Italian water ice, but Antonio remembered how my grandfather was Polish and thought I might enjoy it. It turned out, he was right about that too.

The water ice was delicious. I got bright blue raspberry and pink watermelon, and the woman who took our order was sweet. She filled my cup a little more than regular because she was familiar with Antonio and his business. We scraped our spoons clean onto our tongues while we walked, as the flavors entranced us into conversation about our favorite desserts and the different shore and harbor towns we've been to. I had to try Antonio's cherry ice, and he tried my combo as I learned about how he really hadn't seen much more of the world than I had for an immortal. He had teleported to many buildings in many cities, but was yet to explore the cities outside the walls of the different Immortal Philosopher sanctuaries.

"We'll see the world together," Antonio said. "It'll be the experience of a lifetime."

"I'd love that," I said, biting my wooden spoon and sucking at the sugar syrup stuck inside the grain of the wood. "There are some countries I don't feel comfortable traveling to though, with us being who we are together."

"I know what you mean," Antonio said. "That's something I'd like to change about this world. There're so many of us out there who live in places with no ability to ever be themselves. It's one of the biggest sins of humanity, really."

Our boardwalk walk ended where it began. The day was still bright, and the weight of the night before was less heavy on our minds. My body still ached with the bumps and bruises from battle, but my aura was hard at work healing all the places that needed it. When we returned back to the bungalow, Antonio received a mental message from Zenda that Ikkyu was finally waking up, and we celebrated the end of our weekend with a long hot bath.

The next day Aurelius sent word about the Wednesday date for the funerals for the nine Baileys that had fallen in battle, Joshua included. My parents didn't reach out to me, and I didn't reach out to them. I knew they'd be at the burials, which I intended to attend, and that was more than okay with me.

Aurelius and Antonio were kind enough to join me on the way up north to New York. I drove the Jeep with Antonio next to me and Aurelius in the back seat meditating. It was a solemn drive. Antonio and I had spent the days before together and found peace in the silence we allowed each other and our conversation when it struck. I had a lot on my mind against the music that played on the radio as I maneuvered through traffic on the highway. The song 'Oceans Apart' by Elliot Cutcas cut deep, as the lyrics lulled me to a place where I felt oceans away from everyone else in my life. Antonio was the first person I allowed to get close to the real me, and I had only known him a little longer than a week.

To say the burial was extravagant would be an understatement. The Bailey parents had cleaned up a section in the corner of their backyard and arranged the nine caskets in a row along the tree line. Some of the oldest members of their American heritage were buried in a small graveyard beside the new clearing, and even the older graves had been cleaned up and arranged with fresh flowers for the occasion. Around the nine caskets were bouquets of all types of white flowers, piled up on top of each other to give the effect of a floral wall between the viewers and the caskets, behind which were the dug graves.

Some members of the Bailey family were teary eyed, but Joshua's parents were not. The crowd was too large for me to tell if anybody else noticed, but I did. I wondered if they knew his secret too. The entire town was present it seemed, all taking seats in the sea of plastic white chairs. So many faces I knew from boarding school, the church, and local businesses. But nobody said a word to me, as I had never shared much conversation with any of them. Most of them probably didn't even know my name, but everyone knew the Baileys. Antonio had said he would alert me if he felt any strong auras, but he didn't, which made us think that if Bailey was associated with anyone else with powers like his, they were smart enough not to show up to their ally's funeral. I still had to dig through all of his memories that transferred over to me with my energy before I would find out those answers, I figured. His memory lived in me, like the fading footprints of a past life.

It wasn't until the end of the ceremony, after I had walked up to the caskets with Antonio to place roses, when I first spotted my parents in the distance on the permitter of our yard. I had gotten white roses for the Bailey cousins and a black one for Joshua, that I hid in my jacket and placed down fast when I came to his casket. There was no peace for him to find in this life or the next, but I hoped his cousins found something bearable on the other side of their tortured lives.

I regretted not buying a couple more black roses for my parents after seeing them notice me and start to scurry off back to our house. I couldn't imagine them needing to say anything to me after all of their plans had been buried upon hearing of Joshua's demise. I thought I would have wanted to hear the confession of their desires from their mouths, but watching them cower back home changed something in the dynamic in which I situated myself in relation to them. The threat of them was over, and I was more myself than they had ever had interest in helping me become. I had no interest in opening my new life up to their scrutiny if I couldn't enjoy their support.

"Are you going to follow them?" Antonio asked, watching me follow them across the yard with my eyes.

"No," I said, and with that one word, I felt more clean of them than I had ever before. "I'm good."

"I support you," Antonio said, watching them with me.

"There's one last thing I have to take care of," I said, pulling the last white rose out of my jacket. The one I brought for baby Joshua, the Joshua I never had the pleasure of knowing in my life.

Antonio grabbed onto my shoulder and walked me forward as groups of people started to leave the burial, while a band played a song as the caskets were lowered into the ground.

"What is it?" he asked, turning to me.

"I have to place this rose in the cave," I said.

"You're right," he said. "We need to go to the cave too. We need to do something about it," he said.

"We'll assess it," Aurelius said, behind us. "And we'll see what we need to do about it. Can you take us there?"

"Yeah," I said, knowing the way like the back of my hand. "Follow me."

The three of us crossed the yard and made it to the treeline of the forest behind the houses. After we crossed over into the woods, I didn't need my memory to get us to the cave anymore. My auric senses were on high alert, and I could feel the pull of the energy from the cave. I wondered if this was how even as an infant Joshua was able to find his way to it. We followed the trail that looped around the neighborhood for a number of yards before my internal compass sent us off into the untamed parts of the forest where sticky bushes and vines threatened to rip our clothes and skin. Antonio conjured an auric machete and started thwacking the vegetation out of our way before Aurelius took over and cast a circle of purple energy around us that caused the plants to move themselves out of our way as we walked on.

When we came to the clearing where the cave sat like a misplaced heap of dung, the energy that felt attractive on our walk in had disappeared. The entrance to the cave, where the one stone slab split for people to slip in, was secure in its place, keeping out the mortal world.

"I thought he had taken everything he could from the cave before he drove down to Ocean City," I said, surprised by the pull of the cave's energy.

"I thought so too," Aurelius said. "I felt the cave on our walk in, but something's not right here."

"What should we do with it?" Antonio asked, as we all

approached the rock.

"Well, I had planned on ridding it from this forest," Aurelius said. "Auric sinks like these tempt immortals and mortals alike with powers beyond their capabilities. It will only be a matter of time before the cave finds a new keeper, or a new taker stumbles upon it themselves. We can't risk it causing more harm."

"What did you do with the one on Long Beach Island?" I asked, not daring to get as close to the stone as Aurelius and Antonio. They both stood, staring at the rock and the protrusion where the entrance stood obscured.

"That one, Johnathan Bailey took care of destroying for us," Aurelius said, lifting a hand and placing it against the stone.

"Have you ever seen one with regenerative mucus sliding down the walls?" I asked, as the familiar putrid stench of the glowing jelly billowed out into the clearing as I got close to the entrance.

"Never," Aurelius said, staring into the cave.

"Should we go in?" Antonio asked Aurelius.

"I don't think I can shimmy in," Aurelius said, looking at the size of the entrance and his thicker build.

"We can go," Antonio said, gesturing to me.

"Armor up," Aurelius warned.

"You coming?" Antonio asked, looking back at me.

"I don't know," I said, looking down at the fleshy white petals of the rose against the orange of the pine needle forest floor. I was planning on leaving the rose outside the tomb of terrible memories, but I wasn't afraid of anything associated with Bailey anymore. I couldn't be.

"I'll be with you," Antonio said, holding out a hand.

"I'll be here outside too," Aurelius joined in. "I'll be able to see you inside from here."

"I'll set the rose down, for the real Joshua," I said, activating my auric armor and walking up to Antonio. I grabbed his hand and let him take the lead on the way in.

"Down the rabbit hole we go," Antonio said, activating his aura around himself and squeezing my hand.

I shivered from the feeling that washed over me as I followed him between the tight walls of the crevice.

When we entered the dome of the cave, my body shook with an icy feeling around my back. The mucus that lined the walls before was no longer running in thick clear cascades. It wasn't glowing or pulsing as it had before, it just tainted the air with the eerie wetness of a cemetery on a summer night.

Wanting to get out as soon as possible, I set down the white rose in the center and turned to Antonio.

"There's nothing," he said, touching the inside of the cave wall with his armored fingers.

Something about the touch of energy then activated something within the cave, causing it to shudder and slam shut the cave entrance, and before we could react, the entire cave spun around with us inside, slamming us against the ceiling in a violent tumble that left us both splayed out on our backs with no way out.

THE END

THE *IMMORTAL* PHILOSOPHERS

CHRONICLES OF DYLAN EAGLEGOD
BOOK TWO

LOST BETWEEN THE LANDS OF HERE AND THERE

by

ALEXANDER ANTHONY CASILLAS

OUT NOW

Dylan Eaglegod is on the hunt to save the world from the world famous Popstar and Bro Podcaster predatorial duo and the more sinister foes behind their curtain of toxic popularity. Race across the Mediterranean to save the largest ever, island hopping concert tour, where the Immortal Philosophers must succeed or leave the mortal fans for dead.

Secret forces and hidden magic are just as dangerous as the hearts in our heroes' chests as the romantic and auric taxes of this epic Old World adventure tests their limits and takes its toll. But from the ancient city of Málaga, Spain, to their pasts, the Old Guard of the Immortal Philosophers might not be enough to help Dylan save them all. Especially when on the Mediterranean, nothing is only as it seems.

PROLOG

The black curtains of chest-length hair fell heavy in front of the concealed face of Solomon Ibn Gabirol as he emerged from the shadow of the hall and into the brig of the dry docked cargo ship. His steps were swishing whispers against the grated floor despite the heavy soled shoes and gold jewelry adorned around his tight-cuffed and fitted gray checked suit.

"You called?" Solomon said into the steel walled room, his voice deep with impatience coded into each syllable. The resentment for his association with the selfish American was an aura all its own, emanating from Solomon like a presence difficult for anyone to ignore. But he needed the former FBI Director as much as the American needed his expertise.

"So, you did get my message?" came the slick and eely voice of John Edgar Hoover. "I had to wonder." He leaned across a wooden table engraved with a map of the Mediterranean coast. A number of shining gunmetal gray auric cruise ships floated across the table like ghost ships bobbing in the sea. The darkness of the brig cast Hoover's pale face with a sickly shade of silver in the glow of his auric energy. Behind him was the warm window-framed Málaga bay at sunset, glistening with turquoise waters and catamaran boats where the mountains tumbled into the sea. But nothing could make Hoover appear any less greasy in his navy blue suit with his gunmetal circular lapel pin that Solomon swore he would never wear.

"Must I go through this again with you?" Solomon said.

"I'll work with you, not for you. That includes finishing what I'm doing before rushing over to see what you need of me."

"This job is bigger than the both of us!" Hoover said. "Why does everyone else around here understand that but you? This is no small job. This is the one that will change our lives forever. We'll have the power to do whatever we want. We'd have the power to get to the Moon, Mars, colonize Atlantis or wherever else we might want to go. Do you get that?"

"Atlantis?" Solomon said. "Are we back in the 16th century?"

"We'd have the power to build Atlantis from the very essence of history itself," Hoover proposed. "Our power of limits will be limitless."

"And what good would that do us?" Solomon said, his body still and unresponsive to the Hoover histrionics that Solomon loathed behind the shades of his hair. "I've been everywhere I've wanted to be. I'm where I want to be now, doing what I want to do, aside from right this second and every moment that I spend with you, of course. I am living for what I want, and I'm living for more than what you busy your mind with everyday. With surviving. It's an American curse, of course, survival as a lifestyle. I'm happy with my Mediterranean pace of life and with how I maintain my immortality. I know what I am, and I do what I need to do when I need to do it. Existence isn't my whole identity. My only gripe is with the world infesting my city, and for that, I thought we already had a plan. So, what do you want with me today?"

"Have you always taken for granted the gifts you were given?" Hoover asked, moving his body in a shimmer of gun-metal auric energy as he peered closer at one of the auric ships floating across his miniature Mediterranean.

"My gift came with a heaping of humility," Solomon said, tracing every scar on his boil riddled body with his mind. "But I'm not sure if any amount of humility could counterbalance your American penchant for feeling like you're constantly at a lack of something. I've survived hundreds of years just the way I am, with no need of going to the lengths you feel you must go."

"But you'll do it for Portendorfer?" Hoover asked, staring Solomon dead in the eyes.

"Portendorfer wants a place in this world, not the one you envision," Solomon said.

"Gabirol," Hoover said, laughing. "You're naive even in your old age. This world is an illusion of millions of different forces pulling at the wheel, all trying to direct the way we go. To want to live in this world, is to give up your hand in bending the world to your vision and to accept that of somebody else's. Portendorfer gets that, and if he doesn't, he soon will. I'm ready to start loading the crew. And then the guests."

Solomon couldn't fight the smirk forming in the shadows hiding his face.

"Everything and everyone will be on route," he said. "I'll send Portendorfer over with a list of names and auric levels. We'll soon both get what we want, it seems."

"One way or another," Hoover returned, turning around to take in the view of the orange glowed, crystal blue bay and ship spotted sea.

AUTHOR'S NOTE

Dylan's story speaks to the power deep down in all of us, and how sometimes we're so strong that we keep that power suppressed. Always for too long. Dylan's story is about embracing the changes you want to see in your life and chasing after them until your dreams become your realities despite the chaos of the world around us. Dylan's story is written with magic and the flourish of fantasy, but his struggles and triumphs are not beyond our capabilities when we embrace the bravest act of all and embrace who we are without fear of hate or disapproval from others' oppressive belief systems. Dylan's story reminds us that many of the mysteries of our lives can be explained by reflecting on the memories of the past, and how sometimes doing that is the only way for us to move forward.

Everyday we're met with the feeling of waking up in a world that tells us we're not worth as much as others, and we are confronted with people who genuinely hate us. Their hate makes them menaces against the joyful, and their words are only meant to steal from you the power you've built inside yourself in resilience to their influence.

Look to logic, truth, and to the philosophers, thinkers, and lovers of humanity throughout history. Arm your mind with the tools to maintain the morals, values, and ethics that are so innate in those who love fearlessly. We make the world go round despite the winds of hatred whipping against our faces as we step toward the promise of a world where we all have the power to make our mark. Book One of the Chronicles of Dylan Eaglegod is Dylan's story of self discovery and the exploration of himself in a new life. It's my hope that his story will help propel you to your promised land.

Enjoy, and until next time,
    Alexander Anthony Casillas

THE IMMORTAL PHILOSOPHERS

CHRONICLES OF DYLAN EAGLEGOD

BOOK THREE

MIDNIGHT IN THE CITY THAT LOST ITS SOUL

by

ALEXANDER ANTHONY CASILLAS

RELEASING 2027

SUBSCRIBE FOR UPDATES:

FourElementsPress.com

TheImmortalPhilosophers.com

THE
IMMORTAL PHILOSOPHERS

Aurelius: Stoic philosopher and former Roman Emperor. Founder of the Immortal Philosophers and leader of its members worldwide. Hunter of thieving and murderous predators lurking among us who are desperate to manipulate the innocent to steal the auric life force innate in all of us.

Unique Abilities: Vast Auric Reserves, Teleportation Expert.

Aura: Tyrian Purple

Antonio Antoninus: Adopted son of Aurelius was born and raised on his home island of Puerto Rico. Antonio grew up around extended family and the protective eye of the immortals. His Puerto Rican cafe in Ocean City, New Jersey is his heaven on Earth, until his world is upturned after meeting Dylan Eaglegod.

Unique Abilities: Auric Energy Battery, Fast Regeneration.

Aura: Sky Blue

Dylan Eaglegod: New York born and raised, and one of the newest recruits, Dylan escaped the nightmare of living a closeted life around homophobic friends, who, unbeknownst to him, were predators extracting his energy and who sought to kill him. Until the Immortal Philosophers found him and taught him how to free himself. Now the boyfriend of Antonio Antoninus, and a powerful force within the circle of immortals.

Unique Abilities: Strong Past Viewing, Locating Atraments, Creating Auric Wells.

Aura: Cobalt

Zenda: Oldest of the Immortal Philosophers, and the most in tune with ancient energy. Zenda was a leader of a group of Spirit Warriors in South China, North Vietnam before time was recorded in any organized way. Her tribe was known far and wide as the people to turn to when nothing else worked, or when the danger was too mysterious. They kept centuries safe from demonic predators as far as the Indus Peninsula to the plateau of Tibet. Wife of Ikkyu, Zenda organizes the American based Immortal Philosophers and spent time raising and training Antonio.

Unique Abilities: Conjuring Ancient Bestial Forms, Exceptional Auric Reserves, Healing Expert.

Aura: Emerald

Ikkyu Sojun: Bastard son of an emperor, Ikkyu was sent to become a Zen Buddhist monk as a child. At a young age, he achieved enlightenment and unlocked abilities he was told were legend. After fooling and chastising everyone he met in his life for their hypocrisy and extravagance, Ikkyu took to training his body as well as his mind. Becoming a master of all historic fighting styles over his long lifetime. Husband of Zenda.

Unique Abilities: Hand to Hand & Musical Combat Expert.

Aura: Light Mint Green

Kana: Powerful sibling of Ikkyu and a miracle in her own right. Kana was raised with love and care in an imperial enclave, before her history took a dark turn. She is one of the most battle ready Immortal Philosophers, and always has something to prove.

Unique Abilities: Hand to Hand & Musical Combat Expert.

Aura: Cherry Blossom Pink

Selena Sol-Valencia is an in-denial teenage werewolf battling for her life against family tradition, human traffickers, and teen crushes. But her biggest antagonist might just be her own mind. Could womanhood really be the most dangerous part of a girl's life?

Selena must learn family history, her Tío's rules of survival, and figure out how to make the most of the nightmare situations brought on by teen-wolf puberty and the intrusive world. Secrets lay behind everyone she meets, but once the claws come out, nobody's safe. Especially on the night of the Blue Moon.

Selena Sol-Valencia Episodio 1

Selena Sol-Valencia is off on an institutionalized adventure where breaking free from the psych ward before her full moon transformation is a high stakes journey of self discovery, self control, and the 'pro-social' behaviors she must master as she adapts to her new neurodivergent diagnoses and medications. But the haunting figure of Cualli, La Llorona, is making it more difficult than Selena ever imagined.

Selena must dive deep into her family history and Mexican-Indigenous lore to figure out how and why the haunting spirit is so drawn to her. Friends and family are near and far, and help as they can. But Selena's on her own against the ghosts of her and her family's present and past. With freedom on the horizon is she can win a release before the full moon. While her future, if she fails, promises a life time of werewolf incarceration.

Selena Sol-Valencia Episodio 2

* 9 7 8 1 9 6 5 9 9 6 0 1 0 *